THE
HIGH ONES

a novel

Robert Scheige

ISBN (hardback):   978-1-7345604-0-4
ISBN (paperback): 978-1-7345604-1-1
BISAC: Fiction / Literary Fiction / Historical Fiction

Published by Ashaboo Press
Book design by Robert Scheige
Cover art and dust jacket by Robin E. Vuchnich
Author photo by Michael Wolcott

To Kathy.

Contents

Neanderthal (*Homo neanderthalensis*): An extinct mammal of the genus *homo*, believed to be the species most closely related to modern humans, both genetically and behaviorally. Morphological divergence from modern humans punctuated by a larger cranial capacity, low and rounded braincase, prominent brow ridge, and stockier body. Archeological evidence suggests a potential for sophisticated culture, complex language, and symbolic thought. Habitat included most of Europe and Western Asia. Disappeared from the fossil record ~40,000 years before present. Cause of extinction is unknown but corresponds with the appearance of modern humans in their geographical range.

Where lies the final harbor, whence we unmoor no more? In what rapt ether sails the world, of which the weariest will never weary? Where is the foundling's father hidden? Our souls are like those orphans whose unwedded mothers die in bearing them: the secret of our paternity lies in their grave, and we must there to learn it.

- Herman Melville, Moby Dick

If the eye were an animal, sight would be its soul. When seeing is removed, the eye is no longer an eye, except in name—no more than the eye of a statue or a painted figure.

-Aristotle, On the Soul

PROLOGUE: NINE MONTHS LATER

The Boy and the Man

THE EVERWOOD HAD BEEN RIVEN to its base by a bolt of lightning. Man-sized chunks of wood suspended from its boughs by groaning filaments, and scorched timber, shavings to hulking shards alike, littered the surrounding snows like the wreckage of some feral outburst. The man remembered the very bolt responsible for this destruction. It had been close enough to feel it in his skin.

He limped toward the tree, sundered limbs latticing overhead like the fractured dome of an ancient grotto, shafts narrowing in tortuous curves until they grazed the forest floor. He pushed away the branches and leaned against the shattered trunk, splinters jutting into his handwear as he gripped for balance and bent forward. Standing at this angle meant his rib didn't grate against the one above it, offering a brief respite from the pain. He let go and picked the needles from his handwear before tossing them into the snow.

"What is wrong your chest?" the boy asked.

The man lifted his head and glared at him but said nothing. The boy knew. He'd been there when it happened.

He looked away to survey the landscape before him, taking in shallow breaths through his nose. It even smelled cold. The snowfall from two nights ago had made it easier to see in the dark, the cool light of the sistersun reflecting off every surface. But the snow had also smothered the expanse in a white sameness that worsened the challenge of traveling through lands unknown, even now when a dull light was finally emerging from below the horizon behind him.

"I think it's this way," the man said, pointing away from the coming sunrise. In the distance was a mountain so high it would take days to climb, its summit stark and treeless. The snow line ended where its serrated black walls pitched skyward into the half-haze. He adjusted his shoulderpack and stepped forward, his soles crunching beneath him, his legs plunging into drifts almost to his knees. The verdant peaks of the everwoods teetered above him in the wind, cradling blankets of snow that threatened to suffocate him if they fell.

The boy followed the man.

They reached the edge of a clearing when the man realized where they were. He stopped and unsheathed his blade, his heart rate quickening. He'd meant to go around this place but must have been led astray by the unfamiliar landmarks in these darkward lands. He ducked behind a tree, but it was too late to avoid the clearing. The boy already knew where they were.

"Wait here," the man whispered. "I need to make sure it's safe."

"Is this where—?"

He raised his hand for silence and peeked around the tree. There was no one in the clearing, living or not—even the body was gone. But where was it? The only evidence of habitation was the remnants of a hearth, a dark patch of ash blowing away in the breeze, leaving a pale grey streak on the downwind snows. Three charred logs, each the length of a man's arm, leaned against each other in a jagged arch.

Then the boy dropped his horn and rushed into the clearing. The man tried to stop him but was too slow, the boy's greyfur wearings slipping from his grasp. He chased after him, stumbling in the snow until they reached the depression where the dead man had once lain.

"My father not here!" the boy said, falling to his knees and slapping the red snow with both hands. "He must live!"

The man gripped the hilt of his blade, his stomach churning at the thought of the boy's "father" having somehow survived. He scanned the area for any sign a threat might be near. A great many footprints marked the snow, but none matched the dead man's. His body must have been carried away—but by whom, or what?

"He's not alive," the man said, still not convinced they were alone. "I saw him taken by the forever-sleep." This, of course, was only partly true.

"But his body not here."

"That doesn't mean he's alive," the man said, pursing his lips. He nodded in the direction they'd fled from and shuddered. "You saw what they were doing back there." But even as he said this, he knew he had to return to that horrible place one day. There were things he needed to know, even if finding closure meant facing his worst fears: terrors once unthinkable that now seemed commonplace. The world had become a gelid hellscape; the narrowland itself suspended forever in a profane sea of white, scarlet, and red.

The boy looked back down at the body print, mottled with bloodstains, thick and dark and final. Tears welled up in the eye that wasn't swollen shut. "Those men no do that to him," he said, his bottom lip quivering.

"What I saw back there says otherwise," he insisted. "We have to keep moving before we get too cold."

"We wait to see if Father come back."

"He's not coming back," the man said, raising his voice before calming himself. They both needed to remain quiet in the unlikely case the boy's "father" was around somewhere. "Let's go," he said.

The boy stared at the body print, tears pooling under his chin.

"Well, I'm leaving," the man said. "You asked to follow me. If you want to stay here, that's your choice. No one is forcing you to come."

The boy wiped away his tears and stood. "I go with you."

"Good," the man said. "Get your things, and let's go."

They continued their march forward. Dawn light burst from behind as the sun broke over the horizon, casting shadows through the trees and across the snow and ice. The boy seemed to have trouble navigating the snowdrifts, so deep and dense they threatened to suck off his footwear when he lifted his feet.

"We're almost there," the man said, a mist spilling from his mouth as he spoke. The sounds of carrion birds rose in the distance, suggesting predators had not yet found the carnage he knew lay ahead. He nonetheless unsheathed his blade, unsure what might have changed since the last time he had been there.

They pressed past a thicket to find snows covered in red as if a waterskin filled with blood had exploded. On the ground were the ravaged carcasses of a buck, a doe, and a valleycat—all with eyeless sockets. Carrion birds harried the gore like legion revelers of some grotesque rookery, pecking at open wounds and quarreling over scraps of frozen meat. They flapped their wings, outraged by their new visitors, then lifted themselves off the remains before landing in a riot of squawks and screams. No matter, this was not the bounty the man had come for, especially since the cadavers were now covered in bird droppings.

"What happen here?" the boy asked, his cool response to such a ghastly display perhaps unsurprising after all he'd seen.

"I don't know; it was like this yesterday. But the birds weren't picking at it yet."

A carrion bird flew at the man, hovering in front of him and screeching in his face. He swatted it away.

"Who open doe belly?" The boy pointed at the mangled creature. "It looks like cut by man."

"I did," the man said, eyeing the slate of frozen blood surrounding the doe and remembering why he'd cut it.

"You open belly, but no eat?"

"No. Not exactly."

"What is not exactly?"

"Never mind. Follow me."

He led the boy past the slaughter, the bird cries softening behind them. They pushed into the understory, maneuvering around snowbound deadfall, shaking off the snow to expose the skeletal remains of the branches and brambles within. Soon they reached a rocky outcropping where a valleycat cub, its skin stretched thin over its every bone, lay sideways in the snow, its throat sliced in two.

The boy stopped and gazed at the dead cub. "More foreversleep," he said. He stared at it a moment, then tilted his head and widened his eyes. "That baby killed by man," he said, pointing at the carcass.

"I know."

"You did this?"

The man shook his head but did not deny it. "We aren't here for the cub. It was too starved to offer a meal." He pointed at the outcropping, where a black stone blocked a narrow breach in the rockface. "Help me move the stone."

He positioned himself beside the stone, as did the boy. "Push," the man said, digging his heels into the snow and driving his body against the rock to heave it forward, grimacing as his ribs scraped against each other. The stone ground against the forest floor, leaving a sharp-cut line in the snow behind it. The man held his chest and collapsed, a plume of white powder bursting from beneath him as he toppled over. He wheezed and sat up once the pain lessened.

The man peered into the crevice they'd uncovered, but it was too dark to see. He reached into the blackness and fumbled around until he felt the frozen fawn carcass through his handwear. He dragged the animal out by the neck, contorting his features when his chest again tightened.

"This is what we came for," he said, patting the fawn, hunched over and coughing. He removed the fire pouch from his shoulder-pack and opened it. The embers inside still glowed faintly. "Help me gather wood," he said.

They collected branches from the snows, digging to find ones that had fallen long ago, for any breaks from the storm would be too fresh to ignite quickly. After gathering enough wood, the man mounted the branches in a wedge-shaped formation and filled the cavities between them with thistles and twigs. He placed the embers into the kindling and blew until the first signs of fire appeared, the dark green needles snapping when the flames spread upwards. The fire seethed and crackled and jettisoned pricks of yellow light that flared out at the apogees of their crooked arcs.

"Stand behind me," the man said, tasting the smoke and salivating. "Needle smoke is cruel to the eyes."

Even an obsidian blade could not pierce flesh frozen all the way through. So, once the brushwood produced the orange glow of a settled hearth, the man dragged the fawn beside the flames to thaw. He lifted the carcass so its belly faced the fire, the wind blowing heat against it.

They removed their handwear and held their open palms over the flames. Blood returned to their fingers in a slow burn while they waited. After some time, the man touched the fawn's midsection, which had finally begun to soften. He unsheathed his blade and cut a line from throat to groin, peeling off the skin and reaching with bare hands elbow-deep to pull out the innards. After tossing them aside into a reeking pile of beige and grey, he dragged the rest of the carcass upwind. He carved out a hunk of loin and skewered the meat, held it over the fire until it browned, then cut off a piece and handed it to the boy.

The boy reached for the foodstuff, but then dropped his hand to his side.

"What's wrong?"

The boy shook his head.

"You need to eat. That's why we came here. We don't know when our next chance will be."

The boy again shook his head, this time more adamantly. "Killing baby curse man," he said, pointing at the fawn.

The man snickered. "That's not true. Who told you that?"

"It is known," the boy said, crossing his arms.

"Baby animals are the easiest to kill, if their mother isn't near. We used to target them when foodbringing." The man exhaled, glancing sunward, back to the lands he had once called home. He would probably never see those lands again.

"Killing baby curse man," the boy repeated.

He shook his head. "I've spent the last two sistersuns *saving* a baby. And now I have you. The Gods, wherever they are, will forgive us." He held out the meat again. "Eat. You will be fine."

The boy stared back without responding.

The man shrugged and took the meat himself, warm juices trickling onto his chin as he chewed. The fawn was surprisingly fresh, considering he had killed it the day before. He wiped his mouth and cut off another piece and tried again to give it to the boy.

"See? I'm still here," the man said. "Nothing happened to me. You can eat the meat."

The boy looked away.

"Eat," the man said, shaking the meat at the boy and pleading. "Eat so that we may live."

PART I:
THE FORCE
OF THE SCREAM

1

Ascend

F ALON COULDN'T REMEMBER the last time he had seen the sun.
It has gone forever, some said.
Vul-ka has finally forsaken us, said others.

For someone so unseasoned as Falon, truths were hard to tell
from distortions. He only knew what he saw with his own eyes: the
cycle of light continuing even as the darkness went on. For ages,
the daylight had been cloaked behind the grey waste of the sky, its
unbroken clouds choking the world like it was buried alive. What
once had been a rising and setting sun now ushered in but gradients
of gloom and rain. Yet, here in the downpour was Falon, watching
the aurochs graze upon the steppe, gorging themselves on mud-
soaked grasses while the sky spilled from above like a cataract.

So strange a sight this was, the animals drenched in the field instead of hiding beneath the canopy. But the aurochs knew—
somehow, they knew—the days of sustenance were soon to turn.

A scout had spotted the herd, and the foodbringers were in
position. Felling an aurochs was no small feat; one alone bore the
strength of many men and, over the generations, countless had
suffered mortal wounds in the chase. But still, the *nander* needed

to feed. They needed foodstuff for their families, bones for building and tools, fur for the frozen horror that came with darker purpose when the time of the low sun loomed.

Falon wiped the rain out of his eyes. "We shouldn't be out here," he shouted over the wind.

"We must take the food when it comes," Ber-gul called back. "Which one is weakest?"

"Not the bull whose snout is in the furrow."

"No, not him."

Falon repositioned himself on the ground, mud squishing beneath his knees. "What about that older cow in the back?"

"Her horns are too small." Ber-gul pointed at the largest bull in the herd. "What about him?"

Falon turned to Ber-gul. Surely, he could not be serious. "It looks like it will kill us."

"His stripe is faded. He is old."

Maybe Ber-gul *was* serious. "He looks strong to me," Falon said. "We should kill the cow."

Ber-gul stopped to consider, but then shook his head and stood. Brown clumps of silt dribbled off his bearskin tunic, only to be washed away by the rain. "I made my decision," he said.

Falon was in no position to override Ber-gul, his elder by many hands. While Falon wore a simple weaved-hair necklace, Ber-gul's was full of teeth collected from a lifetime of foodbringing. He was the Kurnisahn's firstmover; he had the aim to hit his target and the strength to impair its flight. Still, as was his way, Falon couldn't resist pushing a little more.

"Are you sure the herd will run to the flowing water? They're facing the wrong way."

"They always run to the water. Now be quiet."

Ber-gul brushed his dripping hair from the ridge in his brow and crept across the plain, his footwear sinking into the mud with every step, sheets of rain pounding his arms and face. Although it was bad luck, no facepaints had been applied this day, for they would have washed away long before the hunt began.

From his waist strap, Ber-gul drew a throwaxe—hilt of bone and shining black obsidian blade—and raised the weapon. The aurochs glanced up warily for a moment before lowering its head back to the greenery. It saw Ber-gul as a man alone, and nander were only a threat when they were many.

Ber-gul stopped a few paces from the aurochs, aimed his throwaxe, and hurled it at the animal. The weapon whipped through the air and struck the back of its knee with the thwack of blade on bone, tearing through hide and tendon alike. The bull stumbled forward and bellowed, a froth of cud and spittle driveling off its chin, the ejecta disgorged by the force of the scream. Alerted by the noise, the herd raised their heads, dark green stalks of grass hanging half-chewed from their mouths. Then, as if called by the want of a collective mind, the herd turned and raced toward the water in synchronized flight, exactly as Ber-gul had predicted. The wounded aurochs toiled behind, desperate to keep pace with its brethren. It snorted and groaned across the rolling plain, the throwaxe dangling from its joint and falling to the ground.

Ber-gul picked up his weapon. Sharper than stone, obsidian was scarce and greatly valued by the Kurnisahn. There was no source of the material other than the j'Lok: the coldland traders who so seldom came through Kurnisahn lands to barter their goods.

Soon, the herd arrived at the shore, the swollen waters splashing skyward, mixing spray with rain. Each aurochs slowed before advancing uncertainly into the rapids. Unable to fight the current, barely able to stand amidst the spate, the animals were drawn under, their legs bashing against the rocks before washing away with the torrent, their eyes wide and panicked when dipping below the surface. They twisted and shrieked and kicked and flailed, bobbing in the whitecaps and purging in terror before disappearing downstream. Not one, it seemed, reached the other side.

A hand of men watched the catastrophe unfold from the waterside, powerless to halt the devastation. Not only would the tribe go hungry tonight, but the entire herd would now be lost forever. But then, at the very moment of the clan's surrender, Bergul's aurochs limped over the hill like a shadow in the colorless scud, its hind leg dragging and mangled from running on a severed knee. It hobbled down the slope and halted when it saw the men, looking side to side to assess the challenge before it. The bull pointed its horns and pawed the mud and tossed its head, then took two steps forward.

"Now, before it goes into the water!" Ao, the eldest of the Kurnisahn, said.

The foodbringers closed in, Ao racing ahead of the others, rain cascading off his shoulders like he'd crawled out of the sea. He gripped his spear with both hands and plunged it deep into the aurochs' neck, twisting the blade after breaking skin. The bull lurched sideways, ripping the haft from Ao's clutches, then rammed its horns into his chest, driving him to the ground. The creature thrashed and bucked in the lateral rain, the spitted weapon swinging from its neck, its hooves bludgeoning Ao before he could roll away.

The other men hurried forth, weapons held high, dodging the beast's horns as it lunged haphazardly at them. They took turns thrusting their spearheads into its ribs, its abdomen, its rear. Finally, Menok brandished a dagger and dove forward, slicing its already injured leg. Crimson sprayed through the rain. The aurochs screamed. It writhed forward, battling to reach the water's edge, its knees collapsing beneath it, its snout and eyes splattering into the muck.

The assault continued, on and on it went, the bull retching and shitting, grunts of rage becoming high pitched cries of pain. By the time Ber-gul and Falon arrived, the perforated carcass was matted and caked with blood, the aurochs no longer breathing. Beside it lay the wounded Ao, staring at the grey sky, his face contorted and his breathing tense. One of his legs was buckled above the knee, bent in a way no bone was ever meant to bend.

"Father, what happened?" Falon said, running to his side.

"The aurochs… I've been trampled." Ao coughed before trailing off and closing his eyes.

"Father?"

A hand gripped Falon's shoulder from behind. "Stand back," Menok said. In his brother's absence, it was he who led the food-bringers today. He knelt beside Ao, wiping his blade with a rabbit pelt. "He fought like a man," he said to Falon, "but this is the price of a hunt."

Falon felt the blood drain from his face. Overhead, the downpour had turned into a lingering drizzle.

"We must bring him to the shaman," Menok continued, "for only he will know if Ao can be saved."

Even then, Falon knew what was to come. He watched his father drift in and out of consciousness, dreading what harm he might have suffered past that which could be seen. There were many organs in a nander body, but few whose roles were known.

"Kurnisahn," Menok said, addressing the group, "direct your ears to me." He rose to his feet. "We are far from the living-place, and there is much to do. We must skin and gut the aurochs before it cools."

Menok looked around, assessing his men.

"Ber-gul, you stay here to lead the cuttings. We must bring the aurochs to the living-place before dark. Falon and Suht will help me carry Ao to the shaman."

Falon and Suht sat Ao up and draped his arms over their shoulders, but even the slightest motion provoked a painful cry.

"He cannot be moved," Menok said. "Falon, wait here with your father. I will fetch the shaman and the Somm from the living-place."

Falon stayed beside his father, holding his hand, begging him to stay awake and not fade away. He spoke of all the things his father had taught him—how to spear a fish, how to skin an animal, how to count, even how to speak. His father would moan, his eyes would flutter; it seemed he could barely hear him through the fog. It wasn't clear how much time had passed before Ber-gul interrupted him.

"Are you going to help, Scarboy, or just sit there?" Ber-gul said.

Falon turned. How he hated being called that.

"Let him be," said Suht, Ber-gul's son.

"I'll let him be when he starts to help. Our hands are slick with blood, our furs soiled with grease. Yet, he sits there clean, doing nothing."

Falon couldn't believe this man's disrespect. If ever there was a time for compassion, it was now. He put down his father's hand and stood, a move that perhaps seemed more aggressive than he'd intended. Ber-gul strode toward him until he stood a breath away, and Falon turned his gaze downward, knowing he'd be beaten if they came to blows. Ber-gul was a man fully grown while Falon still had the slender body of a boy.

"My father is wounded. I—" Falon said.

"You know how this will end," Ber-gul interrupted.

"Well, the shaman might—"

"The shaman cannot save him. Sharpen your blade. It is you who will be cutting. Vul-ka will insist."

"You're not the shaman."

Ber-gul drew his face closer, their noses touching. "You will help us now. We are cold and wet, and we want to go home. There is nothing more you can do for your father."

Falon breathed deep and looked down at his unconscious father. Ber-gul lifted Falon's chin, forcing him to look into his eyes.

"I said now."

Skinning the beast took time, even with many men contributing to the efforts. After removing its head, tail, and legs, they slit the belly clean. This allowed the men to clear out its entrails and peel back its skin from a single place to keep its hide intact. They had just finished the job when the grey-bearded shaman, carrying his coarseoak walking stick and wearing a full array of black beads, emerged from the forest with Menok.

Falon stood. "Where's Somm Ul-man?"

"Few men are left to protect the living-place," Menok said. "Most of us are here."

The shaman walked directly to the fallen man, not bothering to acknowledge Falon. "Ao? Are you awake?" He knelt beside him and patted his cheek.

Ao groaned.

"Where is the pain, other than your leg?"

"Hard to…breathe…"

"Help me take off his furs," the shaman said.

Falon did as instructed, revealing a dark purple bruise where a cracked rib jabbed into his father's breastbone.

The shaman pressed his ear to Ao's chest and closed his eyes to listen. "One of his air pouches is torn."

A torn air pouch meant only one thing. As Falon wiped the trickles off his cheeks, Ber-gul's disapproval of his weakness was practically tangible.

The shaman looked up, turning slowly as he peered into the grey. "The sistersun is not yet sharpened, even if it hides behind the clouds," he said to himself, before looking back down to Ao. "But his injuries will not wait. He can't walk and, soon, he will be unable to breathe." He put his hand on Falon's shoulder. "How ready is your blade?"

Falon unsheathed his stone dagger, still stained by the blood of the beast that had trampled his father.

The shaman stroked his beard. "That will do."

"An obsidian blade will be cleaner. I can use my father's."

"You must use your own blade."

Falon nodded thinly as the others gathered around their wounded kin.

"Our custom is to light fires around the fallen," the shaman said, raising his voice so everyone could hear over the roaring waters behind him. "But the grounds are wet; we'll find no firewood today. Since Ao was wounded while foodbringing, we will spill the blood of the hunted around him." The shaman pointed to the aurochs carcass. "So begins the ascension."

Ascension.

The word Falon feared the shaman would say. Until a few generations ago, the stories said, the Kurnisahn had been wanderers. They, along with two other clans, found a food source in the low-rock valley, allowing what were now neighboring tribes to discard their traveling ways. But relics from their nomadic past still stuck with the Kurnisahn. One such artifact was the custom of ascension—when a nander reached an older age and could no longer keep up with the clan, their spirit was released from their body so it could return to the s'Sah, the lifeblood of the very narrowland itself, the energy that imbued all living things. Instead of being left behind to suffer a fate of nature's choosing, the relative closest to the ailing nander would offer a mercy killing. An old, slow nander would otherwise concede to a darker fate—at best, starvation; at worst, eaten alive by valleycats or howlers.

The men responded to the shaman by carrying over a fist-sized chunk of meat that dribbled pink—blood mixed with rain. They squeezed out the juices around the dying man.

"We have before us bloodstains—symbols of Vul-ka—the sun, the lord of blood and flame," the shaman said. "May his warmth keep Gigas cast down in the belly of the narrowland. Ao's spirit must now flow from his body and return to the s'Sah, where he will remain until the High Ones descend upon us at the end of time."

The mention of the High Ones sent a wave of uneasiness through the men. Although little was known about these fabled beings, legends described them as a harrowing otherness that would one day break the world. The lore of endtimes was passed down from generation to generation, and the mysterious High Ones were somehow present at the end of every tale.

"Falon, you must now send your father to the forever-sleep," the shaman said.

Falon straddled his father's abdomen, drawing forth his blade with a trembling hand. Ao opened his eyes and looked up at his son. "Wait. Not yet…"

Falon looked to the shaman, hoping they could take a different path, but the shaman shook his head.

"But I… still breathe…" Ao said, coughing and gasping, hardly able to form his words. "I will heal… from this. I can still… twist stringrass… build a fire."

Falon turned again to the shaman. "Perhaps it is not yet time?"

"When a man can no longer give to his tribe, his spirit must return to the s'Sah," the shaman said, speaking to Falon as if his father wasn't there. "He is an old man—aged many hands—it is a blessing he was not injured long ago. The ascension must go on."

Falon held out his blade.

"Son, please wait…"

The rain began again, splashing in the bloodstains.

"If there is a reason to save this man's life, Vul-ka, send us a signal now. Tell us to spare his mortal form," the shaman said, looking to the sky.

Silence. The Gods never intervened.

The shaman lowered his chin, his hooded eyes settling on Falon. "Draw the sharpened sistersun across his throat," he said, these oft-repeated words marking the last step of ascension.

Falon's heart pounded as he watched his father's features distort into a panicked horror. Ao tried to sit up, a shrill coming from deep in his throat as he struggled to push him off and get away. Falon's instinct was to let him rise, but Menok held his shoulders down. Ber-gul picked up an arms-length coarseoak branch and handed one end to Menok, and together they laid it across Ao's torso to restrain him. Ao gasped as they pressed the wood onto his broken chest.

"Do it now," Menok said.

Falon had always known this day would come—if not by disease or killing, most nander went to the forever-sleep through ascension.

But not today.

It wasn't supposed to happen today.

"Draw the sharpened sistersun across his throat," the shaman repeated, this time with urgency.

Again, he hesitated as his father squirmed beneath him, his face red with fear and pain as he fought to overcome his subduers.

"By the flames of Vul-ka, I'll do it," Ber-gul said, unsheathing his dagger.

With this, Falon knew the time had come, and when he pressed the blade into the side of his father's throat, crimson surged out in the shape of a crescent.

2

A Good Cut

A FTER DRAINING THE AUROCHS and removing its innards, it
still weighed as much as a small tree, so every man—even
the shaman—would be needed for the haul.

They dragged the animal atop a wooden plank and tied Ao to
the assembly, their bodies fastened together with stringrass
threads. The dead man's blood mixed with the beast's, dripping
from his open throat onto the skinless meat. The foodbringers
carried their spoils out of the steppe and into the forest, stale and
sticky after days of rain, the curdled scent of dead leaves and wet
soils filling the air around them. *unnecessary gore*

Somm Ul-man waited for his men at the entrance to the living-
place—two hands of burdei huts made from strawsod walls and
thatch-bound roofs. Now that the storm had passed, the women
were twisting stringrass and collecting branches to repair their
burdei. Stringrass was a cornerstone of nander tooling when something stronger than hair was needed. It was readily available in the
forests where it clung to the trees, and threads of fiber could be
peeled off and used for binding and sewing and fastening the roofs
of their homes.

Word of Ao's demise had spread, and the women trickled out to see what had been gained—and lost—that day. Every food-bringer was covered in red; the sign of a successful hunt—or battle. Approaching from the front was Falon, head cast down and complexion light as snow. The Somm cared not for the boy ever since he had defiled Una many seasons ago when both children had been nary two hands of age. While Falon had only kissed her, such an act was prohibited without permission from the father, and to this day, the boy wore a terrible scar as a reminder of his trespass. Yet Falon was persistent, still finding ways to speak to her, reasons to be near her. He was a scrawny boy, born of weak parents and stock, unfit for the company of the Somm's daughter. His friendship with Una simply could not be tolerated.

For the moment though, in light of Falon's father going to the forever-sleep, Somm Ul-man had to play the role of a caring leader —not to console Falon but to demonstrate his compassion to the rest of his tribe.

"A day comes in the life of every man when ascension must be faced," the Somm said, putting his open palm on the boy's chest. "We will not forget your father."

Falon let out a long breath with his eyes to the ground, and the Somm pulled back his hand, having done his duty. As he watched Falon walk away, his concerned expression was but a show; he really just wanted to make sure the boy didn't go running to his daughter. Once Falon had entered his burdei, the Somm looked to his own, where Una kneeled atop the roof, holding thatch stripped by the just-passed storm. She met her father's gaze with her sharp green eyes before continuing her work. The Somm did not like the way she looked at him, almost as if she could hear his very thoughts.

He turned his attention to Ao. "It was a good cut," he said, touching the dead man's throat with two fingers. He inspected

Ao's crushed leg and chest, shaking his head. "Prepare him for burial. He must be underground by sunset."

With that, he had fulfilled his leadership role and could now attend to the spoils of the hunt: an aurochs carcass glistening red in the afternoon gloom. It could not have come at a better time, for the clan had not eaten in three days.

"Cut meat for roasting," he said. "We will feast come darkness. Cook and salt the rest, then bury it. At dawn, we will bring some to Bhatt to trade before it spoils." He gripped the aurochs' horns to assess their strength; they were as impressive as he'd been told. Ber-gul targeting this bull had been understandable, even if unwise. The horns mustn't go to waste. "Core the horns before they fester. Now, show me the hide."

The foodbringers brought forth the aurochs hide, caked with drying blood and ravaged by the stabbing it had endured. The Somm poked a finger through one of its many holes. "The hide is ruined," he said, looking to each foodbringer for an explanation. The men turned to one another, no one wanting to be the first to speak.

"My brother," Menok finally said, "after the aurochs trampled Ao, we quickly brought it down so no one else was injured."

The Somm tried not to betray his annoyance, for a leader had to remain steadfast before his clan. "Prepare the hide for drying and tanning. Perhaps we can use it for footwear or handwear, or wrappings for our spears."

He dismissed his men, then headed to his burdei to assess the repairs. Una and his lifemate, the Istri Dam, were placing straw and leaves overtop the strawsod walls and fastening them with stringgrass threads. Una pressed the straw with exaggerated motions as though suppressing a tantrum, refusing to meet his eyes. Not yet three hands of age, she had become more defiant with each passing season.

"What bothers you?" the Somm asked, even though he already knew the answer.

She met eyes with him and turned away, barely acknowledging his question. Although fully flowered a few seasons ago, she still had the soft features of a girl. She was not a woman yet, no matter what their customs might be.

"Is it because of Ao?"

She climbed down from the roof and waved him off in a blatant show of disrespect. Had any of his men been present, he wouldn't have shown patience for her behavior.

"Do not worry. He will be buried today," he said, hoping to ease her discontent before he lost his temper.

She stepped to him. "And what about Falon?" she said, clenching a handful of straw. "He is now alone. He never knew his mother. His father was all he had."

He put his hand on her chest, his willpower focused on staying calm. "Falon is almost a man now, but a few seasons your elder. He will become strong from this. With his gift for aim, he will one day make a good foodbringer."

"You believe him weak, Father."

"Perhaps, with time, his strength will grow."

"Someone should be with him now," she said, stepping back so he no longer touched her.

The Somm felt his face reddening. "With his father in the forever-sleep, Falon's burdei is now his own. He needs time to make it so."

"No, he doesn't, he needs support."

"How do you know so much about what he needs?" the Somm demanded, raising his voice for the first time.

"Falon and I have been friends since we were children. There are too few of us in Kurnisahn to choose our friends."

"And friends are all you will ever be," the Somm said, this time loud enough for the entire living-place to hear. He could feel the fiery humors coursing through his veins. "You are not to be alone with the boy. If he needs company, it will not be you."

She chucked the stringgrass into the mud, her auburn hair bouncing as she stormed away. He watched her closely to be certain she didn't enter Ao's—now Falon's—burdei.

FALON CURLED IN THE CORNER of his burdei, his forehead pressed against his knees, replaying in his mind the chaos of his father's final moments.

The mud-coated coarseoak branch Menok and Ber-gul had used to hold his father down must have felt cold against his skin. His father's tearful expression, as Falon pressed down the blade, burned an image in his mind like he'd been staring at the sun. Beneath him, he'd felt his father's chest heaving, slowing, and at last becoming still. He turned away from Falon and looked into the distance before closing his eyes in that final instant.

Falon forgot to even say goodbye.

No one could survive long with a ruptured air pouch. And yet, his father had wanted to live, his desperation palpable as he fought to delay the inevitable. He battled until his last breath, not unlike the aurochs just moments before. Maybe there wasn't such a difference between man and beast, though men understood the forever-sleep in ways a beast never could.

Falon's numbness choked him like a wet skin as he grieved alone in the darkness. If only Ber-gul had listened to him and gone after the smaller aurochs, none of this might have happened, and Falon would still have a father from whom to learn. Now, only one nander remained in all the narrowland who would comfort him or pay him any heed. But Una was forbidden. Her father had made that clear many seasons ago after opening Falon's face with the crack of his staff. It would take the world breaking to bring them back together.

3

Obsidian

USK HAD FALLEN by the time the Kurnisahn brought Ao to the thuk-tree where his lifemate was buried. A few women stood to the side while the men dug a trench with their hands, the turned dirt releasing the hearty scent of a fresh cut grave. The rest of the tribe remained in the living-place to prepare the aurochs, care for the young, and finish repairing from the storm.

The men lowered Ao into the hollow and piled the dirt—mostly mud now on account of the rain—over his body. The burial would allow his spirit to return to the s'Sah; help his lifeblood steep into the soils and roots of the narrowland and later to the plants and animals living upon it. With Ao now below ground, Falon and the Somm built a knee-high cairn out of water stones to mark the gravesite, completing the ritual. A simple ceremony indeed, the forever-sleep came all too often for the nander, and one could not dwell long on those who'd passed.

When the mourners turned to leave the burial, a stick snapped somewhere near. Somm Ul-man stopped and raised his hand, signaling to be alert for further sounds. Prepared to take no chances, every man unsheathed their blade, for someone—or some*thing*—was approaching.

The Somm had enough men with him that threats from animals were of little concern compared to the danger posed by another group of men. The tribes of the lowrock valley—the Kurnisahn, Bhatt, and Ser-o—had warred for many generations; lifetimes of retribution and blood atonement had endured until at last a truce ushered in an era of peace. To prevent further bloodshed, the tribes had begun inter-bonding—one Somm's child to another's, one high-placed cousin to another's, and so on. Into the fog of time rode most of the actors who'd played a role in this epic struggle of gamesmanship, violence, and folly, and today what remained was an uneasy truce between three tribes who didn't entirely trust—or respect—one another.

Yet, because of the inter-bonding, there was little to fear from the other two tribes; any attack would effectively be against their own kin. There was, however, another group of nander—a much larger and more powerful group—who seemed to flex more strength with each passing season: the j'Lok.

Deep in the coldlands was the living-place of j'Lok (if "living-place" was an adequate term to describe such an enormous congregation of nander). Its origin was unclear and known only from tales; the story the Somm had heard was that it had been founded a few generations ago when many clans united over the black channels in the mountains. These channels were filled with obsidian—that rare rock of the narrowland that was sharper, deadlier, cut better and cut cleaner than any other material. There was no source of obsidian other than these mines, and the j'Lok used their exclusive access as a tool to subjugate the neighboring tribes.

There were also rumors that other clans, even farther away than j'Lok, had been brought in by force or enslaved. It seemed only a matter of time before the j'Lok directed their attention sunward and sought more than barter from the Kurnisahn, who already allotted much of their surplus for when the j'Lok passed through with obsidian to trade.

It was with this in mind that the Somm saw in the dusk light three shadows approaching from the underwood deep. These figures, clearly men, proceeded slowly and, although armed, had not unsheathed their blades. They displayed no markings of any known tribe and appeared worn from lengthy travels—their faces marked with dirt, their hair matted against their scalps, their torsos clad in rust-colored pachydon coats. The man in the center, whom the others seemed to follow, had a crater where an eye might once have been, its fleshy scar textured like a rotten spider. His two companions, bearing stone-tipped spears across their backs, were taller than the one-eyed man and stood as if guarding him.

"Our apologies," the one-eyed man said, revealing a mouth with fewer teeth than most. "We did not want to disturb the burial."

"Thank you for your respect. To whom do I speak?" the Somm asked as the Kurnisahn women took cover behind their men. The newcomers did not appear hostile, but still, they were not known.

"We are simple traders from j'Lok," the man said hurriedly as if to assure they meant to harm. His nascent smile, however, betrayed amusement at the Kurnisahn's defensive posture. "We come from the coldlands with obsidian to trade. My name is o'Fik, and we offer two grassrabbits before any dealings."

The Somm did not recognize the man's strange accent, nor had he ever known anyone from j'Lok to describe themselves as simple. Yet, the newcomer was respectful, so he had to respond in kind.

"I am Somm Ul-man of the Kurnisahn, and this is my tribe. We will share a meal with you, and we thank you for your offering. But you may keep your grassrabbits, for today we hunted an aurochs and offer some to you instead."

"Aurochs is a rare treat," o'Fik said. "We seldom see them in the high hills near j'Lok."

Somm Ul-man met eyes with Menok. The brothers had often spoken about the threat of the j'Lok, but the coldlanders had thus far only ventured sunward seeking trade. It seemed this was not unlike previous visits—assuming these men were actually from j'Lok. But they had no piercings, and j'Lok men always had both brows pierced with wooden pins. And two of the men carried stone weapons; never before had the Somm seen a j'Lok trader armed with anything but obsidian.

"I must ask why you bear no markings of the j'Lok," he said, returning his gaze to o'Fik.

"Our travels have been difficult," o'Fik said after a pause that suggested he wasn't ready for the question. "Just today, our feather headbands were taken by the rain."

The Somm nodded, even though o'Fik's unconvincing response explained only one peculiarity among many. "It was a terrible storm indeed," he agreed, making eye contact once more with his brother. Menok didn't seem to believe their story either, but they'd have to wait until the traders were comfortable and their guard was down before probing any further. He gauged the readiness of his tribesmen, all of whom remained guarded. It seemed safe to offer hospitality to the traders since they were heavily outnumbered by wary men. "So it is then. We invite you into our living-place. After our meal, we can discuss your trades."

THE TOTAL DARKNESS OF THE NIGHT had arrived before the nander returned to Kurnisahn, forcing them to navigate the forest by dead reckoning. No matter though, they had traveled these woods countless times before and knew the whereabouts of every stone and hill and tree. As they approached the living-place, its amber glow swelled behind tree trunk silhouettes and twisted branches. The Somm was pleased that the women had taken the initiative of refiring the hearths—particularly the large central bonfire—for it helped guide the way during the final stretches of their journey. There was something unnatural about all this light; the power of fire perhaps never meant to be harnessed by denizens of the narrowland, for no forest dwellers but nander ever drew a flame.

The Kurnisahn hacked chops of meat from the aurochs' hindquarters and heated them over the central fire, then gathered to roast and eat the game. The evening's fare was brought to the women and children in their burdei, where they'd retreated upon arrival of the unmarked men, knowing not who they were or from whence they came.

"Where were you before coming here?" the Somm asked o'Fik once everyone had settled.

"We did not mean to come this far sunward. First, we went to Bhatt, but no one was there."

"Are you sure you went to the right place?"

o'Fik finished chewing his meat, then looked at the Somm with his head canted toward the missing eye as if compensating for its absence. "We were in the right place. Up the flowing waters, a hand of days darkward. But they're not like you, not organized. And they live in caves."

"Their caves are simpler but of sounder build than the strawsod burdei made by the Kurnisahn and Ser-o. If we had caves in this part of the forest, we would use them too."

"Well, their caves were empty. It seems they left in haste."

"Were they attacked?"

o'Fik bit into his meat and looked at one of his companions while chewing. "Not in their living-place," he said with a mouth full of gristle.

The Somm raised his eyebrows to urge him on.

o'Fik took his time chewing before he swallowed. "Their living-place was empty," he said, licking his fingers between words. "If they were attacked in Bhatt, we would've found bodies. But there were no bodies, only empty caves."

"So, you came here?"

"Not at first. We could see they had not been gone long, and it wasn't hard to figure out which way a group that big went. They were heading toward you." o'Fik pointed in a sweeping motion at several of the Kurnisahn, including the Somm. "But then they turned sunward."

"Into the Sketen?"

"We do not know it by that name. It's the path to Ser-o. The only way through the mountains."

"We call that the Sketen. So, the whole tribe went to Ser-o?"

o'Fik nodded. "Again, it seemed they left in haste. Maybe they fled something—but what? What is to be feared in the lowrock valley?"

The Somm shrugged.

"Well, whatever was chasing them caught up."

"Meaning?" the Somm said, leaning in.

"We found their bodies a half day into the pass. And whoever—or *whatever*—killed them took their ears."

The Somm had never heard of such a practice. "Took their ears?" he said.

"But an ear remained on each of the slain. Some had none. And the killers didn't cut cleanly either."

"Were the women killed too?"

"Some, but their bodies were few," o'Fik said, looking away as if pondering what he had seen. "Whoever killed the Bhatt took their women—all the young ones, anyway."

The Somm looked around the fire to assess his men. They were both captivated and horrified by o'Fik's story. "Tell me more about this killing," he said.

"It made little sense. At first, we thought the Bhatt were attacked by howlers. But when we drew closer, we saw the slain had been stabbed by these." He pulled out a straight stick the length of a man's arm and handed it to the Somm. The object's keen obsidian tip had been fastened to the shaft by hardened tree sap, similar in composition to the baked birch tar used by the Kurnisahn for spear tips. Opposite the obsidian were three evenly spaced feathers tied by some sort of sinew, and a shallow crevice had been carved along the very edge of the stem.

"What type of weapon is this?" the Somm asked o'Fik while handing it to his brother.

"We had never seen anything like it."

"How can this even be wielded? It's too thin and would break in combat or foodbringing."

"From the way they were sticking out of the bodies, they look to be made for thrusting." o'Fik demonstrated with a dramatic stabbing motion, as if the Somm knew nothing of wielding weapons.

"How?" the Somm asked, trying to conceal his annoyance at such an unhelpful display. "The wood would snap before breaking flesh."

"And yet, they had been stabbed with them many times. Some had it in their legs, in their shoulders. Others in their arms or in their stomachs."

The Somm took the weapon back from his brother. "Why didn't the killers collect their weapons?"

"Maybe they fled when the howlers came. Most of the bodies had bite marks; some were missing limbs."

"Maybe a pack found them after the killing."

"No way to know. The howlers left before we arrived. But there were plenty of carrion birds feasting on the bodies." o'Fik paused, holding back a smirk. "They go for the eyes first, you know."

The Somm did not appreciate that unnecessary last detail. He glared at the trader while handing back the strange weapon.

"Can I see it?" Falon asked out of nowhere. The Somm waved off the discourteous boy.

"No, wait. I think I know what it's for."

The Somm wanted to smack Falon, but it would've been poor form considering the boy had just buried his father. Plus, he was curious what he was thinking. Falon could be clever, even if the Somm hated to admit it.

Falon rubbed the wooden shaft before touching the obsidian tip. "It's not made for thrusting. It's made for throwing."

"Throw it how?" Menok asked.

Falon lifted the weapon over his shoulder, aimed at the side of a burdei, and hurled it like a spear. It pierced the strawsod halfway down its shaft before stopping.

"Strawsod and flesh are not the same," the Somm said. "Be seated."

"It's sharp enough to break flesh—if you could find a way to throw it faster."

"That's enough. Be seated, I say." The Somm returned his attention to the traders. "I am sorry for that outburst. The boy should not have spoken."

"It seems it was not the first time he's interrupted his betters," o'Fik said, motioning across his face in reference to Falon's scar.

"Says the man with one eye," the boy countered.

"That's enough! Be seated and do not speak again." The Somm took a breath before turning once more to the trader. "Again, my apologies."

o'Fik grinned without responding.

The Somm gathered himself, veiling his frustration at that fool of a boy. "It is with great sadness I hear your tale of the Bhatt. They share blood with many members of my tribe."

"Yes, it is sad that such a thing could happen," o'Fik said. "But it led us here, to you. If it is alright, we will now speak about why we came: the obsidian." o'Fik lifted his shoulderpack to expose two shiny black stones, each larger than a nander skull. The stones were not cut or shaped, almost as if they'd been ripped from the depths of the narrowland itself. "This is our offer," the one-eyed man said, rolling the stones before the Somm.

"What are we supposed to do with these?" the Somm asked. "They are but blocks of stone."

o'Fik slipped another smile from the corners of his lips. "They are not just blocks of stone. They are raw obsidian."

The Kurnisahn had never seen obsidian in its raw form; they had only seen it already shaped. The Somm raised one of the stones with both hands, using all his strength to lift it, the firelight reflecting off every groove on its surface. "Yes, this is obsidian," he said. "But why bring it to us without first shaping it into weapons or tools?"

"Stone and flint can shape obsidian, and you have plenty of both. What is raw can be shaped to your liking."

Such a stockpile of obsidian was tempting, but many questions first needed to be addressed. Between their sordid appearance and dubious origin, little made sense about these men, and the Somm wanted to hear Menok's perspective before proceeding further. It was seldom he needed his brother's counsel, but the stakes were high given the trader's violent tale, and Menok's ability to judge men was by far the best in the clan. Stepping away abruptly to speak with Menok might draw the traders' attention, but still seemed the safest way forward.

The Somm placed the block on the ground. "We will return in a moment," he said, motioning for Menok to follow him away from the fire.

Both Una and the Istri Dam were sitting cross-legged on the dirt floor of the burdei when the brothers entered. They stood to leave; it was not their place to become involved in the dealings of men. But he held up a hand to direct them to remain seated. He did not want to parade his lifemate and daughter in front of those unseemly men.

"Do you believe their tale of the Bhatt?" the Somm asked.

Menok nodded.

"But why were the Bhatt in the Sketen? A few men might go to Ser-o, but not the whole tribe. Not the women and children."

"It does not make sense, yet I sensed no lies in that tale."

"Nor did I. It sounds like the Bhatt were attacked by nander. They killed the men and took the women."

"But who would do such a thing? The Ser-o?"

"The Ser-o would not have cut off their ears." A heaviness was building in the Somm's stomach. "And why would the Ser-o strike in the Sketen? There's no bad blood between the two tribes. Not bad enough for this."

"And that strange weapon seems like a toy you'd give a boy to train," Menok added.

"Yet they say the Bhatt were slain with it." He tapped a finger against his bottom lip. "What if the fool Falon is right and it's meant to be thrown? Who could throw it fast enough to kill a man?"

"Carn?"

"This is not the time for jokes," he said, glaring at his brother. "Anyway, I don't believe these men are from j'Lok."

"No, they are probably clanless. But they have obsidian—in raw form. What if it's stolen?"

"Then the j'Lok might be following these men. We don't want to be carrying stolen obsidian if they come our way."

"But we can't ignore this much obsidian when it so seldom comes through our lands."

"It is worth the risk," the Somm said, unsure if his words were true. "But could it have been the j'Lok who killed the Bhatt?"

"It could have been them, but then they sent these men to what, warn us? I am not so sure." Menok paused, thinking. "We need to be watchful. There is a threat in the lowrock valley. We should send scouts into the Sketen to see for ourselves."

"I'll send Ber-gul and Suht in the morning." The Somm leaned in to whisper in his brother's ear, not wanting Una, in particular, to hear what he was about to say. "Or maybe I'll send Falon."

"Finally, there will be a use for him," Menok whispered back.

"Well then," the Somm said, pulling away from his brother's ear and returning to normal volume. "Those men wait. What should we do about the obsidian?"

"If it's stolen, maybe we can get it cheap. They won't bargain long if they are fleeing something. They'll collect what they can and be on their way. Carrying those blocks must be tiresome."

"Either way, I want these men out of our living-place as fast as possible without being indecent toward them. Maybe we will find a use for that aurochs hide after all. Let's see if they take it for the obsidian."

The Somm followed his brother out of the burdei, glancing at his lifemate and daughter as he exited. Although they exchanged no words, the Somm's message was clear: they were not to speak of what they'd heard between the brothers. His lifemate could be trusted, for she was the Istri Dam—the leader of the women. A Somm had to put trust in the woman who bore his children and nurtured them into adulthood. But Una was less predictable; it was she who might betray his trust by telling that boy whom she insisted on befriending.

The traders waited fireside with the Kurnisahn. o'Fik was rolling one of the stones back and forth with his foot, and his companions paced with nervous energy.

Menok motioned for a few of his men to set off with him as the Somm addressed the traders. "We accept your offer. My men are bringing a fresh aurochs hide to trade for the obsidian."

"The hide of the one we just ate?" o'Fik said, pointing at the hearth. "That was killed only today."

"That is our offer."

o'Fik waved him off with a snicker. "We won't trade our obsidian for that."

"You would rather return to j'Lok with nothing?"

"We will take our wares to Ser-o," o'Fik said, rising to his feet.

"Ser-o is many sunrises away and past the site of the killing. Do you want to risk going back into the Sketen? The land must now be cursed from all the unburied bodies." As o'Fik considered this, Menok's men returned with the aurochs hide and set it on the ground before them. "This is the hide we offer," the Somm said.

o'Fik glared at the Somm as he knelt beside the hide, only drawing his eyes away after lifting it. He put a finger through one of the punctures. "This hide is untreated and full of holes. No trade."

"This is a good hide. It can be used for foot wrappings or weapon handles."

"Calling it a *good hide* doesn't make it so."

"Then you have two choices, it seems. Return to j'Lok with your obsidian or risk heading even further sunward to Ser-o."

"It will not be the first time j'Lok traders have gone to Ser-o," o'Fik said, tossing the hide into the dirt and standing.

"Let us find a compromise. Your grassrabbits are your only meats. We will add an aurochs leg to the trade. It's already been salted and cooked, and will aid you on your long trip back to the coldlands."

o'Fik walked over to the burdei where his strange weapon still spiked out of the strawsod. He yanked it out and returned to the fire to resume examining the hide. "The hide, an aurochs leg, and someone's hair. For that, we offer *one* block."

Hair was precious, for it was vital for weavings yet grew slowly. Nander were the only source of long hair, save perhaps the mane of a tarpan. o'Fik's offer was the perfect excuse for the Somm to raise his stakes in the trade. "If you want someone's hair, we need both blocks," he said.

"You might want both, but you'll only get one."

"We'll add two flint daggers, but we want both blocks."

o'Fik whispered something to his companions before turning once more to the Somm.

"Agreed."

"Then it is settled. Kurnisahn—wrap the hide and meat, and give these men two daggers of fit quality."

The Somm assessed his men's hair to see whose was long enough to be worthy of the trade. Both Suht and Falon had shoulder-length hair, but Falon's was thinner and thus less useful. "Suht, cut off Falon's hair," he said.

Falon appeared to take this as a personal slight even though the Somm's decision had been purely an objective one. Falon knelt in front of Suht who gripped his hair from the crest in his scalp and sliced it off lock by lock until less than a finger-length remained. He handed the bundle of hair to o'Fik.

"If you will allow, Somm Ul-man, we ask to stay until daybreak," o'Fik said, stuffing Falon's hair into his shoulderpack. "We are not familiar enough with these parts to travel in darkness."

The Somm did not want these men to stay any longer than they had to and would have sent them off if common decency had permitted it. But their caution was wise; traveling in darkness was wrought with peril, especially in unknown lands. "You may stay until dawn," he said. "But our burdei are small and barely enough for even our own. Instead, you may sleep by the central fire, and we will help you collect leaves and straw for beddings to stay dry."

That night, when Somm Ul-man retired to his beddings with his lifemate, his daughter but a step away, he pledged to himself that he'd stay alert, for he trusted not these men. As he lay awake, he rested a hand on one of the obsidian blocks he'd just acquired. And yet, he must have fallen asleep at some point, some passing moment of weakness, for when the dawn broke, the strangers were gone.

4

Envoys

T HEIR TRACKS LEAD down to the flowing water," Menok
said. "They left in the middle of the night."

The Somm curled his lip with unease. "It is as we thought;
those men flee something. Why else leave without warning?"

"And by ridding themselves of the obsidian, they lightened
their carryings."

The Somm crouched, felt the footprints. They were well-
defined; the traders couldn't be far. "We were right to be wary.
Maybe we should follow them."

"Why endanger ourselves? Let them be gone; those were hardened men."

"Hardened thieves, you mean."

"Their ore is now ours. We traded for it fairly before knowing it
was stolen."

The Somm rubbed his fingers together, watching the dirt blow
away. "We should send a party into the Sketen," he said, standing.
"Even if the grounds are cursed, I need to know what happened
there, and I want to hear it from my own men."

"Should I get Ber-gul and Suht?"

"And Falon." The Somm looked away, not wanting to admit he had a use for the boy, but then decided to explain. "He has the best sight in the clan. If there are dangers in the Sketen, he will sense them first, and—"

Something in the underwood rustled. Almost as if they had sprouted from the trees themselves, a hand of men marched into the living-place, each with an obsidian spear strapped to his back. These men were unmistakably j'Lok, unlike the ones who had passed through the night before. Feather bands adorned their sloped-back foreheads and wooden pins pierced each of their eyebrows. They were light of skin, with complexion paler than the Kurnisahn.

"Of what dangers do you speak?" asked one of the newcomers in a thick j'Lok accent. He stood in front of the others and carried himself as if he was their leader. The ridge in his brow was prominent, and his dark brown hair was pulled back in a ponytail that spiked up from the crest of his scalp. The blue pins in his brow signaled he was a man of distinction.

Somm Ul-man had to be careful. The j'Lok were a nander to be feared; they had the numbers, the resources, and the will to destroy any clan that refused to do their bidding. Hopefully, they hadn't heard too much of the Kurnisahn's speakings before appearing. Although the j'Lok had only ever sought trade from the Kurnisahn, that could quickly change if stolen obsidian was discovered, and it didn't seem a coincidence that these men arrived so shortly after the traders.

The Somm raised his hand in salute. "I am Somm Ul-man of the Kurnisahn, and this is my tribe. To whom do I speak?"

The blue-pinned man stepped forward. "I'll be the one asking questions."

This was a bold statement from someone outnumbered more than two times over. Yet, his manner suggested he was not to be reckoned with. The Somm was tempted to ask how the Kurnisahn could be of service, but instead locked eyes with the man, not wanting to appear weak before the newcomers or his tribe.

"We are from j'Lok, as I'm sure you can see," the blue-pinned man said, staring back, undeterred by the Somm's show of fortitude. "And we know who you lot are."

Quite an attitude this man had. If he was in pursuit of yesterday's traders, he might be short-tempered from the long trek sunward, trailing thieves who had managed to stay a step ahead the entire time. Instead of replying, the Somm again offered a stony glare, hoping this continued display of strength would force the man to get to the point.

"We seek three thieves who took obsidian from our mines and went sunward with the ore," the man said, loud enough for everyone to hear. "Do you know of these men?"

This was exactly what the Somm had feared when he traded with the strangers the night before. The Kurnisahn should have known—they *had* known, in fact—that they were trading with clanless men. But if the Somm admitted having the obsidian, the j'Lok would at best demand its return, an outcome he sought to avoid. How would he respond? He wished to consult his brother for a moment but lacked the leverage to break away with Menok as he had the night before. The best thing he could think of was to stall.

"You must be weary from your travels," the Somm said with open arms. "Perhaps we can warm aurochs meat for your men, or share the cho-berries and nuts we've gathered. Over our meal, we can discuss the reason for your visit and how we can help."

The man gave him a sideward glance, savvy to the delay tactic, nonetheless tempted by the offer. "Yes, we are weary. We have traveled for two sistersuns, and the weather has been cruel."

"Then please sit here around the central hearth. My brother Menok will rekindle the flame and prepare an aurochs leg for your men to share."

Menok held his hand out toward the fireside, inviting the men to be seated.

One of the j'Lok whispered in his leader's ear. They were clearly tempted by the aurochs, a delicacy they may never have had in j'Lok. The leader whispered something back before turning once more to the Somm. "We accept your offer. But you and I will speak while your men prepare the meat. We are tired and have no time to waste."

The Somm led the j'Lok man to a fallen coarseoak near the edge of the living-place. The man was strong, with a chiseled neck and broad shoulders, and close to the Somm in age. While they'd be evenly matched if they came to blows, a confrontation had to be avoided at all costs considering who this man appeared to represent.

The man sat on the log, and the Somm leaned against a large stone with level eyes to show respect but not deference. "To whom do I speak?" he asked again.

"I am Sakaq of the j'Lok, first of the Gerent's trust-group."

This was by far the highest-ranking j'Lok man ever to visit the lowrock valley. "It is with great pleasure that we welcome such a man to our living-place," the Somm said. But why would a man like Sakaq come all the way to the lowrock valley? It had to be more than just the pursuit of thieves.

Sakaq nodded impatiently. "We have much to discuss. But first, what can you tell me about the men we seek?"

"Three men came through our living-place yesterday. One was missing an eye, like so." The Somm covered his left eye. "They fled before dawn, and we found them gone before you arrived."

"Did they steal from you as well?"

"Not that we can tell," the Somm said, crossing his arms.

"But you let them stay here overnight?"

"We offered them warmth by our fire but not in our burdei."

"Why offer anything? Couldn't you tell they were clanless?"

"They were courteous and peaceful," the Somm said, realizing his arms were crossed, then uncrossing them. "We offered them shelter, and they were on their way."

"That's because they knew we were coming. They left under cover of darkness."

"Looking back, it seems suspicious, yes. We were surprised to find them gone come daybreak."

"And what trades took place during their stay?" Sakaq asked, leaning in.

"They did not come here to trade."

Sakaq narrowed his eyes. "Did they have obsidian?"

"Only a small obsidian weapon, but its purpose was unknown."

"Explain."

"It was about this long," the Somm said, extending his hands. "Thinner even than a smallfinger. We couldn't see how such a weapon might be used."

Sakaq glanced at the hearth, and the Somm followed his gaze. A few men were cleaning ashes to prepare a rekindled flame. One man carried a charred aurochs' bone out of the ashes and placed it to the side.

"Where did they find this weapon?" Sakaq asked, his eyes for some reason focused on the aurochs bone.

"A sad story these men had. The Bhatt had been slaughtered."

Sakaq's eyes darted back to the Somm.

"Yes, in the Sketen," the Somm said. "The men said they found the weapon at the site of the killing. It had been used in the attack."

"An attack by whom?"

"We don't know. It seems the Bhatt were going to Ser-o." The Somm paused; even after thinking about it all night, the story made little sense. Still, he had to offer an explanation to show he was in control of the situation. "Perhaps the Ser-o saw them coming and were defending themselves," he said, though the argument was unlikely.

Sakaq cocked his head. "Is this your reasoning or that of the thieves?"

"My own. But it is hard to imagine the Ser-o seeing an entire clan—including the women and children—as a threat," he admitted.

Sakaq looked to the ground. He opened his mouth as if about to express his own suspicions about the massacre, but then stopped himself and looked back at the Somm. "Was this strange weapon the only obsidian they had?"

"That is all we saw," the Somm said, hoping the lie went unnoticed.

Sakaq smirked, then walked over to the remnants of last night's fire. He lifted the blackened aurochs' bone. "Where's the hide? It should be stretched and drying."

So that was why Sakaq had taken note of the aurochs bone. How would the Somm explain the lack of hide? He couldn't admit having traded it; Sakaq was already distrustful of everything he said.

"We discarded the hide, for it was ruined," he said, joining Sakaq by the hearth. "It took too many slashes to take down the beast. One of our men was even killed in the hunt."

Sakaq stared at the bone, holding it in one hand and tapping it in the other, the black soot sticking to his palm. It seemed he wanted to believe the Somm but had his doubts.

"We buried him in front of the largest thuk-tree in the forest," the Somm said, hoping to relieve Sakaq's uncertainty. "I can take you there if you care to offer your respects."

"Why would I offer respects to a man I never knew?"

"To see that I speak true," the Somm said, hoping to sound impatient rather than concerned.

Sakaq nodded at the Somm's burdei. "That is your burdei, yes? I'd rather confirm your words by seeing if my obsidian is in there."

The Somm needed to come up with the perfect response, or the consequences would be severe. If he let Sakaq into his burdei, he would discover the obsidian and, with it, the Somm's falsehoods. What might happen then? While Sakaq's band was outnumbered, they represented a larger, far more powerful group—one that might be near. After all, who was it that had massacred the Bhatt? Again, he wished he could consult his brother, who stared at him with great concern from across the living-place.

"I have heard enough," he said. "We have been respectful, yet you speak with suspicion. No, you will not be allowed in my burdei. I suggest we start again. Let us speak as men while the others prepare the meal."

Sakaq stared at him deadpan as if he saw right through his objections. The Somm matched his gaze, and after a few breaths, Sakaq turned his head. "Let us resume our speakings," he said. The Somm followed him back to the log and sat across from him once more.

"I don't know what happened between you and the thieves," Sakaq said, "but we come to Kurnisahn seeking more than just those men."

"We have always been a friend to the j'Lok and will help in any way we can."

Although Sakaq hadn't smiled once, he somehow found a way to straighten his face even further. "The endtimes are upon us. The Gerent herself has said."

"That is a serious matter. What does the Gerent see in her visions to say such a thing?"

"The flowing waters in the coldlands have turned to stone. When the time of the high sun came this year, they did not turn back. Gigas swallows more of the waters each year. His cold has taken the land like a spell." Sakaq lowered his voice. "The legends, you know them as well as I. When the flowing waters turn to stone, the High Ones will rise from the belly of the narrowland to usher forth the end of the world."

The Somm tilted his head. "The waters here still flow."

"But every time the low sun comes, don't they remain stone for longer?"

"They do," he admitted, tapping his knee with his fingers.

"Soon, the waters of the narrowland will be no more. This means the coming of darkness. The arrival of the High Ones. Even fires will cease to burn. The Allseer herself has said so."

"The Kurnisahn do not believe in the visions of your Gerent."

"That will be your undoing," Sakaq said, pointing at him. "While you sunward clans play games with your aurochs and cho-berries, we're hunting pachydon in the snow, tearing obsidian from the narrowland, and preparing for war when the High Ones come."

"So, what do you want from us? It must be important if the Gerent sent the first of her trust-group."

"She sent her *entire* trust-group sunward. All three of us were sent to a sunward tribe with a party like my own."

This was a serious projection of power. The j'Lok had grown so numerous that they could send many hands of their strongest men on a voyage that might last an entire season.

"So the j'Lok are meeting with all three tribes," the Somm said. "The Bhatt, if the stories are true, were taken by the forever-sleep. What then do you offer to the Ser-o and to us?"

"An offer to pay tribute to the Gerent."

"With what?"

"Your men."

The Somm shook his head. "Not interested."

"We are building something great in j'Lok. Many tribes have joined us, but we need more men for the battle to come."

"How many do you suggest we send?"

"At least a hand—from both you and the Ser-o. More if the Bhatt are really gone."

"That's almost half my men," the Somm said, ready to put an end to this conversation.

"That's what she requires as tribute."

"And what is it—exactly—that my men will do in j'Lok?"

"Mine and shape obsidian."

The Somm stopped to consider this. "What do we get in return?" he said.

"We'll let your men send home two hands of obsidian tools of their choosing at each turning of the seasons."

The Somm almost had to laugh at the absurdity of this offer. "You take half our men and we receive so little in return? Why would we agree to that? Who would we have left to foodbring? To protect our living-place?"

"You don't have to endanger your clan. There is another way."

The Somm raised an eyebrow. "A way other than refusing?"

"You can send everyone."

"The *whole* clan?"

"Yes, lead your nander to j'Lok."

"And surrender our self-rule to your Gerent—to a woman?"

Sakaq glared at him. "Be careful with your words, the Gerent is the Allseer. She is our unquestioned leader."

"Yes, I know, forgive me. But what you ask is hard to accept. My tribe looks up to me, trusts me. We cannot just give up our self-rule."

"You won't give up anything. The Kurnisahn can still self-rule in j'Lok. You can live among us but answer only to yourselves."

This was hard to believe. If the Kurnisahn were to migrate into the coldlands, it would not be long before they were taking orders from the Gerent.

"And how will you support so many more nander?" the Somm asked, "Many who are women and children and unfit to foodbring or mine?"

"Our resources are many. One would think in the coldlands, in the mountains, it would be barren. But that isn't so. Strangely, it seems, because of the cold. More large game comes through our lands each season from even farther darkward. We have perfected the hunt of pachydon and tarpan, and our meat never spoils. A single pachydon can feed us for more than a sistersun. The women can attend to children as they always do. There are even nuts and roots for them to gather, at least in the valleys, in the time of the high sun, when the land is not covered by the white. The women can keep fires to melt snow, for the flowing waters are no more. Your best foodbringers can seek game. The rest, we will send into the mines. What we need most of all are workers for the mines."

"Why do you need so much obsidian?"

Sakaq raised his black blade so it stood vertically between his eyes. "To arm ourselves when the High Ones come," he said.

"This is what your Gerent sees?"

"It is," Sakaq said, lowering the blade and attaching it once more to his waist strap. "The end times are upon us. Do not doubt it. Join j'Lok, as the other tribes have done."

This was a critical moment. What would happen if the Somm refused? The Kurnisahn stood no chance against the might of the j'Lok. If Sakaq had told it true, and indeed the Gerent had sent many hands of men sunward, this alone was enough to take the Kurnisahn by force—to slaughter the men and inflict great indignities upon the women. While the Somm's first responsibility was to protect his daughter and the Istri Dam, he too had a duty to his clan.

His options were few. Sending men as tribute was not viable; it would leave Kurnisahn vulnerable and ill-prepared. In truth, he faced a simple choice: send everyone or refuse altogether. And what of the Ser-o? How had they responded?

The Somm didn't realize his brother had approached before he heard him speak. "What did the Ser-o say?" Menok asked, almost as if he'd heard his thoughts.

Sakaq looked at the Somm, unsure if he should feel slighted by this interruption. When the Somm stared back coolly, he answered. "We'll know within half a sistersun."

Somm Ul-man knew Somm Muro well. He was the leader of the Ser-o and had been bonded to Ber-gul's sister many seasons ago. The tie between their clans was strong. It was hard to imagine a man of Somm Muro's temperament surrendering to these extreme demands.

"I suppose we will," the Somm said, looking to his brother. Menok shook his head a single time, almost imperceptibly, as if he wanted no one but the Somm to see. But Menok's meaning was clear: he did not believe the Ser-o would submit to these men. If the Kurnisahn were to stand a chance against the j'Lok, they would have to align with the Ser-o. But preparing would take time, and Sakaq peered at him impatiently as if he wanted an answer now.

"We cannot leave the living-place unprotected by sending half our men. That we simply cannot do."

"Then you refuse?" Sakaq said, rising to his feet. "Is that the answer you want me to bring the Gerent?"

"That is not what I said. I said we won't send half our men."

"Then you will lead the Kurnisahn to j'Lok?"

The Somm had no intention of leading his tribe to j'Lok. But if he falsely agreed, Sakaq might deem the visit a success and be on his way. This would give the Somm time to send men sunward and plan a defense with the Ser-o. "Yes, I will lead them to j'Lok," he said. "If your Gerent sees it true, and the High Ones are coming, we can't stay here."

Sakaq studied his features as if surprised by how easily he had given in.

"But it will take time," the Somm continued. "What you ask requires us to uproot our clan and travel a great distance. But we can be there before the low sun comes if we begin today."

"Good," Sakaq said. "After we eat, my men will see the site of this supposed killing. You should prepare to leave while we are gone. We'll join you on your journey to j'Lok when we return."

5

He Bathes in Blood

U NA COULD SCARCELY RAISE the obsidian off the ground; each stone felt like it weighed more than she. It was hard to imagine those strange men carrying two whole blocks all the way from j'Lok. No wonder they'd been in such a rush to get rid of it.

"Are they still out there?" she asked her mother, who'd been staring out of the burdei for some time.

Her mother turned and pursed her lips. "Put that away. You heard your father. The obsidian must stay hidden."

She placed the greyfur back over the stones.

"Yes, they're still speaking," her mother said. "Now your father brought over Ber-gul. It looks like he's giving him instructions. He points sunward."

"Last night, he and uncle spoke about going into the Sketen."

"That may no longer be the plan. The j'Lok might have changed things." Her mother paused, curled her lips. "Who knows what was said by those men."

"How does Father look?"

"Troubled."

Her mother's knuckles burned white as she gripped the burdei flap. Seeing her mother worry only heightened Una's own concerns.

"Your father and uncle have been speaking since the j'Lok left," her mother said. "They spent time with the shaman as well. Something serious is underway." She raised an eyebrow before turning her attention back outside.

"Is Falon with them?"

"I haven't seen him today. He might be in his burdei."

"Someone should see how he's doing."

Her mother turned to her, straight-faced. "The boy still longs for you, you know."

"Of course, I know."

"You should not lead him on."

"I don't *lead him on*. Falon is just a friend," she said, looking away. "He knows this."

"Does he? The boy doesn't see it that way. He would run off with you if he could. Don't you see the way he looks at you, hoping you notice him?"

"Yes, I know."

Her mother paused as if debating her words. "You never should have let him kiss you."

"We were just children," Una said, sending her mother the iciest glare she could muster.

"It still should not have happened."

"So you've said many times. How long will I be scolded over something that happened so long ago?"

"However long ago it was, Falon has not forgotten it."

"I'm the one who started it," she admitted. "Not him, me."

"Then you should've known better," her mother said, cocking her head the way she always did when reprimanding her. "Why did you do it?"

Una sat on her sleeping mat. "I don't want to talk about this," she said, bringing her knees to her chest.

"You weren't drawn to him?"

"Maybe I was, back then. But not anymore."

"Of course, not anymore. Not with that gruesome scar—"

"Mother!"

She let go of the burdei flap. "You and he had gone off for so long that day. How do you think your father felt when he sent the tribesmen into the forest to find you?"

"That doesn't excuse what he did."

"He was panicked."

"So? Father knew I was safe when he found me. Yet, he swung his staff as if to kill Falon. He scarred him for life; he was just a boy!"

Her mother was about to defend her father again, but then dropped her chin as if recalling her own traumas. The Somm had beaten her many times, and she had the scars to prove it. She looked back out of the burdei, clearly ready to talk about something else. Una welcomed the change; discussing Falon's disfigurement and the events that had led to its creation always sobered her. While it was true that Falon's longing for her stemmed back to that fateful day in the woods, his feelings persisted because she was the only female who ever paid him any heed. In a way, she felt bad for him.

"Falon will be part of your past once you are paired with another man," her mother said. "Your lifemate will be from Ser-o, most likely. Although now I wonder if he will be from j'Lok."

Una swallowed, suddenly queasy. She rose and walked back to the stones, touched her fingertips to the greyfur. "I will not go darkward," she said.

"It's not your decision to make. I didn't want to go darkward either when I was your age, yet here I am. If I had my way, I would have stayed in Ser-o with my family. Instead, I became Istri Dam of the Kurnisahn, leader of the women."

"Ser-o is just like Kurnisahn, Mother."

"It is similar but not the same."

Una paused, stroking her hair. "It's not like they sent you to live in a cave with the Bhatt."

"I was nearly your age when taken from my family."

"You know I'm ready to be bonded," Una said. "I've been fully flowered all season. I want to have a child of my own."

"And you will, but your father will decide when and with whom." Her mother looked outside and raised a finger to change the subject. "Now Suht is there too. It seems he will take part in whatever they're planning."

"Do you think we're in trouble because of the obsidian?" Una asked.

"I don't know. Maybe."

Una peered out alongside her mother, who steered her aside so she'd be less obvious. Outside, her uncle Menok and Ber-gul went into their respective burdei, with Suht trailing his father. The Somm stood there for a moment before turning to his own home. Seeing him approach, mother and daughter alike moved inside and sat down as if they hadn't been eavesdropping.

"I saw you standing there," the Somm said as he entered. He lifted the greyfur and stared at the obsidian with sunken eyes before turning to her mother. "Fill three skins of water for my brother."

Her mother glanced at Una while exiting the burdei.

The Somm picked up the smaller of the two obsidian blocks, grunting as he lifted. With both hands bowled beneath the stone, he balanced it against his chest and carried it outside.

Una reassumed her position at the entrance of the burdei. Across the way, Menok brought over a handaxe. He chipped off a fist-sized chunk of obsidian with a satisfying crack and put the freshly cut stone into his shoulderpack. After accepting three skins of water from her mother, he walked out of the living-place, heading sunward with Ber-gul and Suht, all in silence. Her parents spoke to each other softly while watching the men leave, her mother often nodding with her chin down. They talked for some time before the Somm escorted her back into their burdei, carrying what remained of the obsidian. This time, Una did not bother to hide that she'd been watching.

"Una, we will speak," her father said, covering the obsidian. "I sent your uncle sunward with Ber-gul and Suht."

"And…"

Her mother put her hand on her father's forearm so she might speak. "Una, you are the Somm's daughter and will be matched with a great man. You will one day be bonded to the Somm of another tribe and become Istri Dam of that tribe."

Una was not amused by her mother pretending like they hadn't just been speaking of this, even if it had been in secret. "So you say *again*, Mother," she said.

Her father glared at her mother. Una immediately regretted her outburst, for the consequences could be severe. Choosing lifemates was not a woman's business; it was a pact between two fathers. But the Somm stayed composed—for the moment—and after holding the sharp look, turned back to Una. "As a woman fully flowered, it is time for such a match."

"Why is now the time?"

He groaned under his breath. His forbearance would not last forever. "Your uncle went to Ser-o to offer you to Somm Muro's son and heir," he said.

"You're saying that—"

"Yes, I am offering you to Carn."

Una dropped both hands to her sides. "*Carn?*"

Her mother put her hand on Una's chest. "He is the finest man in Ser-o, it is said."

"He is a killer, it is said. Of all the men, Father, why him?"

"He is said to be the greatest foodbringer."

"It is said he bathes in blood!"

"Those are only tales," her mother said. "Stories told by envious men."

"Even if only one of the stories is true, he is dangerous. No, I think not. I would sooner go to j'Lok."

"I have made my decision," her father said, the words meant to end their speakings.

"No, I will not go," she insisted, trying to sound resolute. But she knew she could never match her father's willpower.

The Somm grabbed her elbow with painful strength and pulled her forward. "I do not need to explain anything to you. That, I do not have to do. This is my decision, and you better pray to Vul-ka that Somm Muro agrees."

"Explain it to me anyway," she said, looking up at him. He was breathing heavily through his nose.

"Just tell her, Ul-man," her mother said.

He let go and looked away, his demeanor instantly changing from fury to concern. "The j'Lok… they are coming."

"They were just here. They—"

"No, I mean they are coming. All of them."

"What do you mean? Coming for me?"

"Coming for everyone in the lowrock valley." The Somm lifted his eyes, wettened in a way Una had seldom seen.

"Because of the obsidian? The three strange men—"

"That's not the reason," he said, rubbing the greyfur-covered stones.

"Then what? Father, explain."

"They have asked us to join them in the coldlands."

"So, tell them no."

"They were not really *asking*," her mother said.

"What she means, Una, is we either join them or become their enemy." He cracked his knuckles. "Did you hear us speak about the Bhatt last night?"

"Yes."

"We think the j'Lok were responsible. We think they offered the Bhatt the same arrangement as us. But when the Bhatt refused to join them, the j'Lok killed them all."

"Uncle believes this too?"

"He does," he said, raising his chin in confidence. "And his instincts are strong."

Her knees weakened. "But what does that have to do with me? With Carn?"

"We cannot stand alone against the might of the j'Lok. That is why we must partner with the Ser-o."

"How do you know the Ser-o won't just join the j'Lok?"

"We don't. But we hope our offer is generous enough for them to side with us."

"The offer being me?" The thought of running out before her father answered crossed her mind.

"You are part of it." The Somm took a deep breath. "There's more. Bonding you to Carn will help bring the tribes together."

"The tribes are already bound together by blood many times over, how does this—"

"What *more* haven't you told me, Ul-man?" her mother cut in.

The Somm raised his palms to silence everyone and then took Una's hand. "All will soon be known," he said. "For now, your uncle goes sunward with my offer. If Vul-ka answers our prayers, he will be back soon with your future lifemate. Until then, we will speak of this no more."

needed a glossary of made up words.

6

The Pachydon

OUT OF THE FOREST walked many Kurnisahn men, their foreheads adorned with black stripes drawn from the juices of fresh-picked cho-berries, a mark of blessing from Vul-ka, under whose dominion foodbringing fell. If the scout had told it true, a pachydon was entrenched in the bog not far from the living-place—the first time a pachydon had been seen in the lowrock valley. While nander clad in their furs, at least from the coldlands, were not uncommon, never before had the Kurnisahn seen one in the flesh. These beasts might not have a taste for blood, but they were creatures of unmatched strength, behemoths far larger and fiercer than any other known. It was fortunate the pachydon was trapped in the slough, considering the challenge it might have otherwise presented.

Under normal circumstances, the discovery of such a bounty would have been met with merriment, but life in Kurnisahn had been tense for half a sistersun. The Somm had told his clan of the j'Lok threat, and it had taken everything in his power to keep them calm. It seemed he was holding information back, some unspoken detail to which only he and Menok were privy. When he insisted

70

the j'Lok could return any moment and the Kurnisahn must be ready to defend their living-place, many questioned his leadership. What if the Ser-o did not agree to bond their heir to Una? What if the j'Lok had gotten to them first?

While Falon shared these concerns, a personal matter weighed upon his thoughts even more: in the coming days, he was going to lose Una. With his father now gone, she was all Falon had, and her companionship meant more than ever given the coming changes. But even if he could overcome being alone for the first time, how could he accept the man to whom she had been promised? Of all the men in the narrowland, why Carn?

Though few had actually met Carn, all the Kurnisahn knew of him. It was said he was two heads taller than any man. It was said he'd wrestled an aurochs to the ground singlehandedly. It was said he'd crushed his brother's skull with his bare hands and now wore a necklace of his bones.

Falon recalled how, many seasons ago, three Kurnisahn men had visited Ser-o with a salt offering, never to return. The Kurnisahn were far closer to the Saltsea than both the Ser-o and the Bhatt, so both tribes depended on them for salt. The Kurnisahn stored great clay trays of water on the sands of the Saltsea, returning in a sister-sun to harvest the mineral once the liquid had evaporated. There was always more salt than one tribe alone could use, so they traded their surplus to the neighboring clans.

When the salt traders never returned from Ser-o, many questioned their fate. The Ser-o claimed to have traded with them and sent them on their way, but few Kurnisahn believed this true. Some even suspected the traders had gotten cross with Carn, who'd then slain them with his own hand. Although there'd been no evidence to suggest this, the rumor persisted simply by virtue of his reputation, and for a time it stressed relations between the clans.

Una had to be protected from him. Falon knew not how this could be done, only that it must.

"The pachydon is in the valley past this hill," one of the food-bringers said, pointing to the buzzards circling above and breaking Falon's stream of thought.

The Kurnisahn scaled the cragged slope, careful to not step in the puddles between stones. From the summit, they peered into a gully where waist-high grasses petered out into a muddy fen, the sun casting shadows across the basin. The pachydon was moaning at the bottom, its front legs, each the width of a thuk-tree, trapped in the muck. Its head alone was the height of a man, and a snake-like trunk rested between its tusks. The beast was surrounded by howlers—one with fangs deep in its hindquarters, another at its side. A third bit down on its neck and jerked wildly to tear open its throat. A couple others traipsed around their prey, glaring at the foodbringers, growling and showing their teeth. One kicked rear-ward with mud-covered hind legs, sending a brown spray into the pachydon's eyes. They weren't going to give up their prize without a fight.

The Kurnisahn held out their blades, ready to strike. "We out-number them," one said.

"They might charge us anyway," another man said, gripping his spear.

"They're only howlers. They'll retreat if we move forward with strength."

The howlers biting the pachydon loosened their grips and turned their snarling maws to face the nander. Now they had the whole pack's attention.

As the howlers stalked up the ridge, the men grabbed rocks and pelted them, wet chunks of dirt flinging off the projectiles as they flew downhill, the beasts yelping each time a stone connected with its target. After halting the howlers, the men descended into the valley, hurling more rocks along the way and lifting their spears once in striking distance. One of the howlers leaped at a food-bringer, its yellow teeth shining out of a blood-filled mouth. The man reared his weapon, thrusting it upward into the airborne howler's throat. The animal's momentum, even as it leaped uphill, knocked the man down, and the others ran in to finish the kill, swiftly turning to the rest of the pack with their bloody blades still drawn.

The howlers continued growling, their bearings now muted and uncertain. The death of their brethren, the knowledge they were outmatched, tempered their movements. The Kurnisahn resumed their approach, waving and hollering to assert dominance. The howlers backed away and scurried onto a bluff, where they perched in stark abeyance while the real killers took their share.

Now the men could turn their focus to the prey for which they'd come. The pachydon's shaggy coat had been torn countless times by the howlers, blood trickling from each of its wounds. It tried to shift as the men closed in, but its front legs were shoulder deep in the mire, its head pressed into the mud. It let out a high-pitched moan, its red eyes peering woefully at the men as if begging for help. The poor creature had just seen them chase off the howlers and probably mistook them for saviors.

The Kurnisahn surrounded the pachydon to assess the task ahead, spreading their weight to avoid sinking in themselves. They had come with little strategy, assuming the trapped animal would be an easy kill, but they'd underestimated just how massive it would be. None of their usual killing methods seemed suitable.

"What do we do?" one man asked.

"Maybe we can cut its throat like an aurochs."

"Do you see how big it is? Its hide must be thicker than our blades are long."

"I will try. Someone watch the howlers."

As the foodbringer approached the pachydon, again it drew out a scratchy whimper. It stared askance at the man, its mouth dribbling mud and mucus, its trunk flopping on the ground. The man laid his obsidian blade against the pachydon's neck, probing past fur to flesh. When he pressed down with all his might, a carmine blot pooled over the incision.

The pachydon shrieked with such power that the men turned their heads and covered their ears, hunching toward the ground as if it would somehow deliver them from this aural battering. The monster knocked down its assailant with a swing of its trunk, sending him face-first into the muck. The fallen man tried to stand but fell to the side, clutching his stomach to regain his wind, the dark brown silt of the narrowland seeping into his mouth and ears and eyes.

"It must not like the taste of obsidian," one man quipped.

At the crest of the hill, a howler bayed.

"We need a longer blade. I'll try my shankhammer," another man said, raising high his blade. He examined the cut the previous man had made, then aimed by touching his shankhammer to the incision before lifting it over his head and swinging down.

When the blade struck with a thud, again the pachydon screamed. The shankhammer's fore was stuck beneath its flesh, and when the monster jerked its head, it lifted the man, still gripping the weapon's hilt, with it. As the man struggled to regain his balance, the pachydon swept its trunk along the ground and threw him off his feet. Its chest pulsed up and down, but despite the dangling blade, no more blood spilled from its wound, and the pachydon let out a painful groan with its head sideways in the mud.

The Kurnisahn stopped to stare at the hopeless animal. It seemed as if the pachydon peered at Falon directly, its eyes forlorn and accusing. In those eyes was an almost singular intelligence, a deeper understanding of what was happening to it and what that ultimately meant. No, this was no aurochs, no tarpan or cavebear. Not even a howler or valleycat, cunning as they might be, could match what Falon saw in those eyes.

"Whatever we do, we need to do it quickly," Falon said. "No need to draw this out."

"Quiet, Scarboy," one of the men said. "What if we stick a spear through its eye?"

"No, you need to cut off its ears," another said.

In the midst of all the noise, Falon noticed the pack had disappeared. "Where are the howlers?" he asked.

"Be quiet. I'm sticking my spear in its—"

Everyone paused when a voice suddenly boomed from behind them, a sound so deep that they questioned, for a moment, if it came from a man at all. "What is the meaning of this?" the voice cried out.

The Kurnisahn turned and saw four men standing at the top of the hill where the howlers had been. Three were familiar—Menok, Ber-gul, and Suht—but one was not. The stranger, standing first before the others, was tall with shoulders round like boulders, and carried a poleaxe with a torso-length haft of bone and a black blade shaped like a sharpened tear. Bare-chested despite the chill, he wore only greyfur breeches and footwear, and as he descended into the valley, his obsidian axe dragged along the ground.

"Why are you torturing this pachydon?" the stranger demanded, a string of valleycat fangs bouncing along his neckline as he stepped to the other men. Nander never hunted valleycats, for they could shred a man with a single swipe. Was this man so fierce that he hunted not prey but the predators themselves?

Having seen his company, the Kurnisahn suspected who this man might be, and perhaps because of this, no one dared to speak. The stranger strode past the foodbringers, the pachydon rasping as he approached. He inspected its wounds and shook his head while smiling. "Don't any of you know how to kill?"

The stranger positioned himself between the pachydon's tusks. He touched it gently between its eyes, caressing it with the back of his hand.

"You poor creature. How these foolish men have pained you so." The stranger pulled back his hand, sneering at the animal before turning once more to the Kurnisahn. "To kill a pachydon, you either run it off a cliff or cut off its nose," he said, his grin transforming into a mien of gravity. He widened his eyes and raised the blade over his head. "Like so."

The stranger swung his axe, landing it with a dull thud across the base of the pachydon's trunk. It blared louder than any time before, jerking its head from one side to the other, spewing a viscid blend of blood and mud and spit. When the axe came down again, the mark exploded in a hot red spray, splattering the Kurnisahn and bursting onto the stranger's chest. He wrestled the blade out and swung again, each strike with greater glee, and in this gruesome revelry, he flexed and screamed as if it was he and not the animal being mutilated. His holler pealed across the basin and echoed off the rainswept bluffs and multiplied until it sounded like the cries of many men. Then he raised and struck anew, ropes of blood flinging off the blade, the obsidian cutting deeper until the entire trunk had been avulsed. The pachydon roared as its very life surged out between its tusks until all that remained was a bubbling stump. The dying beast snorted and gurgled and whimpered and wept, each sound weaker than the one before. It closed its eyes and slowed its heaving long before its trembling stilled.

The stranger lifted the dismembered trunk and draped it over his shoulders as blood poured down his chest, and the creature shuddered behind him. With a crimson veil upon his countenance, his weapon wet with gore and dripping the darkest red, he stood before the men while running bloody fingers through his hair.

"Kurnisahn, do you know who I am?" he challenged.

They turned to one another, each afraid to speak, no one seeking to draw the ire of this blood-slaked butcher, until a boy who stood amongst men finally stepped forward and spoke.

"I know who you are," Falon said.

PART II: CARN

7

Eight Talons

U NA HAD EXPECTED HIM to be big, but not *that* big. Carn stood at least a head taller than her uncle Menok, who trailed behind him as they strode into the living-place. Their marching order alone said a great deal about whatever hierarchy they'd established on the way back from Ser-o, but there was something more. Her uncle's eager-to-please smile conveyed a sense of deference. Deference and fear.

This first impression only reinforced the concerns she'd had since being told of her pairing. She had heard many tales about this man, and here he was, entering her living-place covered in more blood than she'd ever seen. Foodbringers always returned from the hunt with soiled furs, but Carn was so blood-soaked that it formed a crust on his strangely uncovered chest.

As the newcomer strolled into the living-place with Menok at his heels, the Kurnisahn emerged from their burdei to lay eyes on the man with such a fearsome reputation, the man to whom she would soon be bonded. Not a nander remained in their homes, even mothers with babes at their teats and those sewing furs came out to see.

gross

Her father approached the Ser-o heir first. "It is with great honor that we welcome you to Kurnisahn," he said, touching his open palm to Carn's chest. Carn looked down at the Somm's hand, then lifted his chin and glared at him. *I didn't say you could touch me*, his expression seemed to say. The Somm awkwardly withdrew his hand. "I see you joined in slaying the pachydon," he continued after an uncomfortable pause, pointing to the trunk slung over Carn's shoulders and hanging to his waist.

Carn nodded, looking past the Somm to meet eyes with Una. She felt blood rush to her cheeks, then looked away, immediately upset at herself for doing so. She'd been caught staring and only made it worse by averting her eyes so quickly.

"We heard noises over a hill on our way back to the living-place," Menok said. "We found the Kurnisahn working on the pachydon with little progress. But then Carn came and slew the beast himself."

The Somm tilted his head. "By himself? A pachydon? How?"

"All creatures bleed," Carn said, for the first time speaking. "I took its nose and drained it." He raised the end of the trunk, its pink nose bent in death like a half-clenched fist.

"I see," the Somm said. "Surely you wish to rinse yourself of all this blood. My brother and I will show you to the flowing water."

Carn nodded and lifted the Somm's necklace. "Eight goldbeak talons," he said, peering into his eyes.

"I was a fortunate foodbringer that day," the Somm said.

"Yes, that day." Carn released the necklace, letting it flop onto the Somm's chest with a clink, then turned to face the clan. "I am Carn of the Ser-o," he declared for all to hear, "and I come to strengthen the tie between our tribes. You will learn more in the coming days."

No one looked away or uttered a sound. They watched Carn long after he had finished speaking, waiting to see if he'd say more.

He let their anticipation simmer for a moment, then again looked directly at Una, this time holding his gaze. The Somm followed his eyes, realizing he was waiting for an introduction.

The Somm cleared his throat. "I now introduce you to Una," he said, extending an open palm her way, "my daughter and only child."

His eyes still locked on Una, Carn pushed away the Somm's hand and approached her. The closer he came, the bigger he seemed. His muscles, underscored by rifts in the dried-blood crust, were more pronounced than any of the Kurnisahn men. He stepped forth with his chest out, in total disregard of the others, as if no one in the world existed but the two of them. He dropped to a knee and laid the pachydon trunk in a straight line before her.

"Una, my lifemate to be. The stories are true—the most beautiful woman in all the narrowland stands before me. I present to you the trunk of a beast who will feed our tribe for many sistersuns, whose ribs will build us a strong burdei in which to raise our children, and whose fur will clothe us and keep us warm come the turning of the seasons and the setting of the sun."

What could she say? Gruesome though his appearance might be, and as fearsome a reputation as he might have, he now spoke to her so eloquently. Could the stories about him be but tales told by envious Kurnisahn men, as her mother had suggested?

Carn rose and smiled at her, his grey eyes matching the colorless sky, then turned back to her father. "Now show me to the flowing water."

As Carn followed her father out of the living-place, they passed three Kurnisahn men carrying the longest bone she'd ever seen. The pale yellow tusk curled toward its end and was propped on the shoulders of the men below it. Last in line was Falon, who made no efforts to hide that he was eyeing Carn. Once the men set down the tusk, Falon hustled over to her.

"Una, we must speak," he said.

"Come behind my burdei before she sees us talking," she said, noting her mother was distracted by the tusk.

Falon glanced at the pachydon trunk lying on the ground before following her behind the burdei.

"What is it?" she asked.

"This man. Carn. Be careful."

"Why?"

"You didn't see what I just saw. His face while slaying the pachydon—"

"My uncle says he slew it by himself."

"Well, yes—"

"How long were you trying to slay it?"

"There were a few failed tries—"

"So, nothing happened until he arrived."

"Yes, but his face," Falon said again. He paused, exhaled. "It was a look of madness."

"How does one usually look when killing an animal?"

"Not like this. He was enjoying the bloodshed in a way I've never seen. But there's more; something I don't understand. Something in his eyes. When he smiles, when he frowns, his eyes stay the same."

"And?"

"Something is wrong with him, something in his mind. You know the stories—"

"If they're even true."

"They must be true. What I just saw—"

"I just met him, and he was respectful."

"It's not real, Una. He is dangerous. What will happen once he takes you back to Ser-o?"

"What will he do to me? His tales of cruelty were probably made up by envious Kurnisahn men."

He gave her a skeptical glance. "You sound like your mother."

"Maybe because she's right."

"Who will join you on your voyage sunward?"

"I don't know. I haven't talked to my father about any of this. But if he sends someone, it won't be you."

Falon bowed his head, his expression transforming from wide-eyed urgency into hopelessness. This was all very uncharacteristic of him. He had never been an alarmist; he'd always found a positive angle in anything troubling that passed his way. Despite the obstacles in his life and his physical weakness, he'd somehow sustained a cheerful disposition through it all. To Falon, the sun always rose even after the darkest night. Nonetheless, she couldn't be drawn into his mindset, not about her pairing and the fresh path she'd soon be taking. This was a critical time in her life—and one brought about in a decision to which she was not part.

"I have to go," she said. "If my mother sees us back here, or my father—"

"Let them see."

She put her hand on his chest. "Falon, to me you are the most important nander in all the narrowland. But you knew this day would come."

He looked away. "Yes, but not to him. Anyone would be better than him. You have to trust me."

"What am I to do? Tell my father no? Something bigger than a bonding is underway. There is something we haven't been told."

"Your pairing will strengthen the link between our tribes."

"No. There's more, but my father stopped himself before telling me. I don't even think my mother knows what it is."

"Who does know, just your father and uncle?"

"Carn must also know."

"I need to know too. I have to protect you."

She narrowed her eyes. "I don't need your protection."

"We'll be working on the pachydon for days. Tomorrow, when we're out there cutting, I'll find out more."

"You don't need to do that. I'm sure we'll all find out soon enough."

"But we don't want it to be too late."

"Too late for what?"

"Too late..." Falon paused. "Too late to save you."

8

What I'm Going to Do

T HE PACHYDON HIDE alone weighed as much as an aurochs, and hauling it back to the living-place would require fastening it to planks and dragging it all the same. But it was thicker than a bearskin and wide enough to cover a burdei, and thus worth the efforts of so many men.

The Kurnisahn were butchering the carcass for the second straight day, and it had taken most of the day before just to get the monster out of the mire and onto its side. Gutting was never a pleasant task, but the pachydon turned out to be especially awful. It smelled like rot and excrement and had attracted a host of carrion birds that filled the air with their noisome caws. It took the might of many men just to pull out its entrails, some the width of a man's torso. Once the innards had been removed and discarded, one of the men stepped inside the resulting cavity and curled up like an unborn baby. Most of the Kurnisahn laughed, as did Carn. Falon just couldn't get over the stench.

Carn had taken control of the project at first light, and everyone, even Menok, deferred to him from the outset. While he'd already demonstrated his expertise by slaying the animal, it was his bearing that allowed him to take command of his peers. He tromped around the carcass with his chin held high, issuing directives in a steady voice as if he himself was the Somm. It seemed, even without his reputation, he would have quickly taken charge of any group of men.

Falon had been watching Carn throughout the day, torn between awe and fear, always from the corner of his eye to be discreet. It wasn't hard to believe the stories of Carn's violent nature given what he'd already seen. While Falon had sworn to uncover the Somm's secret plans, how could he do that if he didn't even have the courage to speak to Carn?

Then, as if he had heard Falon's thoughts, Carn stopped and looked directly at him. Falon turned away, pretending to be wholly focused on the meat he was cutting, but he could sense Carn walking toward him. "This leg is finished. Well done," he said as he approached.

"Thank you," Falon said, too nervous to look up. Perhaps his staring had been more obvious than he'd realized. He scraped the last bit of gristle off the bone and carried it to the waist-high heap of marbled meat the men had been collecting throughout the day.

"Soon, we will remove the bones and bring them to the living-place," Carn said, following him to the pile. "But first we must take as much meat as we can before it spoils."

Falon didn't know what to say. Here was a chance to speak to Carn—but as much as he wanted to gather information, he was too intimidated to respond boldly or inquisitively. "I don't know if we'll have enough time," he said. "There is just too much."

"No, some will spoil. But that's alright. The Kurnisahn won't be able to eat it all. Some I might take back to Ser-o, but even then, much will go to waste. What's left can be used as bait, perhaps for forest swine. They are not the choosiest feeders."

"No, they're not," Falon agreed, finally finding the courage to look up. Something in Carn's comportment seemed to change when Falon met eyes with him, but it was hard to tell. Although the man betrayed no emotions and his words seemed friendly enough, his sheer presence carried an oppressive energy.

"You are quite the marksman, I hear," Carn said.

"I train with Ber-gul to be a firstmover."

"Then you must have great eyes as well. I want you to help me with something before I leave Kurnisahn."

"Alright," Falon said, curious why a man like Carn would need help from a boy like him.

"When we were in the Sketen, we climbed over the gorge where the Bhatt had been slain. Your kin would not go down for fear of the cursed soil, but we could see the bodies down below. It was a frightful scene, corpses strewn about as though tossed by water and wind. But by climbing so high, I saw a clearing in the forest that had not been there before. It seemed unnatural, like someone had struck down a circle of trees."

"Could it have been the j'Lok? They've been in the area."

"Maybe it was them, I don't know. We were too far away to see. But I want a better look before going back to Ser-o."

"You want me to help you see?"

"Yes. I need you for your eyes."

"Then I will come," Falon said, sensing he didn't have a choice.

Carn stared at him for an uncomfortable time, a smirk at the corner of his lips slowly turning into a full-blown grin even though his eyes remained emotionless. He lifted Falon's weaved-hair necklace and tilted his head down, his demeanor turning quietly serious behind the false smile. "No teeth hang from your neck, I see. Not like mine—full of valleycat fangs. You aren't a strong man, are you? Some might say not even a man at all."

Falon's hands began to tremble. He tried to hide them by dropping them to his sides, then looked around for the other men. Most were busy and not paying attention, although Menok seemed to have noticed the two of them speaking. But Menok couldn't be trusted for protection; he and the Somm were of like mind. Nor could the other Kurnisahn be counted on; the Somm's dislike for Falon had influenced everyone. Who would have the mettle to stand up to Carn anyway?

Carn chortled, still holding the necklace. "You are not fully grown, I know, but still—a great foodbringer you will never be."

"As you said, I'm known for my aim."

"Aim without strength has little use."

Falon tried to pull his necklace from his grasp, but Carn gripped tighter.

"A shame, isn't it? That you resent your betters?" Carn said. He released the necklace and ran a finger along Falon's scar, prompting him to take a step back. "I know about you. You're the one who seeks favor from the Somm's daughter. She who is promised to me. You're the weakling they spoke of."

"Who spoke?"

"It was a long voyage from Ser-o. We had plenty of time, your Kurnisahn kin and I, to discuss a great many things."

"I don't know what you're talking about."

"Yes, you do. I've seen you eyeing me, Scarboy. I see what you are. But I will take her, and there is nothing you can do to stop me."

Falon had never expected Carn to even notice him, let alone for their speakings to take such a sudden and sinister turn. He backed away and started walking back to the pachydon, to be closer to the other men, though he didn't expect their protection. Carn grabbed his shoulder and spun him around, looking down at him from an absurd height.

"A fine girl she is."

Falon stared at the ground without responding.

"But not a woman yet. I'll make one out of her, though. You'll see." Carn lifted Falon's chin until they peered into each other's eyes. Again, the tall man smiled, this time as if in pity, before leaning forward and whispering in his ear. "You have no idea all the things I'm going to do to her."

9

A Presence of Command

BRANCHES WERE CURIOUS THINGS. The youngest rose to the treetops, growing lush from their share of sun. Older branches remained below, passed on over time, in the shade and out of the sun's reach. As the tree rerouted its lifeblood to higher limbs, those below grew dry. Soon, they were no more than lifeless offshoots of an otherwise vibrant being. But these dead branches were once just like the ones above. They too were once the highest. The only difference was that some came closer to the sun than others. But the old always yielded to the new, and every branch would one day grow old.

It was dead branches such as these that were ignited in a pyre to begin the bonding ritual. Somm Ul-man cut both his palm and that of the Ser-o heir, the two men pressing their hands together over the open flame. And with that, ownership of his daughter was passed.

The time had come for the Somm to reveal the truth to his clan. It had been discomforting to keep such a secret, but he couldn't have disclosed every detail until certain the Ser-o supported his plan. But with Carn now bonded to his daughter, no questions lingered about what would come next.

The Somm walked in front of the pyre, his body a silhouette before the flames. "Kurnisahn, with this bonding, our tribe will undertake a great change." He raised his palm for the clan to see the blood trickling down his forearm in a thin red spiral. "A short time ago, visitors from j'Lok passed through our living-place. It was this visit that drove me to offer Una to Carn so the bond between our tribes be strengthened."

He let out a long breath before continuing.

"But I have not told you everything—there is more. The visitors urged us to move to j'Lok, where our men would work in the mines to draw obsidian from the narrowland. This was not an invitation but a demand.

"As you all know, the Bhatt were victims of a great killing. Both Menok and I think the j'Lok were the ones responsible. We believe the Bhatt refused their demands and then bled for their defiance. Their men were slaughtered, their women taken.

"Once the j'Lok departed from Kurnisahn, two choices for us remained. The first was to obey—send our nander to j'Lok, where we would give up our self-rule and face an unknown future. The other choice was to refuse and get ready to fight. We are choosing—we *have chosen*—to fight."

"The j'Lok left here peacefully!" someone called out.

"Yes, but only after we falsely agreed to their demands," the Somm said. "We expect they'll be back soon to show us to the coldlands. We must be gone before they arrive. It is a blessing from Vul-ka that they haven't yet returned."

"What do you mean, *must be gone*?" another man asked.

"You will let me finish," the Somm said, raising a hand for silence. "We have, since their visit, met with the Ser-o. They, too, were visited by the j'Lok and given the same offer. An offer their Somm also falsely agreed to. In secret, he is joining us in our defense, and as a first step, he sent Carn to bond with Una."

"How does that help our defense?"

"Kurnisahn, you will remain silent until I am done speaking," the Somm commanded, raising his voice for the first time.

Carn walked in front of the Somm, shaking his head and motioning for him to step aside. "I will finish for you."

It did not sound like a request.

The Somm opened his mouth, ready to argue that this was his tribe and it would be he who delivered the message. But before the words could leave his tongue, he met eyes with the Ser-o heir, who leaned forward like a man about to strike. The air in Kurnisahn was already stressed, and this was no time to establish hierarchy, so the Somm stepped out of his way. Although the Somm stood before his clan, the nander before which he sought to maintain a semblance of authority, Carn's energy and poise forbade refusal. If the Somm stood his ground, Carn would too.

Carn tensed before the crackling flames, the veins on his arms and neck bulging in the firelight. He pivoted his head to survey the Kurnisahn, his glower met by expectation from the crowd.

"It is time to defend yourselves, Kurnisahn. As it is for the Ser-o. Alone, our tribes lack the strength to fight back against the j'Lok. But together, we might survive. My bonding to Una now brings our tribes together under one leader and in one place."

The Kurnisahn looked to one another in doubt, unsure what to make of this last statement, but no one dared interrupt Carn as they had the Somm. While their comfort with their leader was part of the reason, Carn had a presence of command to him, a physical bearing which the Somm did not have.

"The Ser-o and the Kurnisahn will now bring our clans together to defend against the coldlanders," Carn said, walking back and forth before the tribe. "When the j'Lok return, we must be ready for battle. Both tribes will go to the hills above the Sketen until the threats have passed. There is game in those hills. There are nuts, roots, and berries. There are resources in the ground and in the forest to build burdei.

"But the main reason we chose this place is its location. When the j'Lok come sunward, they will have to go through the Sketen to reach us, and we'll be ready to ambush them when they do. Our new living-place, high in the hills above the pass, will be unreachable without crossing the trap we've planned."

A crinkle in the corner of Carn's mouth revealed an incipient smile as he met eyes with one nander, then another. When at last his gaze reached the Somm, it was clear how he had silenced the crowd so effectively. While the Somm instilled respect in those around him, Carn inspired fear.

"You must wonder who will lead this combined tribe," Carn said, smirking at the Somm before turning again to the crowd. "He who leads must be of both Ser-o and Kurnisahn blood—blood of my father, Somm Muro, and blood of your Somm Ul-man as well. That is the reason for the bonding you saw today. Our son—Una and my son—will be groomed to be the Somm of the combined tribe once born."

Carn paused, giving the Kurnisahn time to think about what he had just said. After a moment of quiet, someone asked, "What about until then?"

The Somm refused to let Carn run away with the proceedings any more than he already had. He stepped forward, retaking the stage. "Bringing our clans together requires sacrifice from both. Somm Muro will step down as leader of the Ser-o, and I will do the same for the Kurnisahn. In our places, Carn will serve as Somm and Una as the Istri Dam."

The Kurnisahn whispered to one another, a wave of restlessness coursing through the crowd. After a moment, Falon pointed at Carn. "That means he's in charge. You've yielded your position to him. That is not equal sacrifice!"

"Una will be the Istri Dam, the leader of the women. Carn will be the Somm and leader of the men."

"That is not equal!" Falon insisted.

Carn stomped over to him and pressed his bleeding palm flat on his face, shoving him into the mud with a splat. The crowd let out a collective gasp, but no one stepped in as Carn retook the stage. They had already been awed by him, but now they'd seen, for the first time, his hostility toward one of their own.

"This is not the time for dissent," Carn said with quiet menace, his chin tilted down, regarding the crowd from the top of his eyes. His fists were clenched so tight that blood squeezed between his fingers. "A great threat comes from the coldlands. Any day, the j'Lok will arrive in Kurnisahn—many hands of men, all with obsidian blades drawn. They will kill you and disgrace your women. Who of you wishes to lie rotting in the soil while your lifemate is filled with the seed of a j'Lok raider?"

The crowd stood silent.

"Yes. That is what we face," the Somm said. "We were once a traveling clan. We settled here, in the lowrock valley, because of its fertile grounds and game. But we must now rethink our ways until it's safe to settle once more. In the high hills over the Sketen, we will find refuge—a place where we can live as we do today, only with greater numbers and in a more defendable place.

"On the morrow, our change begins. You will take down your burdei, collect your belongings. Your best materials—your furs and bones—should come first. Leave what you must. What you cannot carry can be found again."

The Kurnisahn grumbled and spoke amongst themselves, with both Carn and the Somm giving them time to digest the message. As the crowd dispersed and the Kurnisahn withdrew to their burdei for the night, the Somm pulled Falon aside. He had wanted to speak to him before the bonding but hadn't the opportunity. His forthcoming message would not be well received, and in a strange way, he felt compassion for the boy.

"Falon, tonight you will sleep in my burdei along with the Istri Dam and me."

"Why not in my own?"

"Carn needs a place to exercise his rights as a man."

Falon's eyes widened. "What? Why mine?"

"You live alone. Yours is the only burdei in Kurnisahn used by just one man."

"Why are you punishing me?"

"No one is punishing you, but there is no other choice. The bonding must be completed. Tonight, we pray an heir is made."

The blood drained from Falon's face. "How can you do this to me? I know I'm not worthy; you have made that clear so many times. But this—*this*! In my own burdei!"

"It will not be yours for long. On the morrow, we prepare to leave. Over the Sketen, you will make a new home."

"No. I will not accept this. I won't!" Falon said, his lips twitching between words.

He put his hand on the boy's chest. "You must. A great threat comes, and we must all make sacrifices. I am giving away so much for the sake of our tribe. And now you must do your part. Go to my burdei and make Una's beddings yours for the night."

A thin stream trickled down Falon's cheek, his chin quivering from his attempt to hold back the tears. The Istri Dam came out of her burdei and took the boy's hand, sullied with grime as it was from being shoved into the mud by Carn.

"Falon, please. Come with me now." She pulled him gently, and he followed her in.

That night, with fires waning throughout the living-place, the Somm lay awake, listening to cries from Falon's burdei across the way. No one went to investigate the noises, thinking perhaps they were but the calls of a woman for the first time in the throes of passion. But the Somm knew they were not the sounds of pleasure—they were the sounds of pain. And when he looked down at Falon, who too lay wide awake, he could tell he thought the same.

10

The Circle in the Trees

F ALON STEPPED OUT of the Somm's burdei and peered across the living-place, the long morning shadows stretching across his view. On the far side of the central hearth, Una stood in the entryway of Falon's burdei, her wandering gaze soon meeting his. His eyes, he was certain, were underscored by dark circles from a night of little sleep. And hers, he could see even from this distance, were bloodshot from a night of tears. A large hand grasped her shoulder, and the entrance flap fell behind her as she was pulled back in.

The Kurnisahn started gathering their belongings shortly after sunrise. The morning's activities were quiet, with fewer speakings than usual, and those who spoke tended to bicker over even the most trivial matters. Some grumbled about the little warning they'd been given while others lamented their uncertain future.

It wasn't until midmorning that Una emerged again from Falon's burdei, her face awash in pallor, her throat marred by a hand-shaped bruise.

"Are you alright?" Falon asked, reaching for her as she neared.

"He wants to see you," she said, pulling away.

"He wants to see *me*?"

"That's what he said. He's in your burdei." She walked past him and into her mother's arms, eyes to the ground.

Falon took a deep breath before entering; inside was his nemesis who would soon be his Somm if he did not consider himself so already. It was hard to accept apprehension about entering his own burdei, but Carn outweighed him by half a man and every interaction with him thus far had been adversarial. Not wanting to be alone with the man, Falon fastened the burdei flap in an open position before walking in. Carn looked past him, noting his action, then met eyes with him.

"Get ready. You're coming with me."

"Where?"

Carn stood, his legwear unfastened and his exposed member flopping against his thigh. Falon didn't mean to look but couldn't help noticing the dried blood at its tip.

"The circle in the trees we spoke of yesterday," Carn said, fastening his legwear, apparently having waited to dress until Falon was there to watch him do it. "Before we go sunward, I need to see what it is."

"Who else is going?"

"Just you and me."

Falon's stomach sank. Why did Carn want him out of the living-place, alone? "Maybe Ber-gul should come too," he said.

"No. The two of us is enough."

There was nothing Falon could do; if he refused to go, Carn might cut him down right there in his own burdei. "But why me?" he said. He could hear his own defeat as the words left his tongue.

"You have the best sight in the clan, it is said, and we will need a view from afar." Carn grabbed his axe, tapped the flat end of the blade against his palm. "We don't know who or what made that circle."

THEY FOLLOWED THE WATER for half a day, staying beneath the burnt red gloom of the bowers for stealth. Coarseoak roots fanned out in jumbled webs across their path and bored into the sediment. Brown leaves, parched and curled in their death throes, floated off the canopy after every gust of wind. Many landed in the shallows and drifted away with the current, off to some unknown place, swerving around branches and boulders, the water's ebb and flow dictated by the land below it and obstacles in its course.

Not a word was spoken during their journey, the silence deepening Falon's fear that Carn was luring him away for malevolent reasons. The absence of speakings magnified every sound—turbid waters burbling against the banks, litterfall crackling beneath their soles. Carn kept several paces ahead, never looking back. Was this really a scouting mission, or was Carn leading him out of the living-place so there would be no witnesses? He could have said almost anything during their travels to give Falon a clue about their true destination. But no—instead, silence.

Then, out of nowhere, Carn turned to him. "As a child, I saw two rams fighting in the hills near Ser-o."

Falon stopped, waiting for him to say more. Carn looked absently into the distance as if thinking about what next to say.

"A crack echoed through the hillsides each time they crashed," he continued. "But one of the rams was bigger and sent the weaker one tumbling down a cliff. It saddened me to watch the loser crash onto stone, its body drooping on the rocks like a bag of blood and bones. But it was then I realized that, in this world, the strong must kill the weak."

Was this a warning?

"The strong ram took the ewes. The weak went to the carrion birds," Carn said. His story sounded like a threat, but if Falon tried to flee back to Kurnisahn, it wouldn't take long for Carn to catch him. He must have noticed Falon's uncertainty because he spun around and said, "Are my words mistaken? Let me ask you this, boy. When the Kurnisahn foodbring, which animal do you target?"

"The one easiest to slay."

"And which one is that?"

"The injured or the old."

"Said another way—the weakest. And it is the weakest who endure the most punishing fates. How many hunts last a day or more, chasing prey until it collapses from exhaustion or blood loss? Even for nander, the end is often violent, and it is always cruel. It is the way of things. The sooner you admit that to yourself, the more you'll see the world for what it is—the setting for a dark game."

"For the weak?" Falon said, swallowing.

"And who among us will not one day be among the weak? The only thing that separates man from beast is the tip of a spear. Howlers have their teeth, cavebears their paws, aurochs their horns. A man's weapon is his *mind*, and he can do terrible things with it. But we are all made of flesh, and in the end, our spirits always return to the s'Sah."

He stared at Falon as if waiting for a response. When Falon nodded vacantly, unsure what to say, Carn shook his head. "One day, you will lose hope," he said.

Carn continued his march forward, and Falon followed, confused why he had stopped to tell him such a story. His words about the strong versus the weak sounded like something he might have said before striking Falon down, but instead he just walked away without explanation. The more Falon thought about it, the less sense it made.

They started climbing a hill when Carn raised a hand to halt. "You hear that?" he whispered.

Falon shook his head.

Carn motioned for Falon to follow him away from the water. "What are you doing? Let's go," he said when Falon hesitated. "The circle in the trees should be up there." Carn pointed to the top of the hill. "See the sky? That should be forest."

"You think that's your circle?"

Carn nodded. Maybe he was bringing him on a scouting mission after all.

"Let's go see," Falon said, his speech tinged with pep for the first time.

"No. Wait and listen."

With the din of the waters now behind them and no leaves crackling beneath their feet, they could hear strange voices coming from the crest of the hill. They sounded like nander but with a less guttural pitch. Falon turned to Carn and nodded. When the tall man nodded back, a howler barked from far away. It sounded like there were many of them up ahead.

"We shouldn't go up if there's a pack on that hill," Falon said. "There are only two of us."

"The barks are coming from the same place as the voices," Carn said, ignoring his warning.

"Could it be the j'Lok?"

"I don't think so. Let's get closer."

They continued their ascent. Near the edge of the glade, they stopped to hide behind an everwood trunk, peering around it to see the break in the woods. The clearing was indeed circular, almost perfectly so, with many trees lying on the ground inside it. Toppled trees were not uncommon on high ground for they often fell in storms. But these were different, their stumps flat as if upended by false means and their trunks collected in stacks.

Two figures stood in the center of the circle, hacking at a bole with wide black axes. They wore traditional garb—greyfur tunics and footwear—but something set them apart. They were darker skinned and taller than most nander, with narrower shoulders and slighter builds, their movements refined, almost elegant.

"Are those nander?" Falon said.

"They don't look like any nander I've ever seen. They're black-of-skin like they just crawled out of the narrowland itself."

"Their foreheads are not sloped back like ours, and their brows have no ridges," Falon added.

"The High Ones. This is what the j'Lok warned of."

"Why are they cutting down trees?"

"I don't know."

Past the circle up ahead, a howler growled. More low-pitched voices. A man yelling. A woman crying.

Falon exchanged glances with Carn, for the first time feeling as if they weren't adversaries. Carn seemed just as perplexed as he.

"There is something on the other side of the circle, where the forest starts again," Carn said. "Follow me quietly, so those two cutting wood don't hear."

Falon followed him around the clearing, all the while watching the dark figures go about their work. Once they reached the other side, several burdei-like structures came into view.

"There's not supposed to be a living-place here," Falon whispered.

"No, there's not." Carn scanned the area, then pointed at a coarseoak towering over the forest canopy. "Let's climb that tree to get a better view."

The lowest branches of the coarseoak were out of reach, but the thuk-tree beside it was bent and had low branches to climb. Carn went first, and Falon followed, allowing enough space between them so the Ser-o heir couldn't kick him off if he were so inclined. About halfway up the thuk-tree, they shifted onto the coarseoak and climbed the upper branches, rising farther from the forest floor than Falon had ever been. They clutched an upper limb, their feet planted on a thicker one below. Carn pulled down a third branch so its brown leaves wouldn't impede their view.

A living-place stood at the edge of the clearing, full of burdei erected from strawsod, thatch, and bone. Dark figures moved about, performing chores not unlike those in Kurnisahn. Some cooked, others twisted stringgrass. One put chops of wood into a fire. Another walked about as if surveying the scene.

Leaning against a burdei was a row of weapons—spears, clubs, axes, and blades. Beside the weapons were bundles of obsidian tipped sticks, each paired with a thuk-tree stave. There was something curious about those staves—each the height of a man with a stringgrass cord tying the ends, slightly bending the wood.

"I recognize those," Falon said, hardly able to contain himself. "Those are the weapons that slew the Bhatt."

"Shhh."

"There's a bundle of them next to each stave, as if they're paired together."

"I said be quiet."

Falon turned back to his observations. The howlers wandered about as if they belonged there. They played, fought, slept, urinated on a tree. One went so far as to enter a burdei. They were more vocal than any howlers he'd ever seen. One of the—High Ones?— he supposed, smacked a more rambunctious howler on the snout and it scurried away with its tail between its legs. These dark men must have cast some sort of spell over the animals.

"Howlers and nander living together?" Falon said.

"Those aren't nander. What do you see over there?" Carn pointed to the far edge of the living-place where a line of nander women, their wrists fettered with stringgrass binds, were engaged in various activities. One polished a flint tool, another scraped a slate of stone. One sat on the ground doing nothing, staring blankly into the forest. Another, whose rounded belly evidenced she was with child, sobbed beneath a tree with her head in her hands. Every woman's hair had been shorn.

"Those are the Bhatt women," Carn said.

"They could be," Falon agreed, realizing the prisoners, unidentifiable beneath their filth, were the only women in the living-place.

"Don't you see what this is?" Carn said. "Those women were taken from the killing. Whatever those things are over there—be they burnt nander or the High Ones themselves—they're the ones who killed the Bhatt."

The evidence seemed to fit. "And all this time, we've been acting like the j'Lok did it," Falon said.

Carn snarled. "I'm going down there."

"You're doing what? Why?"

"To free them."

This was foolhardy. Despite Carn's undeniable strength, he still was just one man pitted against the many heavily armed ones in the living-place. While Falon welcomed the notion of Carn marching to an early demise, he didn't want to risk his own safety by encouraging him to do so.

"Are you mad? There are too many High Ones. You'll be killed."

Carn paused, reason seeming to prevail. "Then we must go back to Kurnisahn and gather our men."

"We'll still be outnumbered. Not just by the High Ones but by their howlers too."

"What do you suggest then, Scarboy?" Carn spat, grabbing his tunic. "We just let them keep the Bhatt women?"

It seemed like Falon was about to be thrown from the tree, but then Carn let go when children's voices sounded from below. Two High One children, a boy and a girl, ran through the woods toward them. It was strange that there were children here but no women except the prisoners.

Carn put a finger to his lips to silence Falon, then started climbing down. As he shifted from the coarseoak to the shorter thuktree below, a twig snapped, and the children looked up. Carn smiled and held up a hand to assure their safety, but the children bolted away—the girl toward the living-place and the boy away from it.

Carn dropped to the forest floor, his feet thudding into the loam, and ran after the boy. Falon followed from behind once he reached the ground. He ducked beneath branches, jumped over roots, and weaved around the trees, barely able to keep up. In the distance, Carn leaped forward from an arm's length behind and tackled the boy by his legs and pinned him. He smashed him in the temple with his elbow, separating him from consciousness, all with the speed of a cat.

"What are you doing?" Carn said, turning to Falon as he neared.

"I… uh… followed you here?"

"You were supposed to get the girl!"

"She was running to the living-place."

"Gigas' piss!" Carn said, standing. Howlers barked in a frenzy from somewhere out of sight.

"We need to leave," Falon said.

Carn looked past Falon, noting the commotion, voices and barking alike. He slung the unconscious High One boy over his shoulder.

"What are you doing? We need to go, fast!" Falon said.

"He's coming with us."

"He's going to slow us down. Leave him here."

"We're taking him to Kurnisahn."

"Why?"

"To trade him for the women."

"One child for all those women?"

"All of Vul-ka's creatures ignore reason when it comes to their children."

The barking grew louder. The howlers were closing in.

"We need to go! Leave him here."

Carn shook his head. "We can't. He'll go back to his clan and tell them what he saw."

"The girl already went there."

"You have no say in this. Now, follow me. The howlers are almost here. We must cross the water, so they lose our scent."

11

The Captive

U NA KNEW SOMETHING BAD had happened when she heard the noise outside her burdei.

The Kurnisahn were ready for the journey sunward, having fastened furs, bones, weapons, and tools to long everwood planks for transport. The only task that remained was taking apart their burdei—a job that would take some time—but the Somm had said to wait until Carn and Falon returned before commencing the efforts.

How her body ached. Her mother had once counseled that her first night as a woman might be uncomfortable and there even might be pain, but she had not expected *this*. Time and again Carn had shoved his way inside her—splitting her open, grunting and writhing as he clutched her body with all his might. When he wanted to go a second time, she reluctantly consented, and the time after she simply said no. Carn didn't seem to understand or care and, powerless to hold her ground, she was forced to accept him again. It seemed the more she protested, the more aroused he became. But she never should have resisted him at all. Her role was now to attend to his needs and submit to his wants.

When Carn had at last excused her, the first thing she did was run to her mother. The Istri Dam held her close as tears poured onto her bosom. She went so far as to shoo the Somm from their burdei while she cared for her daughter.

Today, Una was raw between the legs and the side of her neck throbbed. Once the Kurnisahn went sunward, she would spend many days walking through the wilderness, traversing forest, hill, and valley alike. She could not imagine such travels when it pained her just to walk across the living-place.

Putting her troubles aside, Una worried about the anguish Falon must have endured knowing what was happening to her in his very own burdei. She'd tried to stay quiet, but no matter how hard she tried, the Ser-o heir would thrust so hard inside her that she could not help but wail and scream so many times.

In hindsight, Falon had been right to warn her. But what could she have done? Her bonding was not something over which she had control. Although at times she'd fussed to her parents, she had always known the decision would never be hers. Especially now, given the importance of her pairing, she would have no say in her father's decrees.

As she reflected upon all this, she heard her father yelling outside. She walked out of her burdei, each bowlegged step aching like her womanhood was stuffed with gravel. The Kurnisahn were in the middle of the living-place, surrounding Carn and Falon—and something else.

She made her way toward the clatter to find a crying boy on the ground, a rabbit pelt gag between his teeth. The boy's features were unlike any nander she'd ever seen; he was black-of-skin, almost as if stained by night, his ridgeless forehead high and rounded. He was young, no more than a hand of age, but his height was hard to tell since he lay sideways with his hands and feet bound together.

"Why did you bring this thing into our living-place?" her father shouted at Carn.

"This is no *thing*—this is a High One child," Carn said, poking the Somm's ribs. The Kurnisahn gasped at both his characterization of the boy and his hostility to the Somm.

The Somm pushed his hand away. "Why bring it here? What did you do?"

"You lead your nander falsely, Ul-man, acting as if the j'Lok were the threat, when everything they said was true. The j'Lok were trying to protect you."

The Somm tilted his head, his eyes locked on Carn.

"The High Ones are here—*here!*" Carn hollered, lifting the child by the back of his neck and shoving him into the dirt. "I saw them. A living-place larger than Ser-o and Kurnisahn combined. They're the ones who slew the Bhatt in the Sketen. Not the j'Lok—the High Ones."

"How do you know this?" Menok asked.

"They had the Bhatt women."

"And the strange weapon the traders showed us," Falon added.

The Somm and Menok looked at one another.

Carn stepped to the Somm. "We must free those women."

"If they outnumber both our clans combined, what can we do?"

"Don't forget the howlers," Falon said.

Carn nodded. "It is true. The High Ones have united with the howlers."

"Howlers can't even speak," the Somm said. "It cannot be."

"We saw it ourselves and barely escaped. The beasts would have followed our scent and torn us apart had we not crossed the water."

The Somm waved his hands. "Enough. What are we supposed to do with this child?"

"Trade him for the women."

The child wailed through the gag, his eyes bloodshot and filmy. Even if he was a High One, Una felt terrible for him. He was just a scared little boy.

"How?" the Somm said. "Once we trade our captives, they'll come here and destroy us."

"We were leaving anyway," Carn said. "Let us go to the Sketen, as planned. Instead of fighting the j'Lok, we'll defend against the High Ones when they come. Only the nature of the threat has changed, not the existence of one."

"And find ourselves confronted with the j'Lok and the High Ones at the same time?" Menok argued.

The Somm turned to the shaman. "What say you? The High Ones are a matter of legend, a matter of faith." He pointed at the child. "Is this a High One before us?"

The shaman knelt to examine the boy, lifting his jutting chin, looking into his eyes. "Before the light split from the outer darkness," the shaman said, "Vul-ka fought Gigas, the spirit of soil and night. Gigas stood in Vul-ka's shadows, squeezing sand into the boulders that would one day become the narrowland itself."

The Kurnisahn were rapt. While they'd heard this story countless times, it seemed more relevant now than ever.

The shaman rose. "As the blackness and the narrowland drifted toward one another, Vul-ka swatted Gigas down, casting him into the ground and beneath the feet of all things living. Out of Gigas' wounds, the blood spilled onto the soils to become the flowing waters of the narrowland.

"So we find it today: Gigas below and Vul-ka shining over our heads. It is Vul-ka's strength that keeps the waters flowing so they do not turn to stone."

The shaman looked at the captive boy again before turning to the Somm. "But Gigas knew Vul-ka was old, his brightness fading. He waited under the narrowland, turning his fingers into black tendrils to poison the land. And he called these tendrils the High Ones, for they would one day reach up from the ground and destroy the s'Sah itself." The shaman closed his eyes, taking a deep breath as if pulling spirits from the air. "One day, when Vul-ka's warmth fades, a coldness will be cast upon the land. The waters will turn to stone, and the High Ones will rise from the belly of the narrowland to bring forth the end of the world."

Everyone stood in silence, waiting for the shaman to reach some sort of conclusion, some sort of answer, but instead, he just stared.

"So, is it a High One or not?" the Somm said, shaking his head.

"Is each year colder than the last?"

"It is."

"Did the j'Lok say the coldland waters had turned to stone and never flowed again come seasons' turn?"

"He did."

The shaman stepped toward the Somm and cocked his head. "And is this child black as if it just crawled from the belly of the narrowland?"

"It is."

"Then you know the answer."

The Somm exchanged glances with Menok. "If the High Ones are here, we must go to j'Lok," the Somm said. "That's the only way to save ourselves."

"The j'Lok might return any time now. We should wait for them," Menok said.

"We don't even know where they are. They should have been back already."

"What about the Ser-o?" Carn said. "I won't just leave my family. If you want to go darkward, that is your choice. But I'm going back to warn my clan."

The Somm shifted his gaze to Una.

"She comes with me," Carn said before the Somm could speak, sending a sharpness to the pit of Una's stomach.

"And what of the High One child?" Menok said.

"If you are afraid of that little boy, I'll take him back to Ser-o, where the men still act like men."

The Somm breathed heavily; Una could see him holding him-self back. There was only so much disrespect he would take before he snapped, and then no one would be safe. She looked around: everyone was on edge, waiting, perhaps dreading her father's reac-tion But then the Somm took a final deep breath before turning to Falon. "You. In my burdei. Now."

Falon's eyes widened.

"Now, I said."

Falon followed him in, and Una stood outside the closed flap so she could hear the speakings within. "I want to hear what hap-pened from you," she heard her father say.

"Carn told it true. The circle in the woods was trees cut down by those dark figures—what we are calling the High Ones."

"How many were there?"

"I don't know. There were many hands, all men."

"And what of their prisoners?"

"Nander women, but I couldn't tell if they were the Bhatt."

"And the strange weapon brought forth by the clanless men?"

"They had more of those than anything else. Whole bundles of them, each paired with a stave."

"What do the staves have to do with it?"

"I don't know, but they were together. Maybe they need the staves to use the weapon. The staves had some sort of cord tying the ends together, bending the wood."

"I don't see the connection," the Somm said, lifting the burdei flap. Una turned nonchalantly as if she hadn't been eavesdropping. Before walking out, the Somm stopped and turned to Falon, ignoring Una's presence. "One more question. Is that a High One child?"

"I... I don't know," Falon said.

The Somm marched out of the burdei with his chin held high. "Kurnisahn, the endtimes are upon us, the shaman has so said. We were wrong to distrust the j'Lok, their belief that the High Ones are coming appears to be true. They are closer than a day away, but we are packed and almost ready to go. Our destination changes but the fact that we must leave does not. At first light, we will take apart our burdei and go darkward to j'Lok."

The Somm turned to Carn. "Our arrangement is over."

Una's pulse quickened. Could this mean that she would endure no more nights with the Ser-o heir?

Carn stepped to the Somm, looking down from a head taller. "Meaning?"

"The joining of our tribes can no longer happen. It was a pact made on false grounds."

"False grounds *you* put forth."

"That may be. But I am taking my nander to j'Lok. If the High Ones have risen, the safest place for my clan is where the most well-armed nander are. That is not in Ser-o, not over the Sketen, but in j'Lok."

"Then our arrangement is over," Carn said, "but my bonding to your daughter is not. That took place under the sights of Vul-ka; we shared our blood over the flames. The girl is mine."

The Somm looked to the shaman, hoping for support. The shaman shook his head and looked away from his disappointed leader.

"Then it is settled," Carn said, smirking, his eyes unchanged in that expression Falon had warned of. "At first light, I will go to Ser-o with Una—and the High One child. Good luck to you all, Kurnisahn. Where you're going, you will need it."

12
She Pulls Away

CARNE ONLY HAD A SINGLE ROUND in him that night, and for that Una was grateful. He climbed up from behind and shoved her face against the beddings, quickly spilling his seed inside her. After resting his heavy frame on her back for a few deep breaths, he rolled over and passed out without a word.

She closed her eyes, trying to clear her mind, fighting to ignore the sticky drip between her legs and Carn's rumbling snores. A drastic change loomed before her, one now even greater than before. As much as her life would have changed in the Sketen, at least her family would have stayed together. But now she would be separated from everyone she knew and loved and go even farther sunward to Ser-o—while her family went as far as possible in the other direction. All the way to j'Lok. She would never see them again.

She feared for the future of the Kurnisahn—her mother, her father, her uncle, and her friends. One day, Falon might find a woman in j'Lok; perhaps Una being taken away would enable him to move on, allow him to erase from his mind the turmoil of recent days.

She couldn't sleep with these thoughts spinning through her head. And that was before the crying began.

The child.

The High One child.

He was bound beside the fire in the center of the living-place. No one had fed him or even bothered to give him water. Instead, he was left out in the elements like a captured animal, his arms tied to a stake. A boy perhaps not even a hand of age. Even the clanless traders had been given beddings.

The child cried and cried, wailing one word—a word with an "mmm" sound that Una believed meant "mother."

Then the crying stopped. She sat up, checking to make sure Carn was still asleep, as if she couldn't already tell from his snoring. She wiped between her legs, rubbed the pink gunk on the wall and stood. After lifting the burdei flap, she stuck her head out to find the child curled around his tethers, Falon standing beside him.

She turned to check on Carn one last time, then walked over to Falon. He noticed her coming but kept his eyes on the child, whose wailing had eased into a sniffle.

"I know what happened to you," he said. He looked at the child but was speaking to her.

"I tried, last night—I don't know what to do, Falon," she said, the words not coming to her. She wasn't even sure what she wanted to say.

He turned to her. "It's not your fault. I just wish it didn't have to be this way. Everything that happened, these past days—"

"Were for the wrong reasons," she finished for him.

He looked away. "It doesn't matter anymore. Your future is set; you'll go sunward tomorrow with Carn, and the rest of us will go darkward."

"And as far from Ser-o as you can go."

Falon didn't respond.

"But what of the dangers?" she continued. "If the High Ones are here, won't we all be taken by the forever-sleep anyway? The stories say nothing of a battle. They sound like we're just going to disappear. The High Ones will destroy the very s'Sah itself."

"I don't know," Falon said, his terseness suggesting he didn't want to say what he was thinking. He shifted his attention to the child with his lips turned down as if in pity. "No one has fed him or even brought him water."

"As if he's some sort of demon," she said.

"He seems just like a child, suffering here in the cold."

"Maybe we should cover him with furs."

"Maybe we should set him free."

Una stepped back. "You can't mean it. Carn would kill you," she said.

"How would he know it was me?" Falon extended an arm to suggest no one was awake.

"Don't. Too dangerous."

The two stood in silent agreement while the shivering child looked up at them expectantly, his lips chapped, his chin tucked in.

"Wait here," she said, before tiptoeing into her parents' burdei. After a moment, she returned with a pair of greyfurs. "My father still wants to hide those obsidian blocks, but it's alright, he'll probably blame you for taking these." She chuckled while placing the greyfurs on the child.

Falon helped cover the boy. "There were no women in the High One living-place," he said. "But there were children. At least two of them."

"In a living-place with only men? Maybe it was a war party."

"Well, they had women, but they were all nander."

Una opened her mouth slightly. "You don't think the children were—"

"I don't know, maybe."

"You said they were the Bhatt women. There hasn't been enough time for them to—"

"We *thought* they were the Bhatt women. But it was hard to see from where we were."

While Una digested this, Falon collected water from a rain pail and brought it to the child. He raised the waterskin to the boy's mouth, who gulped as if he hadn't drunk anything in days. After the child finished the water, Falon stood and met eyes with Una. He raised a hand to touch her cheek. She pulled away.

"Falon—no."

"Let's leave here. You and me."

"Are you mad? And go where?"

"I don't know. But you don't want to go sunward, and I don't want to go darkward. Let's go somewhere else, perhaps to the Saltsea."

"No. That can't happen."

Falon looked at his burdei. "You'd rather spend the rest of your life with him?"

"Under the sights of Vul-ka, we were bonded," she said, so softly she was not sure if Falon would hear.

"And you will suffer for it. You can't stay with the Kurnisahn. Your father won't allow it. But we can escape if we leave now. I can save you from him."

Falon was right. If she accepted the path chosen for her, she would be stuck with Carn, a man who might actually be as dangerous as Falon had warned. The alternative, as mad as it sounded, was to flee, but Carn would surely come after her with deadly purpose. Even if they escaped, how long would they survive out there alone? She had no foodbringing skills, and Falon lacked the strength and experience to do it on his own. What would they live on, cho-berries and roots? The occasional snowbird or mouse? And all this while the days grew shorter, the cold air rising. No, she would not survive out there alone with Falon. Especially not when the low sun came.

"I can't."

"But—"

"No, Falon, I can't," she said again, this time accidentally glancing at his scar—something she had always consciously avoided. Perhaps her eye was drawn to it by the fire-cast shadows rippling across his face, making his disfigurement seem more pronounced than usual. When she averted her eyes and looked back into his, she could tell he had caught her looking.

"It's this, isn't it?" he said, running his finger along the dark purple crevice stretching from his temple to below his eye.

"Why are you asking me that?"

"You haven't looked at me the same since the day your father gave this to me."

"That's not it."

"The way you looked at me before—when we would sneak out into the woods together—your eyes for me were different then."

"You know why we can't be together. Maybe I just hadn't accepted it before that day." As she said this, she knew her words were false, and that everything Falon had said was true. Ever since her father had struck him with his coarseoak staff, she hadn't been able to look at him the same. Underneath it all, Falon had a pleasant face—his features might not be chiseled, nor his brow the most prominent—yet he was handsome in an awkward sort of way. No matter, every time she looked at him, she couldn't get past the grotesque cleft covering half his face. Although she still cared for him deeply, she would never look at him the way she had when they were younger.

Falon stared at the ground with that distracted face he always made when trying to hide his thoughts. "Come with me, Una. We'll find a way. Whatever troubles we face, at least you will be away from him."

"We can't," she said, touching his shoulder. "Our paths have been decided for us already. Come the morrow, we will go our own ways."

Her eyes wettened as she walked away from the fire and back to her snoring lifemate. She didn't know if Falon would set the child free like he'd suggested, but she had to get away from him nonetheless. She couldn't bear to think anymore about what might have been. Tomorrow would be the last day she would see her friends, her family. Of that, she was certain. Of that, she had no choice.

13
Sorrows

M OST LIVES HAVE BUT A FEW MOMENTS where one can say their path truly changed. For some, it might be the passing of a parent or the birthing of a child. Others might say it was meeting their lifemate or their first kill. But then there are times where someone's pivotal event is not reflected in the lives of others. For some, that moment represents something much darker, decisive, and shattering.

Much later, when Falon would look back at everything that had happened both before and after the attack, he would try to identify exactly when it was that everything changed. Was it Carn's arrival, with its bloodlust and gore? Or the moment he killed his father, with its trepidation and torment? Or was it perhaps the visit of the j'Lok envoy and the chain of events that occurred in consequence? No, in truth, it was none of those things. While each of those events had the potential for great changes for the Kurnisahn, none were the catalyst.

What changed things was Carn's stealing of the boy.

The sun had barely risen when the underwood stirred. Rustling emanated from the forest on all sides—sticks snapping, bracken swaying. Whispers. Something had surrounded Kurnisahn and was about to move in.

Yellow howler eyes peered into the living-place from the understory. A few of the animals roved closer, others tramped in with confidence and poise, in total a pair of hands or more. When the predators bared their teeth, the Kurnisahn stood in shock; howlers had never intruded so boldly into their territory. These killers had learned over the generations to fear the nander and their weapons. While a lone howler could defeat any man in weaponless combat, they knew no man was ever unarmed. So, when the beasts entered the living-place and surrounded them, the Kurnisahn saw at once that these were no ordinary howlers. They were under some sort of control, some sort of spell.

"Kurnisahn, to the center, by the fire," the Somm said, lifting his spear. The men steered the women and children to the central hearth, now but a few smoking cinders in the morning gloom. Sensing the retreat, the howlers charged. The men who had time to raise their weapons swung axes, thrust spears, cut with daggers. Others grabbed the nearest object, be it a stick or bone, to use as a club.

Some defenses worked, and many howlers were slain, but many nander were themselves felled. Some bitten on their legs, others on their buttocks. Some were surrounded by more than one howler and never stood a chance. Yet, amidst the violence and horror, the howlers turned out to be the least of the Kurnisahn's problems.

Confusion turned into chaos when the forever-sleep came raining down upon the living-place. Slim sticks, each tipped with an obsidian blade, flew out of the forest in violent arcs. Falon had been right about the strange weapon the clanless traders had brought forth—it was made to be thrown—and the High Ones had found a way to fling it fast enough to pierce flesh. As he watched one man after another fall, he knew only one word to describe such awful weapons—*sorrows*.

Falon was the first to realize the howlers were but a distraction: the real attack was coming from the distance and the sky. He lay on his stomach and crawled to the side of his burdei, sitting with his back pressed against the stretched hide. He peeked around the corner and into the forest. Emerging from the shadows were many hands of High Ones, each man holding a thuk-tree stave in one hand and a sorrow in another, the sorrows pulled back by stringrass cords tied between the ends of the wood. The staves flexed when the men drew their cords taut, sending their sorrows through the air at unspeakable speeds when released.

Sorrows. The ultimate weapon. Thin rods of pain that could slay a man from afar before he even knew his killer was there.

The High Ones marched into Kurnisahn. Menok, a sorrow sticking out of his thigh, fought both howler and High One alike with his spear. Ber-gul and Suht battled back-to-back, protecting the women, one against a howler and the other a High One.

What was Falon to do? He was weak. He was small. And he carried no weapon except his father's small blade. Yet, he had to fight alongside the Kurnisahn. He had to help protect his kin. He scanned the grounds for a better weapon and saw a dirt-covered aurochs horn leaning against the Somm's burdei.

A horn of the beast that killed my father, he thought.

He seized the horn, its texture bonelike in his hand, and stood. As he turned, he saw Carn's silhouette standing black against the rising sun, the flat of his axe lifting off the ground.

"It's because of you this happened!" Carn roared while swinging the weapon.

And that's when the world went black.

14

The Way Her Knees Bent

F ALON HAD NEVER BEEN unconscious before, but now having touched the depthless hollow of the otherworld, he saw what the forever-sleep was like. One moment you're awake, the next you're not. The only difference between unconsciousness and the forever-sleep was that you never rose from the latter.

The first thing he heard in the darkness was women screaming, their cries sharpening as he gathered his senses. Something warm trickled down his forehead, and for a moment, the sensation felt oddly pleasant. He reached up and felt his scalp—wet, hot, and when he looked at his hand, red.

He lifted his cheek from the dirt, the world spinning, his ears ringing. Ber-gul lay motionless in the soil with three sorrows in the chest. Suht, a boy younger than Falon, was face down in a crimson pool with a howler lapping up the blood. Menok was crumpled over with sorrows in his back and his throat sliced open. Most of the men already had their ears cut off, dark holes behind their temples streaming red. Others, like the Somm, were in the process of having them removed—just a few jagged cuts before being peeled away.

Falon felt his wounds again and was relieved to find he still had both ears; all the blood was from a gash in his scalp. The High Ones hadn't reached him yet, but when they came for his ears, they would find him still alive.

Most of the women were in various stages of resistance— screaming and kicking while being tied up and beaten. The Istri Dam, trying to fight off the High One sawing off the Somm's ears, received a knee to the face before splashing into the mud.

As humiliating as a craven retreat might be, what other choice did Falon have? All the men were in the forever-sleep. Some of their bodies were being ripped apart by howlers, growling and snapping at each other while jockeying over pieces of meat. And the High Ones were stalking the grounds, taking ears and making sure no man survived.

Then someone screamed in the forest.

It was her.

Carn must have snatched Una during the attack and run off. Confronting him would be reckless, but it gave Falon a purpose, a sense of courage, an option other than desertion. He grabbed the aurochs horn and crawled into the forest, unnoticed amidst the maelstrom. Once out of sight, he stood and followed Una's screams, pushing away leaves and brush as he pressed forward, his balance slowly returning with each step.

It wasn't Carn who had taken Una, but Falon instantly wished that it was. She stood with her face pressed against a coarseoak trunk and her legwear at her ankles, sobbing as a High One thrust his pelvis behind her. The man pinned her against the grey bark with one hand on the back of her neck, the other on her wrist. The sight Falon would never be able to erase from his mind was the way her knees bent outward and her heels pushed together as if she denied what was happening to her even as it happened.

The High One was lost in such fervor that he didn't notice Falon sneaking up from behind. He raised the horn and slammed it like a club into the back of the man's skull. The man staggered into Una and turned, his glossy, still-erect member pointing at him. Falon swung again, but this time, the High One caught the horn mid-swing and yanked it out of his hands. Still dizzy from being unconscious, Falon tried to hold on but tumbled to the ground, cracking his temple against a root.

He turned onto his back and unsheathed his father's blade as the man pushed him down and straddled his chest, raising the horn for a killing blow. But Falon was faster and drove the dagger into the man's gut and behind his ribs. Blood sputtering from his mouth, the man shrieked something in his strange High One tongue as Falon twisted the blade. The man seized his wrists, trying in vain to wrest the hilt from his clutches, but Falon was too strong. It was a strange circumstance in which to find himself, especially when pitted against a man fully grown. After a moment's struggle, the man released the weapon. Falon pushed him off and plunged his blade into his neck until all that remained was a twitching body.

As he peered down upon the High One corpse, Falon couldn't help but marvel at how much it looked like one of his own. Despite having ascended his father, he felt this was the first time he had killed his own kind. The body before him might be the color of the narrowland, taller and slenderer than a nander. His nose might be thinner and hooked and his brow less pronounced—but still, he was some sort of man.

Una was curled like a baby with both hands cupped over her womanhood. "Una, get up. We have to go," Falon said, crawling to her, trying to catch his breath. He was so bloodied he couldn't tell what had come from the man and what spilled from the rent in his scalp.

She stared blankly past him. He took her hand and stood. In the distance, women cried, howlers bayed, High Ones shouted and laughed in some incomprehensible tongue.

"Una, please. I know you're hurt, but we need to go. They're going to kill us."

He lifted her hand, but she was dead weight.

"I… I can't…Where is my mother? My father?"

"They're gone. They're all gone."

Tears streamed from her red eyes. "I can hear them screaming!"

"A few women are still alive but not the men."

"My mother?"

"She's in the forever-sleep. She was on the ground next to your father when I escaped." Without a way to save her, he didn't want to mention she still might be alive.

"And Carn?"

"Taken by the forever-sleep."

"Are you sure?" she said, tilting her head. Something in his manner must have betrayed the lie.

"Yes, I'm sure." He could not dwell on the fact he hadn't actually seen Carn's body; they had no time to waste. Soon, the High Ones would realize one of their men was missing and come looking for him.

"Let's see what we can take from the body," he said, kneeling over the High One. What concerned him most of all was that he and Una were barefoot, for nander rarely donned footwear in the living-place. But if they were to flee, they had to protect their feet. He pulled off the High One's footwear and unwrapped his leggings and hoisted them over his shoulder. Between the footwear and the leggings, there would be enough material to protect their feet. He also found an obsidian dagger and a waterskin, both slick and red from the slice to the gut. "We need to leave," he said, wiping off the blade. "The High Ones will come for us. We must be gone before they do."

"Their howlers will find us."

"We got away yesterday by crossing the water."

"They still found you."

"They were looking for the child."

She pointed at the dead man. "When they find him, they'll come for us."

He wrapped his arms around her. Her skin was cold. "We need to go where it is safest," he said, putting his chin on her shoulder. "To a place where they know about the High Ones and prepare for them."

She pulled away and looked at the ground, her wearings soiled red from his embrace.

"We know where the High Ones will be," he continued. "Carn and I saw their living-place yesterday. The Bhatt women are there. If any of the Kurnisahn survive, that's where they'll be taken. But we can't save them by ourselves. We need help."

"Help from whom?"

"The only ones with enough men and weapons to fight back."

"The j'Lok," she said, taking his hand.

PART III:
OUR PASSAGE

15

Supply Run

UNA'S EVERY STEP was a struggle as she followed Falon to the flowing water. Already raw from Carn's brutality, she'd been in no state to suffer the humiliations wrought upon her by the High Ones the very next day. By the time Falon had intervened, she'd already endured the ravages of two other men, her willpower crumbling as they pinned her to the tree and struck her with their fists and feet every time she tried to break free. Although her body was bruised from the beatings and her face scored from the bark, her womanhood hurt most of all. It felt like it had been pinched and twisted, the sting reaching deep inside her as she pleaded for Falon to slow his pace.

As if all that hadn't been enough, she wet herself the night after the attack and was nauseous the following morning. Falon rubbed her back as she tried to vomit but nothing would come. Her throat was as dry as she was between her legs—a grim reminder of the violations cast upon her by the High Ones, fevered and lustful as they had been. Now, every time she closed her eyes, she would see the lurid expressions of the High One mankillers, their bulging members thrusting into her as she whimpered amongst the shadows of slaughter.

After the horrors had passed, she stopped to take account of what little remained. In an instant, her family was gone, a new reality she couldn't fully process since nothing had prepared her for losing them so quickly and violently. And the rest of her clan—everyone she knew and loved—gone. The men killed and the surviving women taken. It pained her to think of the indignities her fellow women might still be suffering.

She and Falon hid in the forest across the waters for three days until she felt like herself again. They found a nook under a fallen coarseoak, and Falon built them a shelter using thuk-tree branches and grasses, his movements unusually slow and deliberate all the while. He would stop and put his head in his hands, apparently in a great deal of pain, but every time she asked if he was alright, he waved her off and pretended he was. At least his scalp had stopped bleeding.

They ate nothing the first day even though Falon sought food-stuff from dawn until nightfall. The next day he found a wilted cho-berry vine and plundered its meager yield. While suffering a few days with little food was common, a handful of cho-berries wasn't nearly enough to sustain their recovery. Falon pretended to ignore his headaches both days, imploring her to try to leave, saying the High Ones might seek them still. But she couldn't roam far enough to justify withdrawing from what had thus far been a safe place. By the third day, and in spite of the hunger, she felt she had recovered enough to move on.

"We should go," she said.

Falon stood, refreshed by the prospect of finally leaving. "We should follow the flowing water until it splits, then take the coldlands branch until we reach j'Lok."

His ambitions of going straight to j'Lok did not quite match the reality of their situation. The journey might take a sistersun or more even in the best conditions, and the snows couldn't be far away now that the turning of the seasons was at hand. The grounds in the lowrock valley were often covered by the white for many sistersuns. How long might they be stranded, waiting for the snows to melt, when so far darkward?

If they were to survive such a journey, they needed supplies; without tools, they couldn't spear fish or even trap small animals. They'd have to rely on whatever berries, nuts, and roots they could find, but foraging might not be possible farther darkward where the grounds were less fruitful. And even if they found foodstuff in the coldland forests, how would they stay warm? They had no fire.

"I don't think we'll make it," Una said.

"You just said you're ready."

"I am. But we won't make it all the way to j'Lok."

"Yes, we will," he said, patting his aurochs horn. "If we stay close to the water, we can find nuts and roots, spear fish—"

"We don't have a spear."

"We'll make one."

"And how will we stay warm?"

"We'll build a fire."

"Have you ever built a fire from nothing?" she asked, dropping her hands to her sides. "There's a reason my father always kept hot coals in the hearth and always found ways to keep embers even during storms."

"I know how to build a fire. We just need the right wood."

As usual, Falon's disposition was confident but unrealistic. "It won't be so easy," she said. "Even when our elders traveled to nearby living-places, they always brought embers."

"Then what do we do? The only closer living-places are Ser-o and Bhatt unless we dare go back to Kurnisahn where the High Ones and their howlers might still be about."

"To go to Ser-o, we'll have to pass through the Sketen. That's where the j'Lok went, and they never came back. Maybe the unburied bodies really did curse the soil."

Falon looked darkward. "Then we brave the cold and go to j'Lok. But first, we should stop in Bhatt to see what they left behind."

And so, they headed to Bhatt, darkward and angled toward the setting sun. Although their bellies rumbled, by traveling along the water, they at least were never thirsty. Falon tried to fish, using his dagger like a spear, but spent half the morning in the shallows with no success. These creatures were near impossible to stab, each time slipping away unscathed, almost as if sensing Falon's attack before even he knew it was coming.

Later, they happened upon a waterbird guarding her eggs in the tall grasses by the shore, squawking angrily as they approached. It was strange for a fowl to be nesting this time of year when the days grew shorter, but perhaps its breeding pattern had been disrupted by the unusually cold season. Falon rushed in and grabbed its neck with both hands while it flapped its wings and pecked at the air. The fowl went limp when he wrenched its neck, snapping it cleanly. They collected a few eggs from its dried sedge nest and packaged them for later. That night, they ate the bird raw, thankfully neither falling ill.

After a few days, they made their way up the hillside to Bhatt, now but a few caves littered with abandoned nander effects and oddments. The clan had left behind two bearskins, surprising since such furs were greatly valued. Perhaps they'd been discarded because of their countless tears, either the handiwork of scavengers or evidence of the battles in which the beasts were slain. Tanned hides were also strewn about, and from them they made waterskins large enough to hold a few days of water, using some of Una's hair to tie them shut.

Falon also found a flint spear. With its warped shaft and dull blade, it was obvious why it had been left behind, and Falon laid it out beside the aurochs horn to compare the two. The spear was longer than the horn but also duller. With some clever grinding though, the weapon had potential. The same could not be said for the horn, which due to its hollow center and wide base, could never be wielded like a spear.

"You should leave the horn," Una said. "It's too heavy, and you'll never be able to catch fish with it."

Falon stopped to think about this, lifting the horn to examine it. There was sadness in his eyes as he peered inside the horn, which seemed to mean more to him than a mere weapon or tool. "Let's wait to see if it becomes a burden. For now, it comes with us," he said, packing it away with the spear.

Their search for embers was less successful. The hearths in Bhatt had all gone cold and were but piles of ash and bone. Falon ran his fingers deep into the residue of every firepit, each time finding only powdery coldness.

"There is dry wood here, though," he said. "Their caves have kept out the wetness. The best way to start a fire is everwood for a spindle and coarseoak for the board."

"We'll need a fire pouch to carry the embers."

"My father used to wrap two shells in a pelt. With some lichen and tinder inside, it should stay alight for at least a day."

They found the materials while rummaging through the caves. After packing everything for travel, they gazed out of the grotto and into the forest. Thinking about the journey ahead made Una's stomach turn. No Kurnisahn had ever been to j'Lok, and neither she nor Falon had ever been more than a half day's travel from their home.

"If we head toward the rising sun, we'll reach the coldlands branch of the flowing waters in a day or two," Falon said. "After that, we'll follow it darkward."

"And into the coldlands."

He looked at her but didn't reply, perhaps not wanting to say anything that would change her mind about going to j'Lok.

"Even if we make it there," she continued, "how do we know we'll be treated well—we who deserted our own families?"

"We didn't desert our families. They were killed."

"Still, we know so little about the j'Lok. We know they have obsidian, we know they're in the mountains. But we also know they love to fight."

Falon opened his mouth as if to speak but then looked away.

"Falon, say something."

He rubbed his hands together before turning back to her. "The way to j'Lok will be difficult. Surviving in the mountain snows will be hard enough alone. And we don't know what the j'Lok will do when we arrive. But why would they want to harm us? We know they seek more nander for their mines."

"Yes, but look at us—a stained woman and a…"

She paused.

"You don't need to say it," Falon said, his features slackening. "A weakling."

Una felt terrible for having let that slip, even if she had cut herself off before actually saying it. "I was going to say *a young man*," she said.

Falon nodded, clearly doubting her but wanting to move on. "We don't know what will happen in j'Lok. But what chance do we have here, in the lowrock valley? There are High Ones and their howlers about. We might not see them, but we know they're there." He looked back out into the forest. "You saw what happened to our kin. You and I will fall even faster if we come across those killers alone."

As much as Una had learned to temper Falon's naïve hopefulness, this time he was right. Staying in the lowrock valley was not an option, even if she dreaded the frozen wastes and the great unknown of how the j'Lok would react when two deeply flawed nander arrived in their living-place.

At daybreak, they gathered their belongings, filled their waterskins, and pressed forth with their backs to the sun.

16
Fire Drill

FALON HAD ALWAYS TAKEN fire for granted until it came time to start one on his own. The hearths back in Kurnisahn always had embers burning, even in the middle of the day, since keeping a flame was much easier than making a new one. But he had never appreciated how hard starting a fire would actually be.

More than three sistersuns had come and gone since they'd left Bhatt and staying warm thus far hadn't been an issue. Each night, they built shelters using fallen branches and leaves, and the furs from Bhatt provided enough protection from the cold. They huddled together every night for warmth, and although he never approached her in an untoward way, she always faced away from him. Some mornings, she appeared to have wet herself in the night, but he mentioned nothing for fear of embarrassing her.

The cool air wouldn't last much longer, with each night colder than the one before. The turning of the seasons was at hand, and while they'd gone fireless for reasons of stealth, it would soon be too cold to survive without a flame.

The next night was particularly brutal; they spent the better part of darkness awake and shivering. To make matters worse, they heard what sounded like valleycats near their campsite, craving their next meal. Una screamed and hollered, and Falon waved his aurochs horn to scare them away, but still they could hear the monsters stalking them in the woods.

"We can't go on like this," Una said. "We need fire for warmth and to scare off the beasts. We've come so far and haven't even reached the mountains."

"I thought we'd be in j'Lok by now," Falon said. We should have been there a while ago."

"It was said to be a sistersun away."

"We're moving too slow. Each day, we waste time looking for foodstuff, standing in the shallows and hoping for fish."

"Yet, most days we go hungry."

Falon had foreseen this, even if he'd wanted to believe they could survive the journey. His ribs were more pronounced each day though the lack of foodstuff didn't appear to affect Una to the same degree.

"j'Lok is said to be deep in the mountains," he said. "But all we see are hills."

"Could we be following the wrong branch of flowing water?"

"I thought this was the right one, but now I'm not so sure."

The truth was that his mind had been in a haze ever since being struck by the flat of Carn's axe. Falon had heard many stories about j'Lok, but perhaps there was a detail he remembered wrong or couldn't remember at all. His memory seemed to have holes in it, and often he'd forget what he was doing even while doing it.

"We have to go on," Una said. "There has to be a living-place somewhere along the water. Let's just hope it isn't full of High Ones."

He stared at the flowing water, watching it splash against the slippery rocks by the shore. He strained to remember if there was a detail about j'Lok he hadn't been able to recall, but nothing new would come.

"What is it?" she asked. "You look confused."

"It's nothing."

Her expression hinted that she knew he was hiding something, but she dropped the subject. "I can't go any further today," she said. "Let's make a fire before the sun sets."

He shook his head. "No, too dangerous."

"We're hungry, we're cold. We have to take a chance. It's been long enough. We're so far from home."

"We don't know who might be out there."

"But we know *what* is out there. Soon, one of those valleycats will get hungry enough to charge in."

She was right, but it didn't matter. His fears were outweighed by the comfort a fire would provide. At this point, protection against predators was secondary.

After gathering supplies, they settled beside a thuk-tree and prepared for a fire. He bored a hole into a coarseoak plank, beveling the grain so the hot dust would fall into the tinder pile. He pressed the end of an everwood rod into the cavity and stepped on the slat so it wouldn't turn. Starting the fire was now a matter of drilling the rod into the hole until it generated enough heat to ignite.

But this turned out to be harder than it sounded. Falon drilled and drilled, and although the wood heated, nary a spark or a flicker sprung forth. Soon, his palms began to burn, and he had to ask Una to take over.

"It takes patience and time," he said. "Let's take turns and be careful to keep the rod inside the hole, so none of the heat escapes."

Una drilled, and after a short while, she had to pass it back to him. Her features were sallow as if she was about to heave.

He took another turn drilling until his forearms ached and his palms bled. Still no hint of flame.

At last, he could bear it no longer. Red-faced and hands blistering, he hurled the rod away. "Gigas' piss! How does anyone start a fire?"

"Maybe the wood isn't dry enough."

They stared blankly at the tinder as darkness fell around them.
"Another cold night," he said.

They built a shelter and laid out their bearskins so they could lie between them. Una lay down first, and Falon followed, this time going in front of her so that they faced one another. When he pulled up the fur and wrapped his arms around her, he felt her arm resting between them with a clenched fist.

"Falon, I need to tell you something."

"What is it?"

"I'm not even sure. I…"

He waited for her to continue but she couldn't find the words. "What? Tell me?"

"It's nothing," she said, burying her face into his shoulder. "Never mind."

He pulled away and looked into her eyes. "Tell me."

She took a deep breath and looked away. "The last time I bled, the sistersun was sharpened."

"That's when most women bleed. You still have some time to go then?"

"No. I didn't mean the last sistersun."

"It's been more than two turnings?"

She shook her head. "It's been three."

He paused to take this in, unsure what to make of her words given what she had suffered before escaping Kurnisahn. "The heir to Ser-o is in you then?" he said, hoping the answer would be yes.

Una swallowed. "I don't know that it is."

"I can't think of what else it could be," he said, pulling her close and trying to sound sincere. "We will raise it together, as our own, when it comes."

"Sure we will," she said, her voice trailing off.

They spoke few words after that, and Una eventually drifted off into sleep. As Falon stared over her shoulder and into the blackness, he wondered what this might mean for the days ahead. She would soon become less mobile, more dependent. He would have to provide more foodstuff than he'd expected, and sustenance had already proven a struggle from the outset. And on top of everything, he had no idea how to birth a baby. They needed to find j'Lok soon.

And what of the baby itself? At first, he'd thought it must have been Carn who had seeded her, but he knew there were other possibilities. There had been two High Ones inside her before Falon had intervened and slain the third. Was she flush with the seed that would one day be the Ser-o heir? Or was some sort of abomination—half nander, half High One—growing in her belly?

As he pondered this, a star flickered yellow below the horizon.

"Una, wake up. Do you see that?"

She grumbled and opened her eyes. "See what?"

"Look—over there."

She turned to look behind her, squinting. "I don't see anything, only stars."

"That one star there, you see it? Lower than the others?"

"Yes, I see it now. Why does it shine alone below rest?"

"That's because it isn't a star. That's someone's fire flickering on the hillside."

17
Ashes

T HE SUN ROSE OVER THE HORIZON like a bright red orb, bringing with it no apparent warmth. Una and Falon gathered their belongings and ventured to the hillside where they'd seen flickering the night before. A glaze of unthawed dew coated the soils, making their ascent more treacherous and audible as the gradient steepened. They knew they were close when the scent of smoldering coals wafted over them from up the slope. Past a thicket were the telltale signs of a recently abandoned campsite—a cooling firepit beside a branch-built shelter.

"Stay here," Falon said, his words a mist in the morning air. "The camper might still be near. I'll signal to come over if it's safe."

He unsheathed his blade and crept into the campsite. She watched from behind the thicket, fidgeting and praying to Vul-ka that he wasn't walking into danger, each breath a cold streak down her throat.

Falon touched the ground a few times before holding his open palms over the hearth. "There are embers here," he said, motioning for her to come forward.

"Take what we need and let's go."

"Should we wait to see if the camper returns? They might come back tonight."

"We don't know who *they* are."

Falon pointed at the hearth, noting its size. "It looks like just one man."

"But what kind of man? Do we know he's nander?"

He stopped to consider this, wiping threads of rime off his eyelashes. "We don't. But we don't even know where we are anymore. I'm afraid we might be following the wrong branch of flowing water. The camper might be able to guide us."

Falon was right, even if it was disturbing to think they'd gone this far in the wrong direction. Each day, she could sense her pregnancy advancing, feel the life growing inside her. For the sake of the baby, she had to find somewhere warm and stable.

"So, do we keep going or wait here and hope the camper knows the way to j'Lok?" she asked.

"We should wait. If the camper comes back, it'll be before nightfall. We'll watch from far away to see if he looks dangerous."

"Wait," she said, pointing to tracks almost imperceptible beneath the frost. "What are those?"

"The footprints?"

"Next to the footprints."

He took a step back and straightened his frame. "Those are paw prints."

She nodded.

"Howlers?"

She shrugged. "They're the right size…"

"It looks like a lone howler, not a pack. Maybe it caught the scent of fire and wandered in?"

"Either that or it's someone's companion."

"If that's what it is, we need to leave. The camper probably isn't nander."

She tightened the bearskin around her shoulders. "Let's get the embers and go."

Falon reached into his tunic. At first, she wasn't sure what he was looking for, but assumed it was the fire pouch—the very fire pouch he had asked her to carry earlier that morning. She reached into her waist strap and pulled it out, held it out for him.

"Falon."

"I'm looking for the pouch," he said without looking up, sliding his finger along the rim of his own waist strap.

"Falon," she said again, louder.

His head jerked back when he saw she was holding it.

"You gave it to me this morning," she said.

He held up a finger, mouth slightly agape.

"Are you alright?"

"Yes, I just…" he began, then paused. This was not the first time, since escaping Kurnisahn, that his memory had faltered. She'd been following his lead throughout their journey darkward, assuming he knew where they were going. Now she wondered if they were lost thanks to his muddled mind. "Just give me the pouch," he said.

She considered mentioning that he might be having memory troubles because of the blow to the head, but stopped herself, not wanting to add pressure to their circumstances. She handed him the fire pouch he'd made from the Bhatt leftovers—two shells filled with kindling and mosses and tied shut with a lock of her hair. Falon knelt beside the hearth, scooped up a handful of coals, spread them evenly on the mosses, then closed the shells. With proper attention, he'd be able to keep the embers long enough to start a fire later on.

"We need to cross the water," he said, tucking away the fire pouch. "We don't want the howler following our scent."

THE FLOWING WATER had long ago turned from a meandering flat course to rapids and falls carving through the bedrock, its boulders jutting slick and algae-coated from the spray. The very narrowland itself seemed to rise along the shores, sharp promontories breaking through what once were muddy banks. Out of the riven wall across the waters, a crooked tree grew from a rock crack, fighting outward from the stone for its tiny slice of light. The surrounding forest seemed to thin with every pace, many of its trunks already knurled and limbless, and soon, Una feared, there may be no more trees at all.

They spotted a shallow ford near the cliff base and removed their footwear on the shore before entering. The lapping shallows of the strand soon gave way to a churning overfall, whitecaps teal and baneful in the knee-high spate. She could smell the cold water below, the current threatening to topple and freeze them, every step an act of balance on the sharp, uneven rocks. They issued from the waters trembling, the gravels and sands of the waterbed clinging to their feet. They slid their scraped and bleeding soles back into their footwear and yet grew colder still.

"We need to stop before dark," Falon said, his teeth chattering. "We need to start a fire."

"I know—it's so cold—but what if the camper sees our flames like we did his?"

The bones in her feet throbbed from the chill descending over them. "We've traveled far enough today that we should be safe."

"We don't know which way the camper went," he said, peering at the opposite shore for any sign of the man. "He might have followed the water too."

"There are caves here along the cliffs. One might be deep enough to hide the light."

Falon nodded. He didn't look convinced but probably realized the peril of the frigid night before them.

It didn't take long to find a cave high on a cliff above the waterside, its insides shrouded in darkness only a few paces in. The coarse grey walls domed to a peak just out of reach and tangled rock formations beetled from the gravelly floor. They found a flat stretch deep enough in the cave to conceal some of the firelight, but shallow enough to ventilate the smoke.

Falon went out in the dying light to gather wood and kindling while Una laid out their belongings and stretched the bearskins on the ground. When he returned, he set the lightwood on the floor and arranged the branches into a triangle above it. He emptied his fire pouch into the kindling and gently blew the embers. Soon, the tiny points of orange glow expanded, igniting the straw and brush, and the first signs of a flame appeared. They continued to stoke the kindling, their breaths quickening, the flames spreading to the twigs and sticks, and then to the thicker branches above.

She took off her handwear and opened her palms above the flame. "We did it," she said. This was the first time she recalled smiling since leaving Kurnisahn.

Falon smiled back and put his finger to her lips so she would lower her voice. "Yes, we did it. Now, let's get warm," he said, wrapping his arms around her.

They lay down on a bearskin and bundled beneath another, its oily warmth allowing blood to flow back into their extremities. As twilight gave way to blackness, they huddled together between the furs, warm at last in the glow of the flames.

18

Where is the Child?

UNTIL HIS BRUTAL AWAKENING, it had been Falon's best night of sleep in many sistersuns. He hadn't seen a flame since back in Kurnisahn, and now, wrapped in fire-warmed furs, he slept undisturbed with Una in his embrace. But that was before the sorrow skewered the bearskin, pierced his legwear, and thumped into his thigh.

He jerked up and screamed.

Una slid out from beneath the furs, eyes bleary. "Wait, what?"

"My leg!" he said, yawing sideward, eyes rolling back from the pain.

Her eyes widened. "What is that?"

"A High One must have thrown it! Help me take it out!"

Una pressed her foot on his shin for leverage and pulled the sorrow from his thigh. The weapon slid cleanly from his flesh, its tip thankfully unbarbed.

He flung off the bearskin, hot blood trickling down his leg as he teetered to his feet. He pointed his spear at the black shapelessness outside the cave, his unseen assailant surely watching with another sorrow drawn.

"Stand behind me," he said to Una, the cave slowly spinning around him.

Another sorrow flew from the darkness and thwacked into his thigh, just above the first wound. He dropped to a knee as the cold tip tore through his muscle fibers.

"Get out of the light!" Una said, pulling him to the side.

He wrenched the sorrow from his leg, the slow burn far worse than the shock of the initial strike, then limped behind a ridge and huddled in the shadows. The sound of footsteps grew louder until a High One and his howler resolved out of the blackness and into the firelight. The man was covered in greyfur, tied neatly around his arms and legs, and a ring of dried nander ears dangled from his collar. He stood at the foot of the cave with a sorrow nocked strong against a body-length stave, the weapon pointed at Falon. The howler stood beside the man, snarling and ready to pounce.

"*Veesh ma, ka ka nee sa,*" the man said calmly in his strange High One tongue. He looked directly at Falon, despite his attempt to hide.

"We don't know what that means," Una said.

The man loosened his grip and motioned for them to come out of the shadows. Falon nudged Una to move toward the hearth since the slightest provocation might compel the man to pull back again and release. Once they were back in the glow of the flames, the man signaled to get on the ground. A crimson blot soiled Falon's legwear as he knelt.

The man strode forth with his weapon raised, kicking up gravel with each step. He held a sorrow against Falon's throat, its black tip stinging cold against his skin. When Falon looked up, he saw a man dark as night with fingerbone piercings through each earlobe and oily hair pulled back in a ponytail.

"*Whea—chile?*" the man said, the question more a command.

"What?" Falon coughed, gagging from the sorrow pressed against his throat.

"*Whea—chile?*" the man repeated, the howler drooling beside him, its eyes locked on Falon.

"Where child?" Falon echoed, suspecting the man was asking about the boy Carn had stolen. But wasn't the boy the reason Kurnisahn had been ransacked in the first place? How come the High Ones hadn't found him yet?

The man tilted his head and lifted his eyebrows, urging him to answer. Falon shook his head to signal that he didn't know. The stave groaned as the man nocked the sorrow tighter.

"*Whea chile?!*" the man screamed as the howler barked and bayed.

"He is one of *them*," Una whispered, a few paces away. She needn't elaborate. This man was one of the three who had defiled her after the massacre. Falon shifted his eyes toward her; a thin rivulet streamed down her cheek despite her stoic expression. The man followed his eyes, turned the sorrow toward her, and motioned for her to rise. She stood, and he leaned in, his hooked nose almost caressing her neck as if he meant to smell her. When she turned away, the man shoved her into the wall, and she fell flat on her stomach. Falon tried to stand, but the sorrow was pointed back at him before he could intervene.

"*Kalashima. Veesh nasan ko ma see na!*"

Una whimpered on the floor, her hands tucked under her belly.

"We don't have him," Falon said, angling away from the sorrow's tip.

The man grinned, his uneven teeth shining yellow in the firelight. He placed the stave and sorrow on the ground while the howler stalked over to Falon and perched itself over his head. The man drew a black blade from his waist strap and pressed it against Falon's scar, raising his eyebrows as if to say: *I will not repeat the question.* Falon again shook his head to communicate that he didn't know.

The man scowled and slid the blade across Falon's face, splitting the skin along the course of his scar. He screamed as hot blood flowed over his face like a mask, into his mouth and nose and burning his eyes. The howler roared when the man lowered the blade and pressed its tip against Falon's gut.

"*Hee na slo ma. Kee sah,*" he said, leaning in. "*Whea chile?*"

This was it. The High One was about to drive the blade into his belly and gut him. Una would be next, and who knew what humiliations she would endure before being slain.

Una!

"Move away," Falon heard her say. He wiped the blood out of his eyes. She was standing behind the man, holding his stave with the sorrow drawn tight and pointed at him from an arm's length away. The man snickered as if her threat was meaningless and went to grab the weapon.

She released.

The sorrow struck the High One in the neck with a clap. He collapsed to a knee with pitch white eyes and clutched the shaft. He yanked it out, the wound spewing with a rhythmic pump, spraying the grounds and walls of the cave. The man tried to crawl to Una but crumpled into a dark red pool, his grip of the sorrow never loosening.

Before Falon could grasp what she'd done, the howler leaped at her and sent her tumbling backward. She covered her throat, but it bit down on her forearm. Falon grabbed a log from the hearth and staggered across the cave, swinging it in a spray of orange embers and cracking the howler in the spine with the glowing end of the wood. When the animal wouldn't release, he swung again.

And again.

The third time, the howler let go. It yelped and scampered to the mouth of the cave, hesitating beside the High One corpse and pressing its snout frantically against his chest to awaken him. But the animal quickly realized, it seemed, that its companion was in the forever-sleep, and it scurried out of the cave with its back bent in pain, leaving red paw prints in the gravel behind it.

Una stood, one arm hanging limp, bloody and torn and the other holding her belly. "Falon, my stomach, I…"

But before she could say more, he was unconscious.

19
The Howler

THE GREY SKY ENCASED THE LAND like a shroud. Outside the cave, a gravelly tract quickly gave way to boulders and bluffs leading down to the flowing water. It was there outside the cave the howler rested, lying amongst the scree, staring back at Una with the sharp yellow eyes of a demon.

She tore greyfur from the High One's wearings and pressed them skin-side down on Falon's face to stop the bleeding. By dawn, the flow had mostly ceased, even though his wound was agape and shockingly deep. Even after wiping away the blood, flaky blotches remained on his cheeks and neck, and the collar of his tunic was hopelessly stained. She took off his legwear and stopped the bleeding on his thigh as well. But his sorrow wounds were swollen, the punctures encircled by rosy halos.

Falon wasn't the only one ravaged from the night before. The howler's mauling had left ribbons of flesh hanging from Una's forearm like frayed stringrass threads. She rinsed her wound in the flowing water and placed each strip of skin back onto the exposed pink flesh below. Skin, it was known, had the strange ability to heal itself, a quality she hoped would again prove true.

But she was suffering the aftermath of the High One attack in a different, perhaps more ominous way. She'd landed on her belly when the High One shoved her into the rocks, a sharp pain shooting from her stomach down to her sex, which by sunrise had begun bleeding. And there was pain down there like she had never before felt. She knew a woman with child sometimes did not take and the process of ridding themselves of the deadness was wrought with peril. Many seasons ago, her mother had gone through such a spell, a red profusion washing from her at its culmination. Una's discharge had not reached that extent, but the blow to her belly and the pain that followed made her worry the child inside her no longer remained.

She peeled away the greyfur she'd lodged into her legwear to soak up the blood. The flow had not abated, so she cut off more of the dead man's wearings and stuffed it between her legs. With wet red hands, she threw the soiled greyfur into the growing pile outside the cave.

Falon finally moaned awake. He sat up, holding his thigh. "I don't know what hurts more, my face or my leg."

"Try not to move. Your leg needs to heal."

He picked up one of the blood-stained sorrows. "It looks like the weapon the traders had back in Kurnisahn. The ones that slew the Bhatt."

"And the ones that slew the Kurnisahn." She pointed at the dead man. "He has a whole set of them."

She handed him the bundle of sorrows that had been strapped to the dead man's back. It was a collection totaling many hands, each obsidian-tipped stick carved straight with piebald feathers cleaved to the opposite end.

He put down the bundle, keeping one sorrow. "So, this is how it works." He nocked it tight and pointed it at the dead body.

"That's how it works," she said. When she'd slain the man, it had happened like a reflex, her motions seeming to move through time like a foregone conclusion. She'd seen the man aim the weapon and understood at once how it worked—the taut cord bending the stave so the sorrow would fly forward when released. In truth, she'd been aiming at the man's browless face; the fact that she'd hit his throat had been a matter of luck and poor marksmanship.

"You saved me," Falon said.

"And then you saved me. From that," she said, pointing at the howler, still watching her every move with determined yellow eyes.

"I don't like that it's out there."

"I think it's waiting for its companion."

"He's not going anywhere," he said, kicking the dead man with his good leg.

"What should we do with him?"

"If he were nander, I'd say bury him, but what do you do with a High One?"

"I won't honor him with a burial."

"We're going to be here for some time, at least until I can walk. We can't just let the body rot here." He paused for a moment, then said, "I am hungry, though."

Una glared at him. "That is forbidden. His spirit wouldn't return to the s'Sah."

"Forbidden? He isn't nander."

Una could not bring herself to feast upon his flesh. For all she knew, the corpse was the father of her child, if indeed one still lived inside her. "Our ancestors might have been forced to feed on one another before we settled in the lowrock valley," she said, "but we're not that desperate yet."

"Fine, we won't eat the High One." He pointed at the howler. "But what about that?"

She eyed the animal. "It will give more than a meal, and we could use its fur."

"I'll slay it with a sorrow," he said. He tried to rise but stumbled when his injured leg failed to support him.

"You need to stay down!"

He groaned and adjusted his position on the floor.

"Give me those," she said, pointing at the stave and sorrows. Falon handed her the weapons. She nocked a sorrow and stepped out of the cave. "Just… stay… still…" she said, but as soon as she raised the weapon, the howler darted out of view.

"There'll be other chances," he said from behind her. "Until then, we need to do something with the body."

"We should take his wearings and throw him off the cliff."

"Alright." Falon rose, this time putting as little weight as possible on his wounded leg.

"Get back down," she said. "I'll move him."

"You can't drag him by yourself."

"Well, be careful." She started undressing the body, taking only what remained unsoiled.

He limped over to the High One and lifted him from under his arms. When she grabbed his ankles, a sharp pain shot to the pit of her stomach. She dropped the man's legs and bent over.

"What's wrong?"

She held up a hand for him to wait, only explaining once she had regained composure. He listened quietly as she told him of her troubles, a long pause lingering between them after she concluded. He opened his mouth a few times to respond, exhaling as if he didn't know what to say. Finally, he asked, "What do we do if you pass the child?"

"It has only been three sistersuns. It can't be that big yet," she said, holding her belly. The bump evidencing her pregnancy was barely noticeable beneath her furs.

"So, if you pass it, will it come out… smoothly?"

"I don't know. I'm bleeding, though. You can't see it because I've stuffed so much greyfur down there." She needn't mention the pile of soaked furs she'd discarded outside the cave.

"Una, I'm so sorry."

"I don't know yet if I've passed the child. Maybe I'm just hurt from the fall."

He tightened his features, his gaze doubtful. He thought she was in denial.

"What do we do with him?" she asked, ignoring his uncertainty and pointing at the dead man.

"Let's drag him out of the cave. If we can't make it to the cliffside, we can at least move him far enough so we don't smell him when he rots."

"I don't know how much he'll rot when it's this cold, but we can't let his dead body curse the cave. And we don't want predators picking up the scent either."

Falon grabbed the corpse again from under the arms. He, limping backward, and she, grimacing with each step, dragged it out of the cave. Once far enough outside, they dropped the body. The howler whined and paced down by the water, torn between its desire to accompany its companion and its awareness of the nander threat.

Una followed Falon back into the cave. She'd already felt nauseous and dragging the body only worsened it, an acidic sting glazing the sides of her tongue. She knelt and tried to vomit, her insides thrusting upward, but nothing would come.

"I need to lie down," she said, her belly pain unrelenting. Falon placed his hand on her back and hobbled into the cave with her.

Soon the howler reappeared over the hillside. It crept over to the High One and sniffed. It lifted its head to see if Falon and Una were still in the cave, then bent back down over the body, nudging the dead man's shoulder with its snout and licking his face again and again. *Please, wake up... Just this one time... Please,* Una imagined the howler thinking. After a while, the howler lay down facing the body, rested its jaw between its paws, and stared.

20

An Empty Pit

F ALON WAS HEAVY with the ache of malaise, his nostrils thick like they were stuffed with clay. Even the smallest motions produced shivers on his neck, pangs through his arms, and pains down his legs. Pressure throbbed behind his eyes, which, when he bothered to open them, saw a world in a haze, bulging and coiling like reflections on water. Although he and Una huddled between furs beside the fire, the air blowing into the cave was a cold wave engulfing them from without.

Peeling the greyfur from his sorrow wounds sounded like leaves tearing. The punctures itched and were caked with thick yellow pus, an omen that dark humors had infected his flesh. Each day, his wounds seemed further from recovery, and he prayed to Vul-ka that corruption would not set in. He shuddered at the thought of losing a leg; even in healthier times, it might have resulted in his ascension. Not that Una would have had the strength or the will to dismember him, especially since it would have to be done near the waist where his leg was widest. Above everything, she was unlikely to go on without him, if ever they could leave the cave at all.

Una shivered beside him, her cheeks pallid, her forehead glazed with sweat and tiny beads on her nose. Strips of flesh no longer hung from her forearm, but everything below her elbow was discolored and inflamed. She might have been even sicker than him.

In the first days following the attack, she had ventured out to collect roots and berries, but couldn't go far in her condition. After picking clean the shrubbery near the cave, foodstuff ran dry. Falon had been unable to travel on his wounded leg, and each time they ran out of water, it had fallen upon Una to climb down for more. With each day colder than the last, she had to crawl farther onto the frozen surface to reach the flowing water.

Una had also been collecting brushes and driftwood to feed the flames. Although they now had a decent store, they would be in trouble once it was exhausted. Falon could barely stand, let alone walk, and he couldn't carry a pile of wood limping on just one leg. And now Una's health had worsened to the point where he wondered if she would ever rise at all.

Throughout everything, the howler remained outside beside its dead companion. When Una had been strong enough to leave the cave, she had always brought sorrows with her to scare off the beast, which would scurry away as soon as she held them out for it to see. And yet, every time she returned to the cave and placed the sorrows on the floor, the howler reappeared. It would nuzzle the High One's neck, hoping he might finally spring back to life, but each time it ended up lying back down beside the body, forlorn and dejected.

"We're going to the forever-sleep," Una said, her eyes closed.

"No, we're not."

"We are. I can hardly move."

"We need to feed," he said. Not eating for days had worsened their recovery; his stomach felt like an empty pit consuming itself.

"But we're sick. You have dark humors in your leg, and I think I've lost the child. It must be rotting inside me," she said, cupping her belly.

"It might still be alive," he said. While her belly still had a bump, it might have been distended from the hunger.

"We need to eat the High One," she said, opening her eyes and turning to Falon.

He looked over at the body. A greenish hue had begun to soil its flesh, a sign that the man's spirit was returning to the s'Sah even though he was unburied. "We can't anymore. It's been too long."

"Then we need to eat the howler."

"It's too clever. It scurries away every time we go near."

"And it runs when we pick up a sorrow." She turned, looking farther into the cave. "It's dark back there. Maybe we can fling a sorrow at it from out of sight."

He followed her gaze into the depths of the cave. Past the glow of the firelight was a terrifying blackness. The last thing he wanted was to go back there. "Maybe I can club it with the horn," he said, touching the aurochs horn on the ground beside him.

"The howler will run away before you get close enough."

He hesitated.

"I don't have the strength," she said, sliding a sorrow toward him. "You need to do it."

He waited until the howler fell asleep, then lumbered to his feet and grabbed the sorrows. When he picked up the stave, the howler jerked its head up, ready to run off as soon as he raised the weapon. But when he turned and limped away into the shadows, the howler lowered its head back down between its paws.

Falon turned to the mouth of the cave. Fingers of sunlight snaked over ridges and rocks before fading into the darkness around him. Barely able to see his outstretched hands, he dreaded a sinister presence might reach up from behind and swallow him whole. The hair on his arms stood as he imagined Gigas' tendrils rising from the silent abyss behind him.

He lifted the stave and nocked the sorrow, the blackness of the pit seeming to leak out into the day before him. He aimed the weapon so its tip formed a silhouette against the grey beast. It took all his strength to draw, and even then, the cord might not have been tight enough to hit the target that was now so far away. The howler was dangerous and could easily kill a man, but right now it just looked pathetic and sad, sitting so many days beside its erstwhile companion as if he might somehow, someday rise. But Falon had to ignore his sympathies; he and Una needed to feed. He inhaled the stale cave air, held his breath, and released.

The sorrow whizzed out of the shadows, over the fire, soaring into the day and landing—

—on the High One.

So close and yet a miss.

The howler startled and glared into the cave, showing its teeth when the sorrow thumped into the dead man's chest. It barked twice and ran down the hill, out of view.

Falon hobbled back to the fire with his chin down.

"I don't know what to do. Maybe I can spear a fish." As he said this, his legs gave out, and he nearly fell into the fire.

"You can't climb down to the water like this. You'll fall off the cliff."

"What else can we do?" he said, trying to stand.

"Don't try to get up."

"Maybe we can find some roots or berries."

"I've picked everything clean. The time of the low sun is almost here. There's nothing left to find."

"Maybe there are roots."

She shook her head. "Come under the bearskin. Keep me warm. If we never wake up, I'll at least spend my last moments in peace."

Falon lay back down and held his body against hers. He listened to her breath, felt her torso swell with strength then weakness, their bodies fever-soaked and sticky as they burned between the furs. When darkness fell around them, and the blazes of the hearth settled into coals, their beddings seemed to cool. But was it the natural cooling one might sense as their heartbeat slowed and they drifted into slumber? Or was it Una's body warmth itself that faded? He pulled her closer, the back of her head in one hand and her waist in the other, fighting to stay awake as if it somehow would protect her.

Una's chest rose and fell, and his chest rose and fell, their body rhythms blending like they were motions of a single form.

21

Somewhere in the Distance

W ARM AT LAST, his body healed and strong, Falon curls beside Una beneath the billowing flames. Somehow, he feels—no, he *knows*—a presence is with him, watching him, waiting for him in the darkness.

He raises his head to find his father sitting cross-legged on a boulder at the foot of the hollow. His father smiles at him and looks out into the great wide open. "You're awake," he says with his back turned.

Falon rises from beneath the bearskins and walks over, the cold outside air pouring past him.

"She's still not yours, you know," his father says, calm and unmoving as if frozen in time. "You tell that girl your darkest fears, but for what? You will never have her. She'll never see you for more than what you are."

Falon sits beside his father, the boulder's warmth glowing beneath him. "Where have you been?"

"I've been here all along," he says, his voice distant, transient, drifting like the wind. "And soon she'll join me."

"No, she won't."

"You seek to replace the mother you never knew. The one taken by the forever-sleep to bring you into the world. We drew the mark of the sistersun on her so that you might live."

"That wasn't my fault."

"You were cut from her belly nonetheless. She spilled blood for you alone."

He stares at his father, unwilling to repeat his innocence.

His father lifts his chin to expose the sign of the sharpened sistersun Falon cut into his flesh. The wound pours red as he stretches his throat upward, ceasing when his chin descends and the laceration closes. It is strange that both his parents perished from the same shape of cut.

His father turns once more to Una, who remains buried beneath the furs. "You may not have killed her like you killed me. Yet, you are responsible."

"She won't go to the forever-sleep. I will save her."

"And how will you do that?"

"Foodstuff will bring her strength."

"You have no means to find any foodstuff."

"I have these," Falon says, lifting the sorrows from the gravelly floor.

"Those will be our end."

Falon looks at the sorrows—their obsidian tips have been replaced by desiccated nander ears. He drops the sorrows and screams as the weapons scatter away.

His father shakes his head. "Go back to your bearskins. Bring her peace in these last moments."

Somewhere in the distance, a hooting bird pecks at a carcass, when a goldbeak, its wings spread wider than the outstretched arms of a man, swoops from the sky and clutches its fellow bird with its talons, hoisting it away in a burst of feathers and screams. The plumes land silently on the bent backs of the many aurochs standing amongst the snow-covered stones outside the cave. The bulls stare at his father, whipping their tails over their white dorsal stripes, bowing their heads as if ready to charge.

"If only we had sorrows in the hunt, you wouldn't have suffered so," Falon says.

"Maybe not," his father says, reaching down to pick up the horn of the aurochs that killed him. He rises to his feet and tucks his chin against his chest, the top of his head facing the herd. "Now watch this."

"Don't go out there. They'll kill you again!"

His father scoffs at the warning and charges headfirst into the herd, swinging the horn with reckless abandon. As he exits the cave, he and his weapon vanish midstride into the frosty air. The aurochs are unmoved, and when his father disappears, they look down to the soil where nothing grows.

Back in the cave, Una lies supine in its depths with a bearskin pulled over her head. The blackness is rising around her. Falon approaches, yet she seems to float farther into the darkness, her form flickering in the firelight, the mouth of the cave fading behind him in a cool white dot. She hides beneath the furs and grips from below so he can't lift them.

"I don't want you to see me like this," she says.

"See you like what?"

"I've changed, Falon."

"I don't care," he says, trying to lift the fur.

She grips it tighter. "I've become a monster."

"No, you haven't. You're just not well."

"It's more than that. A demon grows inside me."

"It's just a baby."

"Not anymore. I don't know what it is now."

He again tries to lift the fur, but it is stuck to her.

"No. You can't see my face."

"Let go!" he says, yanking the bearskin with all his might, falling backward from the motion. He sits up and tosses the fur away.

The girl rises from the gravels, her arms drooping to her sides. She stands above him, her unclothed body that of a woman, perhaps flowered but not fully grown, her head that of a snarling grey howler.

"No! What have you done to her?"

The monster shoves Falon onto his back and straddles him, its sandy-haired womanhood smearing ice-cold blood across his chest and stomach. It peers down at him with eyes glowing the ocher of molten stone, its teeth yellow in the firelight. It grabs his wrists with dagger-like claws and holds them to the ground.

"Because of me, she lives," the monster says, leaning in, its wet snout caressing Falon's cheek. Its forked tongue glides out of its mouth, dripping pink saliva and viscera as if flush with the gore of a kill. Its greasy tongue slithers across Falon's scar, over and over until…

22
Target Practice

FALON AWOKE TO A SIGHT he'd hoped to never see—a howler's blood-stained muzzle near enough to taste its breath. He slowly felt around for the aurochs horn so he could beat back the beast, sweeping his fingers along the ground in a gentle arc, keeping his body still so he wouldn't alarm the howler. The weapon wasn't beside him where he had left it, so he felt the other side, his movements turning frantic after finding nothing but rubble and loam. Had he lost the horn?

The panting howler leaned in to lick Falon's lips and nose, and he sat up to face it. When he peered into its eyes, he saw at once that it meant no harm. Something in its expression suggested that it saw him not as prey but as a friend, almost as if asking—perhaps begging—for companionship.

The howler looked to the ground, and Falon followed its eyes. At its feet was a lifeless tree-crawler, its neck snapped in two. The howler whined and lay down before him, its pink tongue hanging out of the side of its mouth.

"Una, wake up," he said, still disturbed by the howler's nearness. She moaned a few times, and he shook her shoulder. Her flesh was hot as coal. "Wake up," he said again.

She turned and looked at the howler. He'd expected her to jolt, but she seemed too hopeless to care.

"Is it going to kill us?" she groaned, closing her eyes. Even beneath the bearskin, her rounded belly was evident; she surprisingly had not lost the baby, despite her tribulations. Only half of all babies survived their first season, so this one's toughness boded well for its future.

"The howler brought us this," he said, lifting the tree-crawler by its puffy tail. He could only hold it for a moment before letting go, having grown so weak from the fever. He had to muster all his energy to skin and gut the animal, while the howler watched patiently as if it had seen the process many times before. He put more wood into the fire and cooked the meat at the end of a stick. In spite of his hunger, he struggled to swallow, and he had to force Una to take her first bite.

They had scarcely begun eating before feeling full. Una couldn't keep her foodstuff down and crawled out of the cave to vomit. The howler darted out of sight when she began to heave.

Once she returned to her bearskins, Falon gave her water and made her eat some more. Throughout the day, they ate a bit, trying to keep it down, sometimes successfully, other times not, until by nightfall they had finished all the meat. Then they dozed off, their bellies full, sleeping harder than they had in memory. Falon didn't know how much time had passed before a bristly nudge awakened him. The howler had returned, this time with a grassrabbit.

And so it went, day after day, night after night—the howler coming and going, sometimes for short intervals, other times for a day or more, always returning with a kill. As the sistersun brightened and waned, the howler slept beside them, and they benefitted from its warmth. And now, with foodstuff in their bodies, energy for their lifeblood, they began to heal, began to grow strong again, began to ready themselves to finally leave the cave and resume their voyage.

On the first day Falon felt well enough to get up and move around, he looked for the aurochs horn that had somehow disappeared during his fever dream. He searched through the cave, behind rocks, in the darkness. He scoured the cliffs and the fellfield sedges, beyond the slopes of talus and the shores of flowing water. But the horn was nowhere to be found. Una had been right back in Bhatt—the horn's utility was limited. While it was sharp enough to draw blood and had the length to intimidate, its hollowness gave it less structural integrity than antlers or even wood.

Looking back, Ber-gul's insistence on attacking the bull with the biggest horns had been purely a product of hubris. And yet, despite the horn's doubtful utility, Falon had been unable to part with it because of what it represented: the last link he had to his forever-gone father. It made little sense to have become so attached to an object, but the horn had achieved a significance to him that he didn't fully recognize until it was gone.

He soon regained enough strength to foodbring on his own. Sorrows were tools of unprecedented power, weapons with a lethal range far exceeding any he'd ever used or seen. He fastened mosses to a thuk-tree and practiced flinging sorrows at it from afar. He'd always taken pride in his marksmanship, and his skill with the stave and sorrows quickly honed. Each day, he set up farther from the target until he was able to hit its center repeatedly, then he'd move back even more. There was a strange connection between the body and the eye—focusing on the target would naturally guide his aim—and he soon flung sorrows from great distances. Hardly a shot was wasted.

One morning while Falon practiced, the howler's white ears suddenly perked up. It raised its snout, sniffed the air, and pivoted its head before darting off in a grey blur. A short time later, it returned, whining and pawing as if signaling to follow. The howler sniffed the ground all the way to the shore where a pair of waterbirds paddled midstream, the only part of the current not yet turned to stone.

The howler stared at Falon from the waterside, seemingly aware the birds would flee if it treaded any nearer. Perhaps it was waiting for him to fling a sorrow at their prey. He wasn't sure if a single sorrow could kill such a large animal, but a wounded bird would at least be unable to fly away.

He lifted the stave and drew the cord deep until it touched his lips, focusing on the bigger bird and waiting for the perfect moment. The fowl dipped its bill below the surface, its backside bobbing in the air. It slung its head back above the water in a fitful spray, a fish writhing in its beak. The bird straightened its neck and joggled its throat, the fish sliding whole down its gullet.

As his prey turned profile toward him, Falon concentrated on the widest part of its body, held his breath, and released. The sorrow landed in a puff of feathers, pinning the bird's wing. It flailed its other wing, hoisting itself onto the frozen surface, screeching and sliding as its companion flapped away. Falon dropped the stave and crept onto the ice, ready to halt if it began to crack. He unsheathed his dagger and grabbed the bird's neck and cut, the frozen water steaming as the blood flowed upon it.

He cut out the fish and fed it to the howler. Then, he carried the waterbird back to the cave, plucked it, cooked it, and ate it with Una.

"With these, we can foodbring from afar," he said, bringing forth the sorrow that had crippled the bird. "With these, a lone man can slay an animal. No longer will we want for food."

"We've sheltered in this cave for more than three sistersuns, but we can't stay," Una said, her hands on her belly. "I can't deliver this child alone." She seemed ready to burst at any moment, though birth should have been a sistersun or two away.

"Once the child comes, we won't be able to leave for some time," she continued. "I can't travel into the unknown with a newborn.

We don't know how far j'Lok is or if we've even been going the right way."

"Then we stay until the child is grown. I'm still limping, and your strength is only now returning."

"But what if the game here disappears? What if we can no longer foodbring? We need to keep moving."

Falon looked out of the cave. "Let's see what the morrow brings," he said. It was darkening so fast that the setting sun alone could not be to blame. He stepped outside and saw a deep black cloud in the darkward skies, ashen whorls rolling off its belly like dust before a rockfall. A cruel flash of light diffused across the thunderhead, so far still that it made no sound.

23

The High Ones

T HE FIRELIGHT FLICKERED in the darkness and exposed the swirling powders of the storm. Una and Falon moved as close to the fire as they could bear, but gusts blew sparks and ash all around them. When a snowbank formed along the rim of the cave, they pushed the fire deeper into the chamber where they hacked and heaved, the smoke consuming them in a black cloud. After abandoning this attempt and returning to their original campsite, neither could find repose, even with their frost-stung bodies huddled against the howler.

Then the animal growled and rose, creeping to the mouth of the cave as if it sensed someone approaching. It swiveled its head with its snout held high, and its back-hair raised when a second howler emerged from the fog and entered the cave. The animals circled one another with their tails stiff, sniffing each other's snouts and hindquarters. Once they settled, the newcomer barked into the tempest as if beckoning someone forth.

Una touched Falon's shoulder, her arms suddenly heavy. "Someone's coming," she said.

He grabbed the stave and stood. "Who's there?" he called, nocking a sorrow and pointing it into the storm.

She squinted, trying to see through the blizzard. There seemed to be several figures out in the snows, floating like apparitions in the void.

"*Kee ma, no ha shee sah*," a voice said.

"Be gone!" Falon shouted. "We seek no trouble."

Silence.

"I can see you out there," he said, stepping forward with his weapon drawn tight.

"*Ho nai po sma. Feeshma kana qah*," another voice said, this time female.

"High Ones," Una said, grabbing a dagger.

"Don't move."

"There's a woman out there."

"I know."

"Maybe they only want to share our flames?"

"We can't risk it."

A High One woman stepped into the fringes of the firelight, her hands held out before her to show she was unarmed. Her wavy hair dripped onto her forehead, her shoulders covered with snowflakes, her nostrils thin and caked with frozen snot. She held out a stack of branches. "*J'ho nasan, fi krah no ess*," she said, pointing the sticks at the hearth.

"I think she's offering wood for the fire," Falon said, his sorrow still drawn. Una warily approached the woman, who handed her the branches and then opened her hands in front of her once more.

"*Ouh phlo qha, ho tai mee san*," she said, on the verge of tears as she nodded at her companions.

"What's she saying?" Falon asked.

"I don't know, but they have children with them."

The woman looked at Una's belly. Then they locked eyes, the woman pursing her lips as though sympathetic to her hardships. A second High One woman emerged out of the darkness, along with two shivering children.

Falon pointed the sorrow at the second woman. "Don't get any closer."

"I don't think they mean us harm," Una said. "They just gave us wood for the fire."

"No. There's someone else behind them."

"The children look like they're about to freeze into the forever-sleep."

"Who's behind you?" Falon demanded.

One of the women gestured for their hidden companion to come forth.

"*Fui navro*," a deeper voice said from the darkness. A man stepped into the light, a headless fawn draped over his shoulders, its neck speckled with blood and rime. He tossed the carcass to the snow and held his hands out as if it was an offering. He pointed to the carcass, to the fire, and back to the carcass.

"He's offering to share his kill if we share our flame," Una said to Falon. "I think you can lower the weapon."

He pointed his sorrow at the man. "Who else is out there with you?"

The man lifted his chin as if confused, his beard covered with threads of ice.

"Who else?" he repeated, nodding at the darkness.

The High Ones exchanged a few words in their strange tongue. The man turned to Falon and pointed to the women, to the children, and finally to himself before crossing his hands as if to say that was all.

"Falon, let them in."

He lowered the weapon and stepped back, still gripping the half-nocked sorrow. After hesitating a moment, the man said something to the women who responded by dragging the fawn into the cave. The children ran to the fire and held their hands over it.

The man took a knee before the hearth, then said something under his breath with his eyes closed as if in prayer. He turned to Falon, showing his open palm to say he meant no harm, then reached into his waist strap with the other hand to pull out an obsidian blade. He turned the fawn belly up and cut.

Falon took his stave and sorrows to the edge of the cave, checking to make sure no threats, High One or otherwise, remained veiled in the blackness. He looked back to make sure the newcomers, who appeared to have come in peace, didn't suddenly turn hostile.

Once the fawn was cooked, Falon helped cut the meat. It was the best meal they had eaten in ages. While Falon had caught the occasional bird or fish, and the howler's hunting had offered some nourishment, nothing could compare to the hearty red flavor of large game.

After the meal, everyone slept, huddling beside the fire—High One, nander, and howler alike. Keeping warm was much easier with the extra bodies. Much of the night had passed, it seemed, before Una awoke, the first of the group to do so. She walked to the mouth of the cave where the wind still bellowed, the snow blowing like a mist whose many shapes and shadows formed from the flickers of the blaze behind her. As she gazed upon the snowy wasteland, one of the women rose and stood beside her. They moved closer to one another, both seeking any semblance of warmth here so far from the flames.

Near the horizon, the clouds split as if sliced sideways by a blade. When they parted, the sistersun shone like a glowing orb fighting its way out of a black wound. The clouds then came together once more, smothering the sistersun and leaving a dull glow in the corner of the sky. Una turned and met eyes with the woman. In that brief moment of understanding between two women unable to speak a common word between them, it was known by both what the other was thinking: the sistersun had now risen twice before Vul-ka himself had been seen.

And then, as if to distract them from this celestial curiosity, a warm wetness flushed down the insides of Una's legs. This was early; this was far too early.

The woman mobilized immediately, leading her back into the cave and urging her to lie beside the fire. She shook the other woman's shoulders to awaken her. A pressure was forming in Una's abdomen, her muscles shuddering and her body clenched.

"Falon—wake up, it's coming!"

His eyes sprung open bloodshot; the howlers barked and bayed.

It felt like a claw gripped her insides, twisting and wrenching at every angle. A layer of sweat formed on her forehead, dripping down her temples and behind her ears. The women pulled off her wearings and opened her legs.

As if she existed outside her own body, she heard herself scream while Falon shouted behind her. She couldn't focus on his words but realized in that moment these women knew much more about how to handle the situation than he.

Something was moving out of her like a bowel movement splitting her apart. She screamed again; it felt like she was being torn inside out by a blade of fire.

And then, when she heard the wailing, the pressure and pain were gone. She raised her head to see one of the women lifting a baby from between her knees—a boy smaller than any newborn she had ever seen, perhaps unsurprising considering how early he had come into the world. The woman bent down and bit the cord, separating mother and child for the first time, a smattering of red on her lips as she lowered the organ.

The woman handed the baby to Una, and she held it close to her breast as it shrieked and jerked its tiny legs. Below the film of blood and fluids, something about the baby was different than any she had seen before. Its features were slenderer, its nose almost hooked, its skin darker than a nander even here in the meager light of the flames.

Falon stood unmoving by the fire, not knowing what to do. Both women stepped back upon sight of the baby, their arms rigid as if repelled.

"*Skeen qro qroh bah fo nashi potra,*" one of the women said, pointing a reproving finger at Una. The man began to pack his effects and forced the children to rise.

"Wait, no. Where are you going?" Una asked. The women's help in birthing the baby had been indispensable—while Falon had stood there helplessly. If he had been her sole companion, who knows what might have happened? The women's presence could only help in the days to come. Una had already been terrified about caring for a baby. What chance would she have alone with this born-too-early, strangely featured boy?

The man ordered the children to gather their belongings. He cupped coals with his bare hands and packed them into a rabbitskin pouch. One of the women grabbed her leftover branches, hoisting them over her shoulder.

"Wait," Una said. "Don't leave us."

The man shook his head and snapped his fingers at his howler. It came to his side at once. He looked into the darkness and back into the cave, a sense of pity in his expression. "*Tro nah ees warakra fa—j'Lok,*" he said, pointing darkward and out of the cave. He paused and said that last word again: "*j'Lok.*"

Falon pointed in the same direction. "j'Lok?" he asked, to confirm what the man had said. The man nodded once before marching out of the cave forever.

The High Ones disappeared into the night, their forms dissolving into the blackness almost as quickly as they had appeared. When something scraped against Falon's leg, he looked down to find his howler pawing at him and whining at him and staring out of the cave. It met eyes with Falon one last time, as if to say goodbye, and then followed the High Ones out into the sheer white fog of the storm.

PART IV: J'LOK

24
The Gerent

I T DIDN'T MATTER IF HER BURDEI was veiled in darkness; the Gerent's world was always black. She had lost her sight so long ago that it was like a distant dream one forgets upon awakening, like faces from the past one cannot recall.

Her home, in the center of j'Lok, had a circular vent at its zenith serving only for the smoke to rise. A column of cold light beamed through the aperture, even on the cloudiest days, and the hearth's orange glow flickered on the pachydon-hide walls. The flames she kept as low as she could bear, balancing a want for warmth with a need for darkness, for light wreaked pressure behind her eyes and in her skull.

She sat upon her coarseoak seat high above the empty room, the rugged armrests beneath her fingertips. She had ordered the seat built many seasons ago so she could peer down dramatically at any nander for whom she held court. They saw her not quite as a deity, yet there was adulation, or perhaps awe, that she sensed whenever they stood before her and listened carefully to her every word.

It hadn't always been this way. It had taken guile and cunning to earn the respect of the j'Lok and to grow into the position she now held. It had begun many generations ago when her family came upon this cratered mountain in the cold hills. It may have been her great-grandfather who'd led her forebears there, or perhaps his father before him; she would never know since the madness took her mother long before she'd told the tale.

Whatever the case, it hadn't taken long for her ancestors to discover what lay in the channels of the mountain's hollow peak. *Obsidian*, they called it, the black rock of the narrowland that could slice with one motion even the toughest of hides.

When the Gerent was barely a woman, back in the days of yesteryear when she could still see, she'd recognized her father's folly of trading with neighboring clans. She knew if they didn't keep their obsidian secret, others would realize what lay in the ground beneath j'Lok and want it for themselves. While there was enough obsidian to share, the outsiders would seek to control it, not just access it through trade. And true to her predictions, the j'Lok thwarted more than one attack in her father's final days.

After her father was taken by the forever-sleep, the Gerent, his only living heir, tried to mobilize her clan, proclaiming they must secure their homes and protect their resources. But the j'Lok paid her little heed since she was but a woman. To earn her nander's trust, for them to listen to her and obey her, she had to turn to faith and fable.

Nander lives were ruled by few concerns—foodstuff, family, and sex. But looming above everything, like a listless cloud obscuring reason, were the myths of origins and endtimes. None of the stories made sense if she gave them any thought; they were legends wrought with holes and inconsistencies. But it mattered not to her nander. Such ancient tales were never to be questioned.

The beliefs that intrigued her most of all, the lore that would be easiest to exploit, were the foolish legends of the endtimes. When the flowing waters turn to stone, it was said, the High Ones would rise from the belly of the narrowland to usher forth the end of the world. To stir her settlement into action, to be accepted as its leader, this was the myth to target. And thus she made a spectacle one night of walking alone and lightless into the deepest of the channels, claiming she'd been led there by a dream. When she emerged at sunrise, her feet bloody, her skin caked with the black soot of the narrowland, she told her tribe she had been touched by fire. She said Vul-ka's flames had swallowed her in the great below and he had tasked her with protecting against Gigas rising from the underworld. She was now the Allseer, she said, and could see the horrors to come and their little means to thwart it.

The flowing waters have turned to stone, she said.

Each day grows colder than the last, she said.

The black channels beneath their feet, the tunnels and corridors of the narrowland from which they wrested tools and weapons were but Gigas' tendrils, reaching up from the belly of the narrowland itself. These channels were the fabled High Ones, their presence a sign from Vul-ka that they, the j'Lok nander of the pitted mountain, had been chosen to protect against the cataclysm.

How irrational men could be when struck by fear. Foolish, superstitious nander, she thought, who see not the reality before them but instead what they are told to see. As her vision began to fail shortly thereafter, she explained that for the sight of the future one must sacrifice the sight of the now. And thus Vul-ka was stealing her vision so she could harness greater powers as the Allseer.

To protect their living-place, she selected three leaders she called her trust-group. With superior weapons to intimidate and obsidian as bait, she sent these men out to neighboring clans, forcing them to trade only with the j'Lok and serve her if called. Those who would not agree were cut off from the obsidian forever.

But still, it was not enough. Stories soon emerged of another people—a slender, tall, and hook-nosed people, dark as if scorched by the high sun—coming to the coldlands in swarms that made even j'Lok seem small. *No-brows*, she dubbed them, on account of their ridgeless foreheads. Nander had kept out the no-brows for generations, it was said, but the number of nander seemed to be dwindling thanks to the growing cold. Soon, there'd be no way of stopping the no-brows unless she grew her numbers even more.

Some of her traders even returned with tales of bartering with these dark people. Others came back with stories about their hoarding uncut obsidian—for what purpose, she was unsure. But uncut obsidian in the hinterland was forbidden; she was firm that only shaped obsidian was ever to leave the settlement. The j'Lok had to control which weapons traveled to the outside world.

Faced with the encroaching dark people, she heightened her efforts. She sent more envoys to visit nander far and wide with demands that all men come to j'Lok to work the mines and shape more weapons. Those who would not capitulate were slain by war parties shortly after their refusal. Word soon spread that the j'Lok were a clan to be feared, and many tribes agreed to serve them or join them simply to avoid her wrath. Over the seasons, the many hands of nander under her purview had gone much higher than anyone could count.

Now, here they were: the most powerful group of nander in all the narrowland—secure and emboldened by their multitudes and their unshared access to the greatest known resource—obsidian.

And yet she now felt as if something ominous loomed in the days ahead. She had sent three bands of men sunward to bring into the fold Kurnisahn, Ser-o, and Bhatt—the last three clans in the region. One band was slain with shocking efficiency after encountering a tribe of no-brows in the lowrock valley. Her first commander, Sakaq, and a few subordinates escaped the slaughter and survived long enough to bring the news back to her. The other two bands never returned; whatever happened to them was anybody's guess.

As the Gerent continued to ponder, the burdei flap rose, sending a wave of light into the chamber. She could see from his stance it was Sakaq who had entered. He sealed the burdei flap behind him, carefully blocking whatever light slivered about its periphery.

"What is it?" she grumbled before he could speak.

"Allseer," he said, approaching. "I know you do not wish to be bothered during daylight, but something has happened."

She replied with silence to urge him on.

"Three nander are at the entrance to the crater," he said. "They are all in a poor way."

"The sick are not welcome," she said. "Leave them outside with the others."

"One of them is an infant."

"It doesn't matter. We seek no plague or tainted spirits in j'Lok."

"They are more worn from travel than sick," he said, speaking slowly as if unsure how to deliver whatever message he came bearing.

"Are they of use to us?"

"Not as they are today, but—"

"Then send them on their way."

"Allseer, there is more," he said. She could hear his shuffling feet, the uncertainty in his tone. Such a display of apprehension was uncharacteristic of Sakaq, even after all he'd suffered in the lowrock valley. "The baby does not look like any nander I've ever seen," he continued.

She leaned forward. "What do you mean?"

"Well the girl says it's not, but the boy…he's not so sure, so even though he says it is—"

"Say what you mean to say, Sakaq."

She sensed his mouth open, but the words wouldn't come.

"What is it? Tell me," she said.

Sakaq took a deep breath. "He says the baby was borne from the seed of a High One."

25

The Crowd Gathers

T HE FRAIL AND UNWELL are not welcome for fear of the
plague and flux."

"We're not ill."

The j'Lok guard planted his spear across his chest and stepped
to Falon. "Down the hill with you," he said, the seams of his pachydon coat poorly sewn and drapes of grotty fur dangling beneath
his arms. "You stay down there with the sick."

Down the slope behind Falon and Una, a few fires burned yellow in the mountainscape, a sea of white broken by black ridges
stabbing toward the sky. Huddled around these fires was the most
woeful group of nander Falon had ever seen. A one-armed man
struggled to adjust his footwear while another picked at angry
lesions on his lips. A red-haired woman clawed her scalp, and even
from this distance, Falon could see the lice tumble onto her shoulders like specks of beige dandruff before scurrying up her neck and
back into her frazzled mane.

"Please," Falon said, turning back to the guard. "We came all
the way from Kurnisahn. Our living-place was destroyed by the
High Ones. We've seen more of them in our travels. It won't be
long before you're found."

The guard snickered. "You two won't make us any readier than we already are."

"But we have with us a newborn, only a sistersun of age." He pulled the rabbitskin off Nunic's head to expose his tiny dome.

The guard rapped Falon's knuckles with his spear handle. "Away! That baby is cursed."

"He's not cursed. He was borne from the seed of a High One."

"Falon, don't say that," Una said from behind him. He held up his palm to quiet her, then widened his eyes to express that he'd only said it to convince the guard to let them pass. Una didn't seem to get the message. Or perhaps she just ignored it, knowing Falon believed his own admission.

"We sent word to the Gerent," the guard said. "Until she says to let you in, you'll remain with the masses below."

The lice-ridden woman had made her way from the fire up to the guards, and Falon stepped out of her way. "Please," she said, raising her hands, "my lifemate and children were taken in. Let me join them."

"Down with the others," the guard said.

"Then let them out! Let us leave this horrible place together."

"I won't tell you again."

"But we didn't come here by choice. My lifemate was forced into the mines when our living-place—"

The guard cracked the woman on the side of her head with the shaft of his spear. She crumpled to the ground and looked up at him, a trickle of blood streaming from behind her ear.

"Down with the others or I strike again."

As the guard said this, a burly figure came forth from the path behind him. Falon recognized the newcomer immediately—it was Sakaq, the leader of the j'Lok envoy that had visited Kurnisahn before the High Ones came. Sakaq had aged terribly since Falon had last seen him; sharp lines stretched downward from the corners of his lips, and dark circles under his eyes evidenced a man whose very character had been shaped by hardship. He scowled at the lice-ridden woman, his miserable expression amplified by the blue pins in his brow. "If you ever want to see your boy alive, get back down with the others. Otherwise, it will be his body we send. We'll let you in once you rid yourself of the plague. Try cutting off your hair."

The woman scowled at him and wandered back down the hill without another word.

Sakaq looked Falon and Una up and down. "Your tale has the Gerent's attention."

"So, you'll let us in?" Una asked.

"She'll hear your story. But what comes next is her decision. You are both unwell, and something is very wrong with your baby. Anyway, come with me."

They followed Sakaq past the guard, who shot them one last threatening glare as they passed him. Sakaq had the conflicted gait of a man gravely humbled—walking slowly with slumped shoulders, but holding his chin high as if it was the final vestige of a once proud man. He led them up a winding path, black rocks jutting from the snow like fire-cracked bones at every turn. After scaling the crest of the hill, the entirety of the settlement came into view. Within the mountaintop crater was a living-place larger than Falon had expected, even after all the stories he had heard. The powdery grounds were covered in crisscrossing paths of hard white snow, beaten under the soles of the men who walked upon them. Many hands of burdei encircled a larger structure in the center of the pit that appeared to be their destination. Unlike the burdei in Kurnisahn, these were made of giant bones—pachydon ribs, it seemed—buttressing one another beneath shaggy red furs to keep out the cold. The sharp tip of every bone met at a high point where wisps of black smoke rose.

They descended a gravelly path into the crater, its sheer black walls towering above them many trees high. The settlement brimmed with activity—men cutting wood, carving staffs and weapons, chipping obsidian shards for blades in a masterful display. Near one of the cliffsides, a group of men carried a large black rock out of a tunnel. Women were nursing babies, warming clay pots, melting snow, weaving hair and twisting stringrass threads.

As Falon and Una crossed the living-place, the j'Lok stopped to gawk and whisper amongst themselves. What they spoke of could not be more obvious—the gaze of every eye focused on the baby—so Una covered Nunic's head with a rabbitskin so no one could see his face.

Sakaq halted in front of the central burdei, multi-domed and by far the largest in the living-place, guarded by two spear-bearing men with feather headbands. Falon was relieved the long walk had ended, for he'd developed a painful limp from his wounds.

"The Gerent is inside," Sakaq said, pointing at entrance to the burdei. Many hands of pachydon tusks spiked outward from the antechamber, the chaos of their coiled shafts like the maw of some otherworldly beast. *Enter at your own peril*, the gateway seemed to say. "But you must leave your belongings before going in."

"Will you give them back?" Falon asked.

"That's up to the Gerent."

Falon looked back at the entryway. The yellowed tusks along its perimeter looked like they had been sharpened. "And if we refuse?"

"Don't challenge me. I'll send you back down to the shivering masses."

Una set a hand on Falon's chest. "Just do what he says. We've come so far."

He knew she was right, even though that burdei looked like the last place he'd ever want to go unarmed. He shook off his shoulder-pack, removed his blades and spear, and tossed them alongside the stave and sorrows into a snowbank. Somehow, the cord had fallen off the stave while climbing the mountain and was nowhere to be seen.

Sakaq raised an eyebrow when he saw the sorrows. "What are those?" he asked in a tone that suggested he already knew.

"Just a set of small blades," Falon said, still wondering what had happened to the stave's cord.

Sakaq held his gaze, clearly not convinced and probably alerted by Falon's puzzled expression. He made eye contact with each of the guards, as if delivering an unspoken order, before motioning for Falon and Una to follow him into the Gerent's burdei.

"Enter quickly, then seal the chamber," said a scratchy female voice in the darkness.

The fusty stench of pachydon hide wafted over them as they entered. Then the flap fell behind them, enshrouding the room in darkness, save the glow from the hearth and a single cool beam shooting down from the peak of the structure. It would take a moment to get accustomed to the gloom.

"Come on then, get closer," said the voice behind the flames. Sitting on a tall coarseoak seat high above the room was a woman older than Falon had ever seen. Her scraggly white hair drooped to her shoulders and had thinned on top like a man's. "You are Kurnisahn?" she said.

"We are," Falon said.

"You are but children. How did you come all this way alone?"

"There were times when we thought we might not make it."

"When was the last time you fed?" the Gerent asked, a flap of flaccid skin quivering below her chin when she spoke. Her eyes were foggy and pupil-less, and never quite faced Falon, as if she couldn't tell exactly where he stood.

"Yesterday. But foodstuff has been hard to find."

"Lift your furs."

"What?"

"Let us see your ribs."

Falon exchanged glances with Una. She too was unsure where this was going.

"Go on, let us see them," the Gerent said.

He swallowed and lifted his tunic to expose his rawboned frame.

"The boy is wasted," Sakaq said. "But that's not all. His face was sliced in half and is poorly healed."

"What happened to your face?"

"It's a scar from when I was a boy." Falon looked at Una as he said this but she turned away.

"The scar is fresher than that. Tell it true," Sakaq said.

"I was cut again on our way here."

"By?"

"A High One."

"A High One," the Gerent repeated, rubbing her fingertips on her chin. "Your passage here must be quite a tale. One for another time, perhaps." She turned to Una, looking in her general direction but not quite at her. "So, it is you who carries the child?"

"I am not with child. It was born almost a sistersun ago."

"Boy or girl?"

"A boy."

"And does this boy have a name?"

"Nunic."

The sounds of a gathering crowd were rising outside. Someone was shouting about a demon.

"Don't worry about them; they won't get past the guards," the Gerent said, somehow sensing Falon's concern. "Now, about your boy. You don't need to hide him from me. Take Nunic out for me to see."

Una looked at Falon, unsure. She, too, seemed to suspect the Gerent was blind but lifted the rabbitskin off Nunic's head anyway.

As the Gerent delicately rose, Falon imagined her bones creaking as if the crackles and snaps from the hearth were the sounds of her every tortured movement. She climbed down from her seat, a few careful steps hunched over like a broken figurine, and ambled over to them. Una tensed while the Gerent felt Nunic's face, focusing on the shape of his forehead and nose. Then, Sakaq helped her back up to her seat where she sat in silence, her hands, covered in brown splotches, perched under her chin as if deep in thought.

"And what color is the child's skin?" she asked.

"Haven't your guards already told you?"

She glared at Falon, clearly a woman unaccustomed to being questioned. He'd need to watch his tongue. "I want to hear it from you," she said.

"His skin is brown like the narrowland," Falon said, looking down at Nunic.

"The ground here is not brown."

"No, it's not," Falon said. "The soil here is blacker than any I've ever seen, almost like crumbled rock. But the High Ones—"

"Have skin like the blackest obsidian," the Gerent finished for him. She turned away from the flames and rapped her fingernails on her armrests, her eyes now closed. "The light bothers me so."

"What happened to your eyes?"

"They were taken long ago."

"In battle?"

The Gerent snickered. "No, not in battle. To see the future, one must forget the now. The sight I lack is balanced by my visions of things to come."

Falon met eyes with Una. Neither of them was sure what the Gerent meant by that. The ancient woman strung words together in ways they had never heard and was clearly of an intelligence they'd not come across before.

Sakaq whispered to the Gerent while pointing at the entrance of the burdei. She muttered something back, and Sakaq walked out, leaving her alone with the Kurnisahn. What had they said? Was it about the crowd outside that even now sounded louder and more disorderly? It seemed something bad was about to happen, particularly after the suspicious way Sakaq had eyed the sorrows.

191

The Gerent resumed rapping her armrests. "Why are you here?"

Falon looked over his shoulder to see what was happening outside, but the burdei flap was down. "Our living-place was destroyed by the High Ones," he said, turning back to face the Gerent. "So was Bhatt. We thought it would be safe to come here."

The Gerent smirked. "Safe from what? The High Ones? Tell me of these supposed High Ones."

"They look like nander, only taller, slenderer. Their noses are hooked, their foreheads high, and they live with howlers."

"Boy, those are not the High Ones," the Gerent said. "They're just another type of nander. We call them no-brows."

As the Gerent said this, Sakaq returned with the bundle of sorrows, tailed by a hand of spear-bearing guards. Falon's hands trembled slightly as the newcomers formed a threatening half-circle behind him and Una, barely leaving room to move.

"These High Ones you speak of," Sakaq said, "my envoy was beaten back by such men. Only a few of us survived."

The Gerent tilted her head toward Falon. "What do you know about the men I sent into the lowrock valley?"

"I recognize him," Falon said, pointing at Sakaq. He hoped his jittering hand didn't suggest he had something to hide. "He came to our living-place and invited our Somm to join you."

"I sent others too."

Falon shook his head. "I know nothing about the others."

"The boy is trembling, Allseer," Sakaq said. "He is hiding something."

The Gerent sat up and lifted a hand to quiet Sakaq, as if she already understood the situation far more than he. "Why should we let you stay in j'Lok?" she asked, her empty eyes locked on Falon.

"We've seen what you do with the weak," Falon said. "We might be weak, but we'll heal with time."

"I'm not concerned about you. Do you hear the unrest outside? That's the sound of the j'Lok calling for the removal of your baby. They say it is cursed."

"He isn't cursed. He's my son," Una said.

The Gerent offered a nearly toothless smile. "Did your father bond you to a no-brow?"

"No, it was to a nander."

"To him?" the Gerent said, stretching her hand toward Falon.

Falon let out a long breath, remembering the night Una had been bonded to Carn. He wasn't sure how, but the Gerent seemed to notice his discomfort. "No, not to me," he answered for her, guessing the Gerent already knew what he would say.

"Then where is your lifemate?"

"He was killed in Kurnisahn."

"But the baby is his?"

"Yes," she said, looking away. She didn't even believe her own words.

The Gerent shook her head. "Child, you cannot lie to me. Or to yourself. We all see what the baby is."

Una stared back at her without responding.

The Gerent sat silently as Sakaq approached her. He lifted a sorrow from the bundle and handed it to her, again whispering in her ear. She caressed the sorrow's tip with a gnarled finger.

"This obsidian was not shaped by us." She turned to Falon. "Did you make this?"

"No. It belonged to a High One."

The Gerent threw the sorrow on the floor and turned to Sakaq. "It is as we feared. Thieves are trading stolen obsidian to the no-brows. You, commander, need to stop this leakage or I will find someone else who will."

Now it was Sakaq's turn to stiffen as the Gerent directed her ire toward him. "We will better protect the mines," he said.

The Gerent stared at him, waiting for more.

"Allseer, it is as I said before," Sakaq continued, his tone unsure. "I know these blades. They were used by no-brows to kill my men."

"Your men were killed by *these*?"

"Yes. They came like flying daggers. Unlike anything we'd seen before."

"How is that feeble weapon thrown?"

"I don't know. They came at us from afar, and we couldn't tell how the no-brows threw them with such speed. There was too much confusion as our men fell."

The Gerent turned to Falon. "And you, I suppose, know how to use this weapon?"

"I do."

"How did you come to have it?"

"We were attacked by a High One in the mountains—"

"Stop calling them High Ones."

"Right," Falon said, pausing to think. "A *no-brow* attacked us in the mountains. He was the one who opened my face. We saw him use the weapon, but then Una seized it and slew him with his own blade."

"You slew a no-brow?" the Gerent asked her.

"I did. With a sorrow."

"That's what you call these blades?"

"Yes," Falon replied. "It seemed fitting after what they did to our clan."

"My girl, you impress me so," the Gerent said as if she didn't quite believe their story. She straightened her features. "Show us how to use the weapon."

"Will you let us stay?" Falon said.

"We'll come to an agreement."

"We need to agree on something now."

The Gerent leaned forward. "You come into our living-place, carrying a newborn no-brow and armed with no-brow weapons.

Weapons, I see, that were carved from obsidian stolen from our mines. You, boy, will accept whatever terms we offer."

"Nunic is not a no-brow," Una snapped.

Falon swallowed when the guards gripped their spears. "What are your terms?" he asked.

"Sakaq told me what this weapon can do. If you show us how to use it, we'll let you stay."

Una and Falon exchanged glances. She shrugged, her mouth slightly agape as if surprised how quickly they had come to terms. "Then we agree," Falon said.

"Good," the Gerent said. "But there is one condition. Your baby cannot stay in j'Lok."

"What do you mean? Why not?"

"My nander believe it cursed."

"Do you believe that?"

The Gerent stared at Falon for a moment before responding. "I do not have faith in much, you see. No, I do not think the child is cursed. But that doesn't change the fact that everyone else does. You can hear for yourself what is happening outside."

"What are we supposed to do? Leave him in the mountains for the forever-sleep?"

"No. We will ascend the baby."

"No," Una said, shaking her head, holding Nunic tighter.

"Perhaps you don't understand the situation. You have two choices. Show us how to use the weapon and stay. Or show us nothing and leave. Either way, the baby goes to the forever-sleep."

"We're leaving," Una said, her voice breaking. She rushed toward the entrance of the burdei, clutching Nunic to her chest.

"Guards, stop them!" the Gerent commanded. "Sakaq, take the baby."

"No!" Una screamed, pushing past the guards and running out. Falon turned and followed. The crowd gasped upon sight of the baby, everyone backing away. In the middle of the confusion, Sakaq hurried out and grabbed Una by the shoulder. He spun her and ripped Nunic from her arms and carried him back into the Gerent's burdei before the crowd could reach him.

"Give him back to me!" Una cried, striking Sakaq's back with a flurry of hammerfists as he withdrew. The guards threw her to her knees and kicked her spine, sending her face-first into the gravel and snow. Falon swung at the guard who'd kicked her but was himself thrown to the ground. It took only a few breaths before both their wrists were tied with stringgrass binds, while the entrance flap fell behind them, muting Nunic's cries.

26
Imprisoned

OW QUICKLY UNA'S HOPES had been trampled. When she and Falon had first approached j'Lok, she'd thought their travails would at last be rewarded. But she had been foolish to believe they'd be welcomed unconditionally. Had they arrived healthy and unencumbered, they might have been allowed to enter and become productive members of j'Lok. But that was not to be. That path had closed the moment the High Ones filled her womb with their progeny.

Even if she insisted outwardly that the baby was Carn's, inside she knew it wasn't. Nunic looked nothing like him, even at this infant age. Thinking back, she wondered if Nunic's early birth had been due to her hardships while with child or the heinous union in which she'd been seeded. Perhaps her body was not meant to carry a half-breed.

"You'll stay here until the Gerent decides what to do with you," Sakaq said after the guards threw her and Falon into a dark, heartless burdei in the shadows of the cliffsides. They were seated back-to-back with their wrists tied to a stake in the rock and their ankles bound.

"What about my baby?" she cried.

"It will be ascended on the eve of the sharpened sistersun."

"The sistersun will not be sharpened for many nights. My baby must be fed!"

Sakaq let out a long breath. "I'll talk to the Gerent."

"Please, it's been since morning!"

"One of the milk mothers will feed it."

"They think he's cursed. I'm the only one who will do it. My breasts are painful and swollen already."

"I'll do what I can," Sakaq said, walking out.

They fell into darkness when the burdei flap descended. She wept, her chest heaving, her thoughts spiraling. The stringgrass wrenched into her wrists, not far from the bite scars that mangled her forearm.

Falon turned his head as if he wanted to rest his chin on her shoulder. "Una, please calm."

"How can I calm when they're going to kill Nunic?"

"They aren't going to do anything until the sistersun is sharpened. We have time to plan."

As usual, his view was skewed by the unrealistic notion that somehow, someway there'd be hope. Throughout their voyage to j'Lok, she had tried to temper his outlook and keep him focused on what was possible given the realities they faced. This balance between his hopefulness and her doubt had been effective; without it, they might not have made it all the way here. But now, imprisoned by the j'Lok and her child torn from her arms, she saw no way forward.

"Time to plan what?" she said. "What can we do?"

"Maybe we can wrest our hands from the stringgrass."

"And then? How are we going to rescue Nunic?"

"Maybe we wait until dark, then sneak into the Gerent's burdei to take him."

"That isn't a plan. How will we get past the guards?" As if on cue, she heard a guard position himself outside the burdei.

"Quiet," Falon said. "Let's cooperate for now and see what they want us to do."

"We don't have anything to trade."

"We know how to use the sorrows."

"And if they figure it out on their own? Then we have nothing."

"They won't figure it out."

"We did, didn't we?"

Falon, already whispering, lowered his voice further. "Did you see the stave when I gave it to Sakaq? The cord was missing. It must have fallen off on the way up the mountain."

"So, it just looks like a long stick?"

"A *really* long stick, yes. It has notches where the cord was tied, but that doesn't tell them anything. Without the cord, there's no way for them to use it. The Gerent said she'd let us stay here if we showed them."

"But she also said Nunic couldn't stay. Are you saying we leave him?"

"No, but if I'm going to teach them how to use the weapon, first they'll have to let me hold it."

"Then what—you kill them all? That isn't going to work. You're brave, Falon. Brave and stupid."

He shook his head. "You're right. We'll never make it out of here alive. At least not with Nunic."

Then, Una had an idea. A crazy one, but there might not have been another kind given their predicament. And while she recognized how impossible it would sound, she also knew Falon's naïveté would take hold, and he'd be roused into action as soon as she said it. While she felt remorse for provoking him into what was likely a suicidal gambit, she could think of no other way to save her baby.

"Do you really think you can grab the sorrows?" she said.

"If I get close enough."

"How many of the j'Lok do you think you can wound before they stop you?"

"One. Two, maybe. Why?" He paused for a moment, then turned his neck, trying in vain to see her. "Are you thinking what I think you're thinking?"

"What do you think I'm thinking?"

"You want me to kill the Gerent."

"No. But maybe you can take her hostage. Trade her life for Nunic's."

27

For Him to Break

T HE GERENT HELD THE BABY to her breast. It was warm against her bosom, and for a moment she regretted never having one of her own. But as the Allseer, she had no patience for the time-consuming foolishness of a child. Too much had to be done to grow her power and protect her nander.

The baby's head seemed so normal as she caressed it with her fingertips, even if it was unusually small. Its features were sharper than you'd expect of a nander, but still, they didn't seem that strange.

"This creature I hold against my breast," she said, "how odd does it truly appear?"

"The strangest thing is its color," Sakaq said.

"This is no demon child."

Sakaq stood before her, unsure what to say.

"What are the j'Lok saying about it?" she asked.

"They still believe it cursed. The girl hid it as she crossed the living-place, leading to rumors about its face and form."

"Such as?"

"Some say it has the horns of an aurochs. Others say the face of a bat."

She shook her head. "This baby is not cursed. A no-brow forced himself upon its mother."

"As you say, Allseer. What do you wish for us to do?"

"I don't want to ascend this baby. It seems a disgrace to do so."

"Should we cast the Kurnisahn out of j'Lok with the baby?"

Almost as if it understood what Sakaq had said, the infant let out a shriek. She lifted it to him. "Take it. Take it from me."

He took the baby, carefully lifting it from under its buttocks and the back of its head. "Allseer, it must be hungry. Its mother—"

"Then bring it to her to be fed," she snapped. "But I want the prisoners guarded. Both of them."

"And when she's done feeding it?"

"I have no patience for the wailing of infants. Bring it to one of the milk mothers."

"The milk mothers won't come near it."

"We're not in the practice of starving children, Sakaq. Keep the baby fed until the sharpened sistersun."

"We just took it from its mother. Now you want to give it back?"

The baby shrieked again and jerked in Sakaq's arms.

"I don't know. Figure it out. Now get it out of here."

"Guards!" Sakaq shouted. Two guards, Frohk and Kao, entered at once. "Bring the baby to its mother to be fed."

Kao took a step back, shaking his head.

Frohk pointed at Kao. "He's stronger than me, make *him* carry it."

"Take it now!" Sakaq said, clearly annoyed at their cowardice. "And I want a hand of guards protecting the baby. It is not to be harmed." Frohk mumbled under his breath while taking the baby, and Kao followed him out, the entrance flap falling behind them.

"It doesn't matter if I *want* to ascend the baby," the Gerent said after the guards were gone. "But if we don't, it'll be killed in a far less forgiving way."

"We can still send the Kurnisahn away. All three of them."

"If we do that, some fearful fool would chase after them, seeing it as his duty to rid the narrowland of the 'accursed' child."

"If you say it must be ascended, it will be done."

"But not until the sharpened sistersun," the Gerent said, holding up a finger.

"Allseer, if we're going to do this, we should not wait. The living-place grows restless."

"No. An ascension must take place on the eve of the sharpened sistersun, for that is the time of bleeding as every woman knows. There must be consistency in our rituals. It is belief that has brought j'Lok to where it is today. It is belief that allows us to control the lives of so many. Without belief, we have nothing."

"Yes, Allseer."

She stared down Sakaq to keep him uneasy. He'd lost some of his mettle since returning from the lowrock valley, his waning confidence making him easier to manipulate. "Now, we will speak about security," she said. "Those strange weapons the Kurnisahn carried. This is not the first time stolen material has been used by no-brows. Whoever is stealing our obsidian seems to know exactly who to bring it to."

"Perhaps."

"The thieves must be many. Do you think they're organized?"

"No. But there are many bands of them. Some we've caught, either in small groups or alone. If there was more to know, we would have made them tell us."

"How are they getting the ore out of j'Lok?"

"Not from the tunnels inside the living-place," he said, adjusting his posture. "It must be the other one."

"The tunnel outside the crater is not used for mining. How far have we advanced in there?"

"We've gone deeper, to no end. It just goes on, getting warmer as we descend."

She tapped her armrests. "It makes sense that thieves would target that channel. They wouldn't have to get past our guards. It seems the way to avoid future thefts is clear."

"Yes, Allseer. I will put guards at the mouth of every tunnel." Sakaq waited for her to respond but she stared back at him straight-faced. "Is there anything else, Allseer?"

"I'm not done with you. I don't think you recognize how serious our situation is."

"I do," he said, confidence returning to his tone. "We must control our obsidian. This resource is what sets us apart from other nander."

"It is more than that. Those who steal our obsidian are arming our enemies."

"We ourselves have traded obsidian to the no-brows."

"Yes, but always in a form of *our* choosing. The no-brows now make a new kind of weapon." She pointed at him. "Need I remind you how quickly your envoy was destroyed?"

"You don't need to remind me."

"Until we figure out how to use the weapon and can make it ourselves, we're at risk for slaughter. Tell me of your progress."

Sakaq paused. "We haven't figured it out yet," he said.

"Gigas' piss, Sakaq. Bring me the prisoners' effects."

Sakaq walked out of her burdei, returning with a couple guards carrying the prisoners' belongings. She heard them lay everything on the ground.

"They had waterskins and bearskins," Sakaq said, pointing at the items. "Of interest, though, are a few obsidian daggers, a broken spear, the sorrows, and a thuk-tree stave."

"Like a branch?"

"No, it's been shaped. More like a staff, but it isn't that either."

"Why would they need such a long piece of wood?"

"It might be connected to the sorrows."

"Let me see it."

Sakaq handed her the stave. It was heavier than she could hold on her own, so she rested the ends on the armrests of her seat. She felt along its length, noticing how smooth and straight it had been carved, almost like an absurdly long walking stick with notches on each end.

"I don't see how the stave connects to the sorrows unless something is missing," she said.

"The stave is probably just a club. They must use something to throw the weapon so fast, but the only unusual item they had was the stave."

"Unless they hid something."

Sakaq shook his head. "They came here as if we were some sort of refuge. They didn't have the mind to do something like that."

"The boy knows how to use it. Make him tell us."

"Should we question them until they break?"

"I don't know if they *will* break, not while we have the baby."

"You've seen my questioning. If the boy knows how to use the weapon, I'll make him tell us."

"I'm not so sure. Something about the boy tells me his will is strong."

"Then we'll trade the baby for the information. That would be the fastest way."

Sakaq was right, but letting the baby live was too risky considering the disruption it would cause across the living-place. "No," she said. "Unless the Gods themselves send us a message to spare its life, I will ascend it."

"What then? Tell the boy we'll give back the baby, then betray him once we have what we want?"

"No. Not that either. They both seem clever. They managed to make it all the way here alive. I don't think he'll be so easy to fool."

"We can try, though."

"There is another way," she said, lifting a finger. "The boy longs for her, do you not see that?"

"I assumed they were lifemates until she said hers was killed in Kurnisahn."

"Yes. She was bonded to another, yet the boy provides for her as if that baby was his own. He wouldn't do that unless he cared for her." She nudged the stave so Sakaq would take it back. "Let the girl feed her baby. We don't want it wasting away into the forever-sleep before we can ascend it."

"Yes, Allseer."

"And the boy—put him to work. Give him hope. And after they're both comfortable, we'll tear everything down."

"I can send him into the mines at once."

"Good. But keep them guarded. The baby too. After the sister-sun is sharpened and the baby is ascended, we strike."

"Torture the boy for the information?"

"No. We see how long it takes for him to break while he watches us torture *her*."

28

Into the Narrowland

S AKAQ ENTERED THEIR FIRELESS BURDEI, flanked by a pair of
guards, each with his spear facing forward. Sunlight blared
from behind them, casting their forms in stark relief upon
the entryway. "She stays here with the baby," he told the guards,
then pointed at Falon. "If we untie you, I don't want any trouble.
Understood?"

Falon nodded.

"Tell me you understand."

He stared back at the j'Lok commander, his body tensing.

"Or we can leave you here, tied up in the dark. Your choice."

"Are you letting us go?" Falon asked.

"No. You're going to work in the tunnels."

Falon looked at Nunic. He was asleep in Una's lap, his little
nose twitching, his brow wrinkling as he dreamt. "What about the
baby?"

"You're in no position to bargain."

"Falon, just go," Una said. "They're leaving Nunic here with
me, right?"

"Yes," Sakaq answered.

"What about everyone out there who wants the baby taken by the forever-sleep?" Falon said.

"Your being here won't protect it," one of the guards interjected.

Sakaq raised a hand to silence the guard, annoyed at the interruption. He looked back at Nunic and Una. "Nothing will happen until the Gerent commands," he said quietly, a tinge of regret lurking beneath his words. "I have my strongest guards defending them. Now I tell you again: no trouble when we untie you. Understood?"

"Understood."

Sakaq signaled a guard to untie Falon from the stake. He sat up and rubbed his wrists, red and scraped from the stringrass.

"What about giving us fire?"

"You're asking for too much now, boy."

Falon gestured at Una. "She has a baby, early-born. They need to stay warm."

Sakaq exhaled. "Put them in a burdei with a fire pit," he told the guards. "But it must be at the edge of the living-place."

The guards exchanged glances.

"That wasn't a request," Sakaq said. When the guards walked out, he turned back to Falon. "Is there anything else we can do for you?" he asked sarcastically.

"We'll take a fresh chop of aurochs meat, if you're offering."

Sakaq glared at him before ushering him out of the burdei. His vision blurred from the brightness of the day, and he shielded his brow to protect against the glare.

"You've been in darkness half a day, I know," Sakaq said. "But where we're going, you'll have to get used to the dark again."

"Are we going to the tunnels?"

"Follow me."

He followed the j'Lok commander to the rim of the crater, two torch-bearing guards flanking their front and back. Falon's legs were stiff from being tied up for so long, worsening the pain that already came with every step.

"Why are you walking like that?" Sakaq said.

"A few sistersuns ago, I took two sorrows to the thigh. I fear I might never walk the same."

"The wound didn't corrupt?"

"It started to, but... well, a howler saved us."

Sakaq burst into laughter, jerking his head back and looking skyward as if it was the funniest thing he'd ever heard. "A howler!" he repeated. The guards took his cue and snickered too. "Thank you, boy, I haven't laughed like that in ages."

Falon didn't doubt it; he wouldn't have been surprised if this was the first time Sakaq had *ever* laughed. Nevertheless, this moment of merriment seemed like a good time to find out where they were headed. "I thought we were going to the tunnels," he said, pretending to chuckle along with his captors. "Why are we leaving the mountain?"

Sakaq's features returned to their default brooding configuration. "Keep going," he said, pointing forward.

"Are you casting me out?"

"I said keep going."

They passed the crater rim and turned down a winding path Falon hadn't noticed before. Down the mountain, the shivering masses huddled beside their fires. They looked even more pitiful than he remembered.

"There are many black channels below j'Lok," Sakaq said, breaking a long silence. "But only three are wide enough for a man to enter."

"Those are the mines?"

"The two big ones in the crater are. There is a third, whose mouth is on the side of the mountain. But we don't mine it. We learn from it."

"Learn what? I thought the Gerent said they were Gigas' tendrils reaching up from the underworld."

"That is what she says, yes. But she still wants us to dig as deep as we can." He held out a hand to urge Falon forward, apparently not ready to explain further.

They clambered up the bend, bringing into view a windswept plain in the distance, its white expanse broken by a sheer black cliff. At the bottom, a pile of maroon furs appeared to project from the snowdrifts, guarded by a couple men. Carrion birds circled the scene from high above.

"What is that?"

Sakaq stopped to look into the distance, squinting.

"Over there, at the bottom of the cliff."

"Oh, that." Sakaq turned to him with a closed-lipped smile. "You can see that far?"

"I'm not sure what it is, but I see something."

"Those are pachydon."

Falon furrowed his brow. "Why aren't they moving?"

"They're in the forever-sleep." Sakaq started walking again.

"Why are they piled up like that?"

"Because that's where they landed when we ran the herd off the cliff."

"But what a waste," Falon said, dropping his arms to his side. "How much of the meat spoils?"

As if in response to his question, a stiff wind blasted a puff of snow in their faces, forcing everyone to turn their heads and shield their eyes. "Do you feel how cold it is here?" Sakaq asked once the gusts subsided, brushing powder off his wearings. "Our foodstuffs never spoil."

Falon recalled the day he had ascended his father. How he hated thinking about that day, a day that seemed a lifetime ago. "Back in Kurnisahn, we drove a herd of aurochs into the rapids where they drowned," he said. "It saddened us because we knew the herd was gone and would never return to our lands."

"More pachydon come from deeper in the coldlands as the days grow colder," Sakaq explained. "They are a resource that never ends. Now, let's go over this next ridge. We're almost there."

Climbing over the summit revealed a slope half the height of the mountain itself, tapering below them into a cave mouth littered with obsidian spalls. A few men, their faces and furs covered in grime, carried black blocks out of the shaft before tossing them down the mountain, where they rolled and bounced out of view. Falon wondered if these men were here by choice.

"This is exactly what we need to stop," Sakaq said to the guards. "The thieves don't even need to go into the tunnels, the obsidian must be piling at the foot of the mountain from all this waste. Starting now, all obsidian will be brought back to j'Lok for shaping."

"As you command," a guard said.

"You wait here at the entrance," Sakaq told the guard, before addressing another. "And you—gather men to clean up the rubble. Any rock bigger than my fist must be saved."

Sakaq returned his attention to Falon. "Below us is the channel where we study the obsidian. Where we learn. The Gerent wants to know how deep the veins go."

He followed Sakaq down the hill and into the hollow, its ebon walls smooth at its mouth and cragged a few paces in. No natural light remained once they passed the first bend, but the tunnel's every groove and rimple glittered in the torchlight. The cave soon narrowed into a corridor so tight that he had to squeeze around its corners. The space became stuffy and thick, torch smoke choking the air. He waved his hand over his face to breathe.

The channels went deeper, cramping further, sloping down-ward, to the side, even upward at times. It seemed they were entering the gullet of a black serpent carved into the mountain, the floor sometimes so steep that Falon had to hold onto the walls to keep from tumbling forward. Every so often, emaciated men would cross their path carrying obsidian blocks, Sakaq warning them not to throw them down the mountain.

On and on the tunnels went, their sable walls scored by thin cracks fanning out like fibers of a web. After some time, the air grew warmer, almost as if flames billowed beneath the tunnels. Even the rocks beneath their feet were heated.

Then Sakaq stopped, looking over his shoulder at Falon. "Do you feel that?"

Falon nodded. The soreness in his thigh radiated to his hip now that they weren't moving.

"Outside, it's cold, the ground frozen," Sakaq continued. "Yet the deeper we go, the warmer it becomes. It's as if Vul-ka himself heats these tunnels."

"Perhaps he's fighting to keep Gigas below ground."

Sakaq raised an eyebrow. "That's what some say."

"What does the Gerent think?"

"I don't know what she thinks. It's always hard to tell." He touched the wall, examined the soot on his palm. "When she speaks to the j'Lok, she seems to believe in nothing but her visions." He wiped his hand on his tunic. "But when you're alone with her, she says things that make you question if she has faith in anything."

"What's the real reason she's making you dig here? You said it was to learn."

"She wants to know how deep the obsidian goes," he said quickly, as if it was something he'd repeated many times.

"I don't believe it; that isn't the real reason. How does knowing that help anyone?"

Sakaq cocked his head, considering the question.

"You never thought about this until now?" Falon said.

Sakaq looked back at him, his deep-set eyes revealing the sadness of a man forced to fight for something he didn't believe in. "Maybe she wants us to find a place safe from the cold. It's no secret that each season is colder than the last. We often wonder if the thaw will ever come."

"And yet, here we are, warm underground."

"Perhaps the Gerent seeks a place to hide until the battle of the Gods is done."

"What makes her think that place is here, under the mountain? There are no legends of such a place."

Sakaq shrugged. "Only she knows what is legend and what is true."

"I don't know why you put such trust in your Gerent."

"Careful, boy. She is the messenger between the worlds of Gods and men."

"If she can see the future, why didn't she warn you about the no-brows in the lowrock valley?"

Sakaq narrowed his eyes.

"What?" Falon said, breaking an uncomfortable silence.

Sakaq pointed at a guard. "Give me a torch, then wait for me at the mouth of the tunnel." Falon sucked in a breath. Had he just earned a beating?

"But, commander, we must guard the boy at all times."

"I'll watch the boy."

"But your own safety—"

Sakaq yanked the torch from him. "He's no threat to me. Leave us. That's an order." He waited for the guards to disappear up the tunnel, then turned back to Falon, the lines of his weathered face deepened by the torchlight. "You seem like a smart boy, and I don't want you to get hurt. So, do the smart thing and answer me: how do you throw the sorrows?"

Falon wasn't fooled by Sakaq's display of concern. "I'm not telling you anything until you promise our safety. Especially the baby's."

"And if I make such a promise?"

"I'm not talking about your word."

"Then what?"

"Let us leave j'Lok," Falon said, hoping to sound resolute. "And you can send one person with us—*one*. It can be you, if you like. Once we're far enough away, I'll show you how to throw the sorrows. Then you can leave us and take what you know back to j'Lok."

Sakaq smiled. "You're a clever boy. But that won't happen. You'll have to tell us here."

He studied Sakaq's features for any sign of compromise, but the commander stood in austere silence. "How do I know you won't betray us?"

"Why would we betray you?"

"The j'Lok think Nunic is cursed. Letting him live will cause unrest. The Gerent said so herself."

"Maybe she'll change her mind."

Falon crossed his arms. "Our speakings are over."

"Do you know what will come of your defiance?" Sakaq stepped forward, the torch's heat radiating onto Falon's cheeks. He lowered his chin, his eyes darkening. "We will do terrible things to make you speak," he said, each word articulated slowly.

Falon's stomach sank. He stared back with the most adamant expression he could muster, despite Sakaq's harrowing words.

Sakaq tilted his head, adding a look of frustration to his repertoire of grim expressions. "I shouldn't tell you what I'm about to tell you. But I don't want you to suffer the way you're about to."

Another threat, this time touched with sympathy. Falon wanted to appear unshaken but knew his eyes betrayed his fear.

"Only a few nights remain before the sistersun is sharpened," Sakaq continued, the flames reflecting off his eyes. "The baby will be granted ascension on that night. What you should worry about now is your own safety, and that of your woman."

"She's not my woman."

"But you care for her. She's in even more danger than you."

Falon shifted his feet and swallowed.

"Show us how to throw the sorrows. It's the only way to make it out of this alive."

"I will, but only in the way I offered."

"We're not going to accept that offer." Sakaq placed his hand on Falon's chest, leaning in. "I'm trying to protect you. I'm putting myself at great risk and going against the orders of the Gerent."

Falon lifted his chin, looking at Sakaq from the corner of his eye. "She who knows everything already?"

"How do you throw the sorrows?" Sakaq demanded, raising his voice.

"I told you our terms."

"We know you use the stave. How do you use the stave?"

Falon didn't respond.

Sakaq exhaled. "For your sake, boy, I hope you reconsider." He stared at him gravely for a moment before pointing past him. "Keep going down the tunnel. There's plenty more to see."

29

He Looked to the Man

T HE SHARPENED SISTERSUN approaches its highest point, Frohk thought while watching the dark night sky. It was frustrating to be stuck at the entrance of the crater when it wasn't his turn to guard, but the commander had thrown everyone's schedule awry by increasing security in front of the mines and tasking so many men with cleaning up the rubble at the foot of the mountain.

Of all nights too. Tonight was the eve of the sharpened sistersun, the bright grey slice shining like a troubled smile over the mountainscape. Tonight, the demon would be ascended; a ritual to be performed before witness of all the j'Lok. All except Frohk, of course, and a few other unlucky soldiers who had been given duties outside the living-place.

Could he watch the ascension from the pass? He could still stand guard from there. He didn't need to be stationed at *this* particular place, did he? But no, if he left his station, Kao would surely report him. Kao was such a bore, yet Frohk somehow always found himself working alongside him. Sakaq could have at least partnered him with someone who spoke. All "speakings" with Kao were just one man talking, interrupted at best by grunts and one-word replies.

Yes. No. Ugh. Hmph. Yet another inspired performance by Kao. Frohk wondered why Vul-ka had even bothered to give him a tongue.

Down the mountain, the shivering masses huddled beside the fires. The wind swept in from deeper in the coldlands, the chill rising fast. This might have been the coldest night of the season. The guards should've had more fire than just torchlight; they were the ones out here working. Time and again, Frohk considered moving down to the fires—wasn't he protecting j'Lok from the shivering masses anyway? It was much warmer down there than here at the edge of the pass, where the wind screamed from behind him. But going down there was a bad idea. That fool Kao would surely report him. The mute would finally find a reason to speak.

Even if he could trust Kao, Frohk shuddered at the thought of stepping too near the pestilence. The shivering masses were down there for a reason; their afflictions could not be allowed into j'Lok for fear of dark spirits spreading. The Gerent even allowing them to shelter close to the living-place had been a gesture of kindness. It would have been easier just to ascend them all, even if it meant getting close enough to strike them down.

Then a shadow fluttered down the mountain. Someone new approached. Someone huge. Could the man really be that big, or was it a trick of the flames?

And with him was a child. A young one.

Was the newcomer from j'Lok, for some reason outside the living-place in the middle of the night? Perhaps a trader returning from a long voyage? No, a trader would have been carrying goods and joined by other men rather than a child. If Frohk's sight told true, the newcomer wore greyfur, uncommon for the j'Lok.

"Kao, what do you make of that man?"

The mute shrugged.

"Down there. The one talking to the shivering masses. Now he's pointing this way."

Another shrug.

"He isn't one of us. We don't wear greyfur."

Kao shook his head.

"You're useless. Here he comes."

Kao nodded, contributing to the speakings yet again.

Frohk narrowed his eyes to better see in the darkness. The newcomer was indeed walking toward them, and Frohk could be cast down into Gigas' darkest pits if that wasn't the tallest man he had ever seen. And there was something strange about his companion—his skin dark, his features uncertain in the shadows of the night. Could the tall man be accompanied by a fledgling no-brow?

"Get ready, Kao. They're almost here."

Kao finally showed a semblance of emotion, lifting his spear across his chest.

"Who comes?" Frohk shouted, the wind rippling behind him.

The man continued his ascent without responding.

"Who comes? Answer!" Frohk repeated.

The man lifted from across his back an axe with a blade shaped like a sharpened tear.

Frohk and Kao exchanged glances, then pointed their spears forward with both hands, ready to defend their position. The man was almost there, his axe dragging on the ground as he approached. He stopped just outside the reach of their spears, the child standing behind him. Although the newcomer stood a few paces downhill, he looked Frohk eye to eye. Outnumbering him two to one might not be enough.

The tall man turned to the child and signaled for him to come forward. The boy's features were strange, his forehead high and ridgeless. He lifted a hand toward the guards, his palm facing forward. "We come to j'Lok from lowrock valley," he said in a strange accent, almost an elegance to his tone and voice. He looked to the man after he spoke, as if for approval.

Frohk ignored the boy and studied the man. "Why are you with a no-brow?"

The man motioned for the child to retake his position behind him. He gripped his axe tighter and lifted it off the ground, the wind roaring in his face. "j'Lok is behind you, is it not?"

"Answer the question. Why are you with a no-brow?"

"I don't answer to you."

"Then turn around and leave the mountain."

The man stared back, his sockets black pools in the torchlight. "I didn't come here to fight," he said.

"Then answer the question."

The tall man looked at the bonfires below, clenching his weapon with resolve. "The nander by the fires, do you keep them out so they won't carry dark spirits into j'Lok?"

"That is not your concern. Who are you and why are you here?"

"I already said I don't answer to you."

"Then go. You're not welcome here."

"Get out of my way, and I'll let you live."

Frohk's heart pounded. He was used to bullying the shivering masses, but they were sick and weak and unthreatening beyond their afflictions. Before him was the most imposing man he had ever seen. And yet, he could not show any weakness. j'Lok had to be defended.

Frohk and Kao clutched their spear handles and lifted their blades at the axe-bearing man.

"Answer the question, or it's down the mountain with you," Frohk said, doubting the man would back down and turn.

"You are a brave lot," the man said, his lips curling upward while his eyes remained unchanged.

"We don't care about your opinion. Turn around, tall man."

"Once I strike you down, nothing will stand between j'Lok and the afflicted."

"This is the last time I'll say it, turn and leave."

The tall man's smile disappeared. Frohk was right; it was the last time he said it. It was the last time he would say anything.

30

A Dying Heartbeat

N UNIC STARED AT THE WOOD SMOKE in a post-meal daze. Una put her breast away and placed a foxskin over his head, hoping he would close his eyes and slumber yet again. Soon, she hoped to do the same.

Many nights had passed since their arrival in j'Lok, and it had been many sistersuns since she'd slept well. Her living conditions had improved since being tied up with Falon; Sakaq moved her into a burdei with a hearth and allowed Nunic to stay with her so she could care for him as a mother must. His soldiers even brought her meals and fresh skins for Nunic daily.

But no matter how well Sakaq treated her, she sensed his kindness was but a ploy to achieve his ends, for Una was not a guest but a prisoner. The only time she was allowed outside was to relieve herself, and it was always under heavy guard, the process awkward with so many men surrounding her. But the guards were there to protect her and her baby. Without them, her burdei might have been stormed by a mob swearing her child was cursed.

And what was to be Nunic's fate? The last she'd heard, he was going to be ascended on the eve of the sharpened sistersun. Was that still to be? The way the j'Lok treated her suggested otherwise. Why guard a baby so earnestly only to kill him shortly thereafter?

How she missed Falon. She hadn't seen him since Sakaq escorted him away and she had no idea how he was doing or even where he was. "He will work underground with the other miners," Sakaq said, "until he earns our trust and is given other duties." But Falon was not likely to be given any real opportunities here, given his lack of stature and strength. Still, at least he hadn't been cast out.

Once Una was separated from Falon, Sakaq asked her many times how to operate the weapon. But she was no fool; their separation was clearly intentional, and if Falon hadn't revealed how to use the sorrows it was because that knowledge was their only leverage against the Gerent. If Falon was still alive, of course. Since he'd been led away, Una had no choice but to trust what little Sakaq told her of his whereabouts.

"I'll show you how to use the sorrows once he returns," Una said, hoping Sakaq would say something—anything—that might prove Falon was alive and well. But the man shook his head and walked out. Not the response she'd hoped for.

But now, other worries clouded her mind. Tonight was a different sort of night; she could feel it in the air. It was the eve of the sharpened sistersun, the clamor of voices rising even over the wind that beat against the sides of her burdei. It was unlike the sounds she'd become accustomed to—men joking crudely with one another, guards shooing away curious nander who sought a glimpse of her child, men returning to the living-place with pachydon, felled trees, or obsidian. No, tonight there was something more. It sounded as if the whole living-place was in motion, as if all the j'Lok were congregating in a single place, as if something extraordinary was about to occur to which they all sought to be witnesses.

"What's happening out there?" Una called to the guards.

No reply.

Again, she asked, but no response. It sounded like Sakaq was giving orders and the guards were making way for someone to enter. Now shuffling. Someone new approached. Una recognized those footsteps.

It was her.

A guard lifted the flap, and the Gerent entered, Sakaq on one side, holding her hand, another guard palming the small of her back as if to prevent her from falling. She looked so frail that she might collapse at any moment. It was a testament to her power that she hadn't been ascended long ago. But the j'Lok saw her as the Allseer, touched by the Gods, the one woman chosen to foresee the futures and fates of those over which she had province.

The ancient woman stood before Una, a hand over her brow to deflect the firelight, her blank grey eyes affectless. "It is time," she said in her raspy voice.

"Time for what?" Una said, her heart sinking. It couldn't be a coincidence that the Gerent came to her now on the eve of the sharpened sistersun after so many days of silence. Una stood, holding Nunic as tightly as she could without hurting him. "Time for what?" she repeated.

Two guards escorted the Gerent out, leaving Sakaq and a few other men with Una. When she looked at Sakaq, his eyes shifted to the ground. He nodded to the guards and they marched over to her.

A guard raised his open hands before her. "The baby," he said.

Una turned away, clutching Nunic and sobbing.

"Don't make this any harder than it needs to be," Sakaq said.

She squeezed Nunic closer to her chest. One guard peeled her arms off the baby while another ripped Nunic away.

"No!" she cried, falling to her knees, grasping the guard's legs.

"Take her too," Sakaq said. "She must attend, or the ascension will mean nothing."

She screamed, a cry so loud that her voice cracked, leaving her shrieking silence as the tears streamed from her eyes. This could not happen. This *must* not happen. When the guards grabbed under her arms, she jerked to shake them off. She kicked with one leg, then another, then slammed her foot into the hearth, ejecting sparks and flames into an ashy cloud.

Sakaq grabbed her cheeks, pulling her toward him. "If you don't stop fighting, we'll restrain you."

Una hacked up as much phlegm as she could muster and spewed it in his face. He wiped the saliva off his cheek and onto his tunic, leaving a drop on the tip of his nose. He looked over to the hearth, and Una's eyes followed. A swath of debris was strewn beside the fire, a single ember glowing orange over a streak of black ash, pulsing calmly like a heartbeat fighting to live on. *Soon it will turn black like the rest of it*, she thought.

Sakaq turned away as if ashamed of what was happening, of what was about to happen. "Do it," he said, shaking his head as he said it, refusing to look at Una.

The guards shoved her to the ground, tying her hands and legs with twisted stringrass whose splinters and spines scraped against her skin as they tightened. Then they carried her out of the burdei and into the night, where all of j'Lok waited for the ritual to begin.

PART V: KILL THE BOY

31
Silence, of Course

I T WAS NOT OFTEN the Gerent presented herself before all the j'Lok, especially now in the twilight of her days. The whole living-place was in attendance, from the way it sounded, all facing her and awaiting her words. Some of the audience, she knew; they had been residents of j'Lok for generations. Others were more recent additions, brought into the fold by invitation or by fear. Those from parts afar had been taught to respect her, look up to her, even to revere her. Those who hadn't were swiftly shown the error of their ways, either shorn from the living-place or cast into the mines.

The crowd grew silent as she stood aloft on the everwood platform, for any affair administered by the Gerent commanded their undivided attention. They stood in adulation of her, content with just a glimpse of the woman touched by the fires of Vul-ka and who so rarely left the shadows of her dark burdei.

The demon child, as it had been dubbed, had been the topic of many speakings since the Kurnisahn arrived. She had sent some of her strongest soldiers to protect the girl and make sure the baby was not torn asunder by a frightened mob. Although its gruesome fate was certain, a "demon child" could not just be butchered; it had to be ascended. There had to be a ceremony. An audience. A *system.* To control her nander, she had to adhere to the tenants of her faith. Or at least to the faith she imposed upon her subjects.

Her efforts to extract information from the boy Falon had proven futile. She'd sent him into the channels and separated him from his companion, but the halfwit refused to speak until the baby's safety was assured. It seemed like a fair trade, one she might have agreed to if she hadn't faced such fright and choler from her nander. Allowing the demon child to live might have raised questions about whose interests she truly served. Such doubt could not be allowed to creep into the minds of her followers, for a seed of disbelief might blossom into mutiny.

She dreaded what she was about to do. Slaying a baby would not be an easy burden to carry. But the baby must be sent to the forever-sleep; there was no other way.

She had done worse before.

Once she carried out this final deed, she could focus on the two Kurnisahn fools. Losing their baby would shatter them, and with no more reason to resist, drawing information would simply be a matter of course. The love-struck Falon would not last long watching them cut fingers off his companion. And if somehow he endured, other body parts would follow.

The baby's mother screamed in the distance. An uneasy chatter rippled through the crowd, so the Gerent held up a hand for silence. Una, she could hear, was being carried toward her along with the wailing infant. The guards dragged her to the foot of the platform and threw her to the ground with a thump. On and on she went, her cries heightening the restlessness of the gathering.

"Silence her," the Gerent commanded, indifferent to which of her guards responded. They quickly muted the girl's screams (beneath a rabbit pelt gag, no doubt).

She shuffled to the girl, each step a delicate act of balance. The tragic march of countless seasons weighed upon her every bone. "Be calm," she said. "It will all be over soon."

The girl shrieked beneath her gags, kicking wildly. She would end up injuring herself if not better restrained.

"Sakaq, do what must be done to silence her."

She heard the guards hold her down, most likely tightening her restraints. The girl's bawling turned into a sob, almost as if her face was being pressed into the ground.

"Is the child ready?" the Gerent asked.

"He lies unclothed on the pedestal," Sakaq said.

"And the boy Falon?"

"Restrained in the channels, as you ordered."

"Good. We don't need him causing any trouble."

She touched the crying baby's midsection. It was soft and warm, and she stroked from its belly to the throat she would soon be cutting. Una's breath quickened behind her. Although the Gerent sought to inflict no trauma by forcing her to watch the murder of her baby, the ritual was supposed to be performed by the relative closest to the ascendant. Since Una would never send her own child to the forever-sleep, she at least had to be present to give the ceremony meaning.

The Gerent faced her audience. "My nander. The j'Lok. We are the chosen," she began, trying her best to be heard over the wind. Her voice was brittle, and she could only speak so loud and for so long before losing it. In the days of yore, her sheer presence had been domineering, but today she relied on the respect earned through a lifetime of soothsaying and prophecies.

"We have been chosen by Vul-ka to defend against Gigas. The battle for the narrowland itself. Vul-ka has led us here, to j'Lok, where we arm ourselves with Gigas' black shards to prepare for the fight to come."

Even as she said it, she knew how little sense it made. But it mattered not; belief had a course of its own. No one would question the Allseer.

"And now," she continued, motioning for Sakaq to lift the baby, "Vul-ka sends us a message—a demon borne from the womb of a Kurnisahn nander."

She gave Sakaq a moment to hold the baby up dramatically before motioning to put it down.

"The demon child is yet another sign of the endtimes, Vul-ka testing if we will fight for him when the battle reaches the rim of our crater. Tonight, before the sharpened sistersun, we ascend the monster. Guards, light the fires."

The guards carried roaring torches onto the platform, their heat warming her cheeks as the fires around the baby were lit. The infant continued wailing in the glow of the flames, its mother blubbering beneath her gags. The Gerent needed to get this dreadful business over with.

"We have before us four fires—four symbols of Vul-ka, the lord of blood and fire and food and flame. May his warmth shine on us and keep Gigas cast down in the black channels beneath our feet."

Sakaq handed her an obsidian blade.

"The demon spirit shall now be released from its body and returned to the s'Sah."

She ambled to the side of the pedestal, gripping the cold bone of the hilt. Vortices of frozen wind clashed against the flames around her, whipping her hair into her degenerate eyes.

"I now draw the sharpened sistersun across its throat," she declared in her creaky voice, the blade heavy in her hands. The baby kicked and cried beneath her. "If there is a reason to spare its life, Vul-ka, send us a signal now—show us that plans remain for its mortal form."

Silence. Of course.

"Your will, Vul-ka, will now be done," she said, touching the blade to the baby's throat.

A rustling in the crowd. Something was happening. She drew back the bloodless blade.

"Sakaq... Sakaq, what is it?"

"I'm not sure, Allseer."

The commotion grew louder.

"It is a sign, a sign!" someone hollered from deep in the crowd.

"Tell me now, Sakaq. What is happening?"

"Guards, protect the Allseer! Take her away at once!" Sakaq shouted.

She felt two men surround her. One grabbed under her arms and the other took her ankles, and together they carried her down from the platform.

"Tell me what is happening!" she demanded.

"Allseer, I don't know what to make of it," one of the guards said. "An axe-wielding giant just entered the crater."

"What do you mean 'a giant'?"

"It is the biggest nander I've ever seen, a head taller than any man. He is joined by a child, a *no-brow* child!"

She sensed the crowd scattering, women screaming about the end of the world, soldiers readying to fight.

"Allseer," the guard continued, "behind them are the shivering masses. They have breached the entrance and are entering j'Lok!"

32
Tell the Gerent

T HE GUARDS HURRIED Una and Nunic back into their burdei
at the edge of the living-place when the fighting began.
Outside, men shouted. Women screamed. Weapons struck
flesh. It was strange to be protected so intensely by the guards
whose own kinsfolk were being thrust into the bloodletting.

There was no doubt it was Carn she had seen striding into j'Lok
and leading the shivering masses to their slaughter. Yet another
entrance drenched in red. While less grotesque than his blood-
crusted march into Kurnisahn, this time the gore was fresher, the
streaks on his neck glistening in the torchlight. But how could
Carn be in j'Lok? Falon had seen him killed. If Falon had been
wrong—or lying—about Carn, what about her mother? What
about her father? Were they alive too?

It didn't take long for the havoc to subside; the j'Lok soldiers
must have been remarkably efficient in their training. They may
have even struck down Carn like they had the shivering masses.
After a time of calm, the burdei flap rose, and a guard shoved Falon
in. He was covered in filth as though he'd been underground for
seasons. Soot knotted his hair, penetrated every pore of his face.

"Are you hurt?" she asked, holding Nunic to her chest.

He shook his head.

"Did you see what happened?" she said.

"Yes." He brushed off his wearings to little effect. His tunic was sullied with black streaks, his footwear matted with grime. "The shivering masses killed the guards and ran into j'Lok."

"Is that what the soldiers told you?"

"That's what it looked like when I saw the bodies. I even recognized someone—the lice-ridden woman—from when we first arrived."

"It wasn't the shivering masses that killed the guards. It was Carn."

His eyes widened.

She nodded, waiting for him to respond. His eyes darted around the burdei. "Where is he?" he said.

"I don't know if he's even alive anymore. He entered j'Lok with the High One child he stole back in Kurnisahn. The shivering masses must have followed them in after Carn killed the guards."

He tilted his head back, a hand over his mouth.

"The confusion stopped Nunic's ascension," she said. "When the fighting broke out, the j'Lok threw us back in here. And now they brought you here too, but why?"

"I don't know. There are many bodies out there, but I didn't see Carn's. Are you sure it was him?"

"It was him," she said, narrowing her eyes. "You told me he was killed back in Kurnisahn."

"I thought he was," he said, betraying the lie by looking away.

"Who else isn't in the forever-sleep?"

Falon paused, patently aware that his earlier falsehood had been exposed. "No one, just him. But I thought he'd been killed."

"You thought?"

"I guess so."

"You guess?"

He wrung his hands together. "Everyone was killed, bodies everywhere. What else was I to think?"

"What about my parents?"

"Your father was in the forever-sleep, I'm sure of it."

"And my mother?"

He again looked away.

"And my mother?" she repeated, raising her voice.

"She was on the ground when I escaped. I don't know if she was in the forever-sleep or captured."

Una felt her face redden. "So, she might still be alive?"

"I don't know." He dropped his hands to his sides. "She might be."

"The High Ones might have her prisoner like the Bhatt!"

"Una, I don't know. I…"

As he struggled to find the words to defend himself, the burdei flap rose. The Gerent hobbled in, propped up by two guards, dragging her soles with every step. She studied Una and Falon as if she could actually see. "Do you know how lucky you are?" she said.

"Why are we lucky?" Falon asked.

"I looked up to the sky and pled for a sign to spare the baby. And then, as if Vul-ka himself heard my call, a blood-covered giant enters with a no-brow child, both trailed by the shivering masses which we were forced to strike down. The mess out there is unthinkable, and we must clean it quickly before their dark spirits spoil the land. You, boy, will be helping with the labors."

"What happened to the giant?" Falon said, ignoring the fact that he'd be on clean-up duty.

"He was captured along with his no-brow companion, but not before slaying four more of my men with that axe of his. He killed more than a hand of men tonight, as I hold him responsible for the guards outside the crater."

It wasn't surprising that Carn's arrival had involved such bloodshed. Una exchanged glances with Falon, who seemed to be thinking the same thing.

"Wait," the Gerent said, somehow sensing their eye contact. "What do you know about this?"

Falon shook his head to suggest they deny knowing Carn. But Una wouldn't plead ignorance when the Gerent was clearly so perceptive.

"His name is Carn," she said. "He's the heir to Ser-o. What are you going to do to him?"

"We will send him to the forever-sleep," the Gerent said without hesitation, as if answering a foolish question. "He killed my men. Some good ones. And he risked us all by letting the shivering masses into j'Lok. I don't know how many men it will take to hold him down, but his fate is certain."

A mixture of feelings washed over Una about Carn's reappearance—and death sentence. On one end, he was vicious and rough and had carried out many acts of violence in the short time she'd known him. On the other end, he was her lifemate, bonded to her under the sights of Vul-ka. But what would happen if he learned of Nunic? She knew the baby wasn't his, even if the truth was hard to accept.

"How do you know him?" the Gerent asked.

"Everyone knew each other in the lowrock valley," Falon said, glaring at Una to once again urge her to say no more. This time he was right: she'd said enough, and it might be best for the Gerent not to know the extent of their ties to a man marked for the forever-sleep. The woman was hard to fool, but Falon's response sounded convincing.

"I see," the Gerent said. "Now, I come to you for another reason. Do you know what it is?"

"You need to finish the ascension?" Falon guessed, swallowing.

"There will be no ascension. The j'Lok believe the giant was a sign from Vul-ka that your baby's life is to be spared."

All of Una's tension seemed to vanish. She breathed in slowly, then exhaled. "What do you believe?" she asked, a warm wave rushing into her arms, up her neck, and to her head.

The Gerent paused before answering. "It doesn't matter what I think. But I never wanted to kill your baby. It was just something that had to be done." She seemed to speak true, but blank eyes were hard to judge.

"So, we can leave?"

"Yes, if you choose. But if you stay, be wary. Your baby attracts attention."

"Because he's a demon?"

"I will hear no more of that," the Gerent hissed. "You laid with a no-brow. Tell it true."

Una didn't respond, but Falon opened his mouth as if about to speak.

"What is it?" the Gerent said.

"Nothing," he said, leaning back.

"Tell me."

"It… it wasn't by choice."

The speakings paused while the guards placed more wood in the hearth. The Gerent rubbed the tips of her fingers together, focusing on Una with a hollow, yet penetrating gaze. "With women, it rarely is."

Silence again. A block of wood snapped beneath the fire.

"But before you go anywhere, you still have something we want." The Gerent called for the guards to bring in the stave and sorrows. They placed the weapons on the ground.

Falon picked up the stave, the guards watching closely. He studied it before turning back to the Gerent. "How do we know you won't send us to the forever-sleep as soon as we show you?"

"You ask me that after what happened here tonight? I might not believe the giant was a sign from Vul-ka, but the j'Lok do. I no longer need to murder your baby."

"What about us?"

"Why would I want to kill *you*?"

Una again met eyes with Falon.

The Gerent stepped forward. "You will tell us what we want to know. And you will do it tonight. Final warning." She turned and exited with the guards, leaving the Kurnisahn alone beside the crackling fire.

After the j'Lok were out of earshot, Falon turned to Una, still holding the stave. "I was right. The cord is gone. That's why they can't figure out how to use it."

"What should we do?"

"I don't know. I didn't tell them how to use the sorrows because I wanted to trade the secret for Nunic's life."

"And they only kept us alive so we can tell them what we know."

He rubbed the sorrow's tip. "What's to stop them from killing us once we tell them?"

"There's no way of knowing that they won't."

He peeked out of the burdei. "They're not even guarding us anymore. We could leave right now if we move fast. There is a lot of activity out there."

"What does it mean that they've left us unguarded? And armed! Soldiers haven't left our side since we first arrived."

"I don't know," he said, still looking outside. "Maybe they're just busy."

Nunic was getting fussy, whining and squirming in her arms. "There's something else to consider," she said, rocking him gently.

Falon let go of the burdei flap and turned to face her. "Let me guess. Carn."

"Yes, but not for the reason you're thinking. He was there, in Kurnisahn, when the High Ones came. He might know how to use the sorrows."

"And the High One child will also know." He prodded the dusty ground with the sole of his foot. "We're no longer the only ones with a secret to trade."

"We'll risk everything if we show them how to use the sorrows—but our only other option is to run."

"Then let's run," he said, putting his hand on her arm.

She pulled away—just like she had their last night in Kurnisahn. His arm flopped between them. "No," she said. "You saw what it's like out there. In the cold. In the snows. We won't survive."

Falon lowered his head, his posture slackening. He muttered something under his breath, then turned around and lifted the burdei flap. After watching for an awkward moment, he called for Sakaq. The commander pushed him aside and entered, wiping sweat from his brow. "What is it?" he said. "Don't you know how busy we are out there, what we're dealing with?"

"We do. But we're ready to help. Tell the Gerent."

"Tell the Gerent what exactly?"

Falon raised the stave. "We'll show you how to use the sorrows."

Sakaq lifted an eyebrow.

"But the weapon's not ready," Falon said. "First, we'll need to fix the stave."

33

His Name is Kaa

T HE GERENT LISTENED TO FALON fling sorrows into the targets he had made. It seemed so simple now that he had shown her how to use the weapon. He would draw the cord taut, she was told, bending both ends of the stave before letting go and sending the sorrow through the air at an incredible speed. The j'Lok would have figured it out themselves if only the cord had been intact when the Kurnisahn arrived.

Killing would be so impersonal if one could do it from afar, and war parties equipped with such weapons could inflict carnage never before seen. No wonder her envoys had been crushed in the lowrock valley. How could one defend against such a threat unless similarly armed?

The path forward was clear. She would send men into the sunward forests to gather thuk-tree branches for staves. And then shape sorrows. Many, many sorrows, for the weapons were so slight they might be usable only once. They could be crafted from any type of wood, but the j'Lok would have to refine their carving techniques to make shafts lean enough to fly. The obsidian tips might be even more lethal if they were barbed. Her shapers would have to look into that.

As she listened to the sorrows whiz through the air, she realized how even a light breeze might affect their travels. At first, she'd thought the feathers were just an adornment, but perhaps they were needed to fly straight. It was unsurprising, she supposed, that to fly like a bird one must wear their feathers. She would have to send trappers and foodbringers to collect as many snowbirds as they could find. She didn't care about the meat; she just wanted their feathers. The weapons had to be made.

But weapons were only part of the security improvements needed for the living-place. By positioning j'Lok in the center of the cratered mountaintop, she'd once thought the towering black walls were impervious to attack. Aside from stones, the only projectiles she had known of were spears and throwaxes, neither of which could travel farther or faster than a man could throw. But now she imagined raiders standing along the rim, flinging sorrows into the living-place and picking off her nander one by one. j'Lok was an easy target for a massacre, a fate sealed by its setting. Once she'd crafted enough sorrows, she would deploy guards along the rim to seal the weakness.

She summoned Sakaq and told him her plans. Although she'd lost some confidence in him as a commander—after all, it was under his watch the shivering masses had breached the crater—he was the best man she had, and the only member of her trust-group to survive the lowrock valley. Her soldiers looked up to him and respected him, and he remained a valuable instrument to achieve her ends.

Now—onto other business. That beast of a man was restrained under heavy guard at the edge of the living-place. The time had come to find out exactly who he was and why he was here. The girl Una had said he was the heir to Ser-o. But why come all the way to j'Lok, with a no-brow child in his company? It was all too curious to not know more.

"Are you sure he's restrained?" she asked a guard before entering the burdei.

"We're sure, Allseer. His wrists are fettered with our strongest binds, and his feet are tied. We collared his neck and fastened him to a stake plunged deep into the stone. He is gagged with a rabbit pelt so he cannot bite. He will not escape or harm you."

"And the guards?"

"Two inside the burdei, two outside. And me."

"Very well. Walk me in and stand between the prisoner and me at all times."

The burdei's interior formed a gentle blackness when she entered, the only source of light coming from the entrance behind her. Although she would have preferred the flap down, she needed the guards to see if the prisoner became aggressive.

"Ungag him," she said.

Her guards did as commanded. The prisoner coughed.

"Tell me your name."

"Tell me yours, you ancient pile of howler shit," the prisoner said, his voice deep and hoarse.

"You are *my* prisoner. Now tell me your name."

"Give me water."

"You'll have water after we talk."

She could feel his glare. "I'm going to kill you," he said.

She turned to one of the guards. "Do it."

The guard slammed the butt of his spear into the prisoner's skull with a thwack, and he responded with a strange groan as if in glee. "Hit me again," he said.

The guard hit him again, harder.

The prisoner laughed.

The guard hit him a third time, even harder.

The prisoner coughed and took a deep breath after spitting. Blood, she assumed. "Again!" he shouted after a moment's pause.

"That's enough," she said, lifting her hand to pause the beatings. "You'll answer me, or we start cutting limbs."

"Come try. First, you'll have to untie me."

"I'm not talking about yours. If you keep fighting, I'm going to drag your child companion in here and start chopping. We'll take his balls first, I think."

She sensed the prisoner's face straighten. She gave him a moment to digest the threat, and he remained silent. "That's better," she said. "Now, I asked your name as a courtesy. I already know who you are, Carn of Ser-o."

"The bitch told you."

"Who?"

"The Kurnisahn girl," he said, clearing his throat. "The one screaming on the platform when I arrived. Why was she up there?"

"I'm the one asking questions. Where is your father, Somm Muro?"

"In the forever-sleep."

"How do you know?"

"I saw his body," he said after a pause suggesting either sadness or deceit.

"So, you're the Somm of the Ser-o now, no longer just the heir?"

"There is no Ser-o." He coughed, then wiped his mouth on his shoulder. "It was destroyed by the High Ones."

"The High Ones? Let me guess: a horde of men with dark skin and high foreheads?"

He looked up; she could sense his surprise. "Those are the ones. Their killings are marked by flying daggers and stolen ears."

"Stolen ears?"

"They cut them off their victims. It's just one of the many strange things they do."

"I see," she said, rubbing her chin. "Did anyone survive, other than you?"

"Maybe some of the women. I don't know." She heard him shift his weight, hardly able to move thanks to his binds. "It all happened before I arrived."

"Why weren't you there to protect your kin?"

"Why do you care? They're in the forever-sleep."

"Answer the question."

"I was in Kurnisahn," he said, spitting more blood.

"So that's how they know you."

"They?"

"Una and Falon. If you've been to Kurnisahn, you must know who they are."

He tilted his head as far forward as his collar would allow, suddenly very interested. "Did you say Falon?"

"The boy with the split face," she blurted out, immediately upset with herself for saying more than she needed to.

"So that's why I couldn't find her during the attack. She ran off with the weakling."

Interesting. There was more to Falon and Una's relationship with Carn than the youths had admitted. But to maintain control of this exchange, she had to question him carefully. The full story would come with time. "I don't know about that," she said to get back on topic. "Why did you come here?"

"There was nowhere else to go. Everything in the lowrock valley was destroyed."

"By no-brows?"

"By who?"

"The High Ones," she clarified so the superstitious fool would understand.

"That's what it looked like in Ser-o," he said. "And I saw it happen in Kurnisahn."

This at least validated the Kurnisahn's sorrowful tale. But it did not explain why Carn traveled with a no-brow child in his company. "And who is your companion?"

243

"Kaa."

"What did you say?"

"His name is Kaa."

"I don't care about his name," she said, waving him off. "Why are you traveling with a no-brow child?"

"The tale will take too long to tell," he exhaled, as if he had better things to do. She could feel his discomfort; he was obviously not used to being in a position of weakness.

"Do you have somewhere else to be?"

"I took him from them," he said with a snarl. "From the High Ones."

"During the attack on Kurnisahn?"

"Yes." Although his tone was firm, she sensed hesitation in his delivery. There was more to this part of his story.

"I was told the boy speaks nander."

"I taught him." He shifted again, tensing, bringing his bound wrists to his chest. "Where is he now?"

"He's safe."

"Have you harmed him?" he said, aggression returning to his tone. The guards tightened their spear grips with light creaks.

"No. And if you want it to stay that way, you'll stay calm."

He hocked out another glob of blood and spit. "I taught him how to speak nander. We've been traveling together for many sistersuns. Kaa loves me, sees me as a father. I've protected and nurtured him since we escaped Kurnisahn."

"The stolen boy has grown fond of you?"

"He has no one anymore. Only me."

"Strange how a prisoner can learn to love his captors."

He snickered with smugness unbefitting his predicament. "Then you better let me go before I start having eyes for you."

"No," she said, refusing to play his game. "Tonight, we send you to the forever-sleep."

"Why? For bringing in Kaa?"

"For killing my men and letting the shivering masses into j'Lok. We pray the plague and flux do not set in within the walls."

He straightened his legs, trying in vain to find comfort. "I suppose it doesn't help that I ruined the ascension."

"I don't care about the ascension."

"You ask questions about my High One child," he said, "yet you were about to ascend one yourself." His boldness was stunning for a man just told he would be killed. "A baby, no less."

"The baby is a half-breed," she said, correcting him.

"A what?"

"The girl Una, it is her son."

"Her what?" he said, his voice again rising. "That is not my son."

"I said *her* son, not *your* son."

"If not mine, then whose? Falon's?"

"No, it was borne from the seed of a no-brow."

"That disgraceful bitch!"

The guards stepped between them, their spear tips just out of his reach. She gestured for them to back off. "Why such anger?" she said.

"She is my lifemate, you crone."

The Gerent paused. This she had not known. Why had the youths hidden this detail when she'd questioned them earlier? Had the Kurnisahn and Ser-o been plotting against her? "So that's why you were in Kurnisahn," she said.

"Yes."

"And I suppose your bonding was arranged after my soldiers visited your living-place?"

Carn stopped to think before answering. "Everything was fine until the High Ones came," he said, confirming her suspicion by sidestepping the question. But it no longer mattered if the Ser-o and Kurnisahn had conspired against her—assuming the tale of their demise was true. And Una's half-breed child was a strong indicator of its verity.

"Why didn't you protect her?"

"I looked for her, but she was gone. Escaped, I now see, with the weakling. I'm surprised they made it here alive."

"If you'd paid attention to her instead of that child, perhaps she wouldn't have been seeded by a no-brow."

He let out an angry breath. "That baby is probably Falon's spawn, cursed and deformed by the flames of Vul-ka!"

"There are no Gods, you superstitious fool. The baby is a half-breed. Nothing more." She turned to leave.

"Wait, where are you going?"

"You've made many things very clear."

"Kill me, and you'll regret it."

The Gerent spun around as quickly as her brittle bones would allow. "Again, you threaten me?"

"You think you know what's coming, but you don't."

"You don't frighten me, tall man,"

"When the High Ones descend upon j'Lok," he said, cracking his neck, "you'll wish you had me fighting on your side."

"If you mean the no-brows, we already prepare."

"You don't realize how many of them there are."

"Then one more man won't save us. I don't care how big you are," she said, walking out.

The formless daylight made her wince as she shuffled outside, where Sakaq and several guards awaited. She lifted her chin to assess the air. "It grows colder," she said. "A storm is coming."

"So say the guards outside the crater," Sakaq agreed. "They say the snow piles high in the darkward valleys."

"Have you finished throwing the bodies off the mountain?"

"Yes, Allseer."

"Good," she said, sniffing the breeze. Cold humidity. A light draft but getting stronger. This was going to be a bad one. "We won't want to bother with them after it snows."

"And the prisoner?"

She lowered her chin. She could barely make out Sakaq's form in the sea of grey. "Nothing changes," she said.

"The sistersun will not be sharpened for many days."

"This is not an ascension. I want it done quietly. In this very burdei, if we must." A single snowflake landed on her cheek. She wiped it away. "I don't want the living-place panicking if there are any problems. Not after what happened a few nights ago. Slit his throat and be done with it."

"As you command, Allseer. When should this be done?"

"Wait until dark, after everyone is in their burdei." More snowflakes. A gust of wind. "But it must be done before the storm worsens."

34
The Storm

T HE BURDEI FLAP BILLOWED to the beat of every gust, and Falon could only hope it would last the night. Although the flap was fastened to the gravels by heavy stones, the frozen air continued to seep in below it. The vent at the tip of their burdei dripped from the snow piling above, each drop rising in a puff of steam when touching the flames. As the grey wisps snaked upward and away, it was impossible to tell what rose as smoke and what as steam.

Clad in greyfur, huddled beneath a pachydon hide and beside the fire, he and Una had thus far stayed reasonably warm. But the heavy air now pressed from beyond the bone-built walls, and he had to keep feeding the fire to fight the cold. What would they do if they ran out of wood before dawn?

Una suddenly perked up. "Did you hear that?"

"Hear what?"

"Someone's out there."

All he could hear was wind beating on the walls. "How can you hear anything over that?"

She paused, listening. "There it is again!"

"Are you sure it's not the wind?"

"It's not the wind!" she said, looking up at him like he was crazy. "It sounds like a child screaming for help."

He still didn't hear it. But maybe if he went out to check, it would calm her down. "I'll go see," he said.

He grabbed the cold end of a burning log to use as a torch, recalling how he had done so when beating back the howler in the cave. How long ago that now seemed, and he wondered where the howler might be and why it had left him. There had been some sort of bond there, some understanding between him and the beast. But then the howler left him and joined the wandering High Ones, shunning the warmth and security of the cave for the darkness and uncertainty outside it.

He lifted the flap, a torrent of frigid air rushing over him. Outside in the blackness, a powdery mist swept sideways with the speed of a tarpan, and the wind deafened it all.

He leaned back into the burdei. "No one's out there," he said, closing the flap behind him. But then, as he fastened it down, he heard it: a cry for help, high pitched, calling out in the night.

"You must have heard it that time."

He grabbed his dagger.

"Wait. Don't go out there."

"You just wanted me to check!"

"I said I heard a sound. I didn't say to go out there."

"Someone is calling for help."

"Yes, but we don't know who it is."

He held up his blade. "That's why I have this."

"I'm sure someone else heard it. Let them go see."

"If everyone said that, no one would go," he said, sealing his footwear around his ankles to keep out the snow.

"Then take sorrows, not just a dagger."

"I need a free hand to hold the torch. Besides, it's too windy to use the sorrows."

He nestled into the depths of his headwear and walked out, letting the flap fall behind him. In the darkness, the voice cried out again—but what was it saying? He couldn't quite tell over the gale, nor could he see more than a pace or two ahead. The hot end of the log devoured the wind, growing brighter as he pressed forth into the strange white blackness.

Again, he heard the call—like a child in distress. There it was, just up ahead, a little boy huddled in the snow. The boy buried his face in his hands, guarding it against the wind. Falon tucked his blade into his waist strap and reached out to him.

"What are you doing out here?" Falon asked.

The boy didn't move.

"Where's your mother?"

The boy looked up, his features unclear in the shadows of his headwear. Falon knelt and clasped his shoulder. "Come with me. You shouldn't be out here. I'll take you somewhere warm."

The boy pulled back his headwear and met eyes with Falon, his features unusual. Falon leaned in and saw he wasn't a nander at all.

Before Falon could stand, something pounded into the side of his head. He fell over, his face crashing into the snow. Everything around him spun fast and suddenly.

He tried to rise a second time, but his legs were kicked out from beneath him. His torch fell into the snow and puffed out in a hiss of steam, plunging him into darkness. On his hands and knees, he tried to rise again, but another kick crushed his stomach, driving the air from his body. He collapsed, clutching his midsection.

Again, a kick.

Again.

He writhed on the ground, unable to breathe in, pain coursing through his body and his arms falling limp. He tucked his knees against his chest and looked up to see the shadow of the biggest man he had ever seen.

"You piece of aurochs shit," Carn said, bending over and squeezing his face with wet hands, snowmelt smearing against his cheeks. Falon reached for his dagger, but Carn grabbed him by the back of the neck and forced his face into the snow. If he had trouble breathing before, that was nothing compared to this. He tried to inhale but instead drew in snow. It filled his mouth and nose and seared cold against his open eyes.

He tried to move his arms.

Tried to move his legs.

His face turned numb.

He couldn't breathe.

He couldn't see.

His arms weren't moving.

His legs weren't moving.

Darkness. But he could still hear. Hear the wind.

The wind.

Beating against his ears.

The wind died down. Slowly, it died down.

The storm went on while the world grew quiet.

Silent.

This was it. This was it. This was...

Gasping. Someone was gasping. A long single gasp.

My spirit has not yet returned to the s'Sah, Falon thought as he raised his head from the snow and wiped the powder off his face. Slush and blood drooled out of his half-open mouth in syrupy threads. His stomach felt like it had been impaled by a spear but didn't appear to be bleeding; whatever injuries he'd sustained during the battering must have been internal. He tried to rise, keeping one hand on the ground to balance his frame, then straightened his back and stood on wobbly knees. The world around him reeled as he careened this way and that to regain his composure. How long had he been out?

Carn must have gone after Una. When he found her, he would see Nunic was not his, lift him by his tiny ankles and beat his head against the rocks. Falon had to get there before the killing began.

His head cleared more with each step, but the pain in his chest grew worse. His bottom rib grated against the one above it, the scraping so acute he could almost hear it when he moved. It would be many sunrises before he healed from this.

His burdei was up ahead, its flap unfastened and rippling in the wind. He gripped his dagger and rushed in to find Nunic wailing on the ground beside the hearth, his tiny hands grasping at the air. Praise Vul-ka, the baby was unhurt—but where was Una? Had the butcher gotten to her already?

He held Nunic to his chest, careful not to pressure his throbbing ribs. He laid the baby beside the fire, pulled the pachydon tightly around him, grabbed another burning log and looked outside. There were footprints in the snow—two sets—a man and a child. Carn and the High One boy. But where were Una's? Was Carn carrying her?

With a hand over his eyes to block the blowing snow, he followed the footprints until he saw they were headed out of the living-place; Carn was fleeing j'Lok and taking Una with him. He stood no chance against Carn alone, so he screamed for help while trudging through the knee-high snow. He stuck his head into the first burdei he passed and saw a man, a woman, and a child huddled by the fire.

"Lower the flap," the man said. "It's freezing out there."

"Please, he took her. He took Una!"

"Who?"

"The giant!"

"We're not going anywhere until the storm passes."

"But—"

"Out, boy."

"Please—"

"I said out!"

He slogged over to the next burdei. They, too, refused to help. Then the next. Same response. No one would brave the storm. He needed to find help. Now.

Sakaq. Sakaq would know what to do. Sakaq would help!

He hustled to Sakaq's burdei, his makeshift torch offering just enough light to see the way, snow creeping into his footwear and numbing his heels. He lifted Sakaq's burdei flap and stepped inside to find a lone woman huddling beside the hearth.

"What do you want, boy?"

"I need Sakaq."

"He went to see the prisoner. But that was before the storm strengthened. I don't know where he is now."

He thanked her and plodded across the living-place to where Carn had been detained. Although the butcher wouldn't be there anymore, Sakaq and his soldiers might be searching for him nearby.

As he approached Carn's burdei, something about it wasn't normal—its roof had collapsed and bowed over on itself.

And there was blood. All over the snow.

Gods, there was blood everywhere, stark against the white drifts, a spray of red and black. Three guards were scattered in pools of slushy black blood, their limbs bent and broken beneath them. Was Sakaq among the slain? No time to tell—the wind blew swaths of white powder across the grounds, filling every footprint. Soon, there'd be no trail to follow.

But even if he caught up to Carn, what could Falon do? Fighting him man-to-man would be suicide. The only chance he might have was to use sorrows. It would have to be daylight, and the wind would have to calm, but with sorrows, he could slay Carn stealthily and from afar.

He returned to his burdei, exhaling when he found Nunic warm and safe. He had to take the baby with him; no one would care for him in j'Lok, not even the milk mothers. While they might have sympathy for an infant's plight, they still saw him as an abomination. Besides, there was no time to seek out a reluctant caretaker. He had to follow Carn's footprints before they disappeared forever. Bringing Nunic along for the pursuit was the only way.

This was going to be dangerous. He might not make it through the night alive, let alone the baby.

But Una.

He couldn't let her get away.

He dreaded what Carn might do to her once they escaped j'Lok.

What he might be doing to her already.

He wrapped Nunic in greyfur, followed by a second layer of pachydon, leaving just enough space for him to breathe. He traded his greyfur footwear for pachydon which would hopefully hold up better in the snows. With each motion, his ribs scraped against each other, sending a pang through his body, forcing him to pause and straighten until regaining his strength. With the shrieking baby swathed in his shoulderpack, he carried him like a cavebear mother with its cub, unsure from where his resilience came. He grabbed the stave and sorrows and followed the fading footprints to the entrance of j'Lok. The guards that should've been there were gone, perhaps having taken cover from the squall.

He peered into the yawning darkness when lightning streaked above him, so close he could feel it in his skin. Its flashes brightened the mountainscape, revealing peaks and valleys smothered in the white, each summit buffeted by swirling brumes of powder. The boom that followed echoed off the crags and surged through his body and shook him. He had to be careful not to tumble—he had a baby on his back, and his balance hadn't yet returned. He descended the mountain in Carn's footprints for fear of voids beneath the snow, barely able to see a pace ahead when the wind would gust, blowing snow around him in a great white fog.

At last, he reached the foot of the mountain, tree stumps before him like a field of stunted cairns. The everwoods were more evident in their vacancy than ever by their presence, their splintered bases like gravemarkers of those who'd stood for generations before being torn from the forest like the j'Lok had torn obsidian from the ground.

He crossed the field and entered the forest. The everwoods at its edge would feed the j'Lok fires next, he thought. On he went, trudging through the woods, the always-green trees towering above him like needled sentinels blanketed in the white. Here, Carn's footprints were distinct since the treetops collected the snow in an endless white mezzanine suspending from above.

His toes were numbing, his feet felt like frozen blocks—the pachydon footwear had outlasted the greyfur but wasn't impervious to the cold. He needed to build a fire before the blue corruption set in, but all he carried was the glowing log he'd taken from his burdei. Countless branches scattered about him though, their dark green needles carpeting the forest floor, most surely fallen from the storm. A fire was his only option, even if it might reveal his position to Carn. They would freeze out here if he didn't, and Nunic's wailing might draw attention anyway. He never should have left j'Lok, and now he'd gone too far to make it back alive.

He kicked away the snow to uncover the black soil below, then collected branches and piled them over the torch in the clearing he'd created. He looked to the sky and almost prayed for Vul-ka to bestow him with even a meager flame. But the sky was empty, the sun nowhere to be seen, and it was uncertain to ever rise again.

35

The Cub and the Fawn

SILENCE.

Had Falon fallen asleep?

The fire still burned, and the needle smoke whipped his weeping nostrils.

He sat up and hocked a wad of snot and scab which hardened upon hitting the snow. He could finally feel his feet again, having rested them beside the hearth. But he could also feel his ribs, the pain dull and shapeless while supine but acute when rising. He had been so focused on his ribs that he'd forgotten about his leg, which now throbbed with every step. No matter, he had to go on.

Scattered gusts remained, but the wind had otherwise settled. Carn's footprints had survived the night; they were faint but could be followed in the dim light emerging from the lands of the rising sun. The forest thickened around him as he limped forth, Nunic crying all the while. Snow-bent branches cracked in the distance as the weight sent them plummeting to the ground.

Wait, what was that up ahead?

Out of sight, a man spoke loudly as if berating someone.

The voice of his enemy.

He couldn't get any closer while Nunic was crying. To stand a chance against Carn, he needed to catch him by surprise.

The rocky outcroppings behind him might offer a safe place to shelter Nunic while he handled Carn. He tightened the baby's furs and placed him deep in a gap between two boulders, then rolled a third rock in front of the crevice so no predators could reach him.

With the baby hidden, he followed the scent of smoldering coals back to where he had heard Carn. The tall man was on his knees collecting embers across a clearing, Una and the High One child both in his company. The boy carried himself strongly, clearly emulating Carn's bearing, while Una gazed at the ground with deep circles under her eyes, holding onto a tree as if she needed it to stand.

Falon slid behind an everwood trunk and laid a sorrow across his stave. He closed his eyes, breathed deep, and peeked around the tree to gauge the distance to his target. He nocked the weapon and aimed at Carn's heart—the sorrow's black tip against his form—planted his back foot for better purchase...

...and a dead branch, hidden by the snow, crunched beneath his sole.

Carn lifted his chin and looked right at him.

Falon's hands began to tremble.

Carn dropped the embers and stood, staring into his eyes with his chin down and brow furrowed.

Falon had been ready to release, but now couldn't still his quivering hands.

Carn clenched his ash-covered fists, grey dust filtering through his fingers like a sieve. He started walking toward Falon.

Falon stood tall, moving out from behind the tree, desperate to steady his aim. He drew the cord taut as Carn continued his fearless march forward, his pace quickening with each oversized step.

Trembling hands or no, he had to release before Carn got too close. This was his only chance.

And then came a thud when a sorrow flew in from *somewhere else*, piercing the side of Carn's abdomen. He grunted and grabbed the shaft, breaking it in half and leaving the rest inside him. When he turned, a hail of sorrows soared at him like a sheet of rain, striking him in the chest and legs and others flying past him. The High One boy screamed. Una stood frozen. Falon ducked behind a tree, hoping he hadn't been seen. Carn stooped to a knee and wrenched a sorrow from his leg.

A hand of High Ones ran in from the forest shadows, screaming war cries with their spears held high. Carn tried to rise, but the men thrust their blades into him, blood pitching skyward in beady strings as they pulled out and reset and stabbed again. Carn lunged at an attacker and wrestled him to the ground, but the others yanked him off and beat him with their fists. He looped a disoriented punch at the air and toppled face-first into the snow, the High Ones kicking and stomping him long after he'd stopped moving.

One of the High Ones straddled Carn's back and grabbed his hair, lifting his face from the blood-soaked snow. He sawed off his ears with a black dagger, sliding the cartilage into the folds of his tunic. The men tried to lift Carn's body but quickly waved off the efforts, as if whatever they had planned wasn't worth the struggle of carrying his massive frame.

The ear-cutter issued some sort of command while pointing at Una and the child, who was on his hands and knees screaming. They stood the boy and questioned him, but he shook his head like he didn't understand what they were saying, as if he spoke a different tongue altogether. The men turned the child around and urged him forward, forcing both he and Una deeper into the forest. Una faltered with every step, scarcely able to stand, but the men pushed her forward mercilessly. As she disappeared into the trees, she glanced at Falon, then turned away, perhaps not wanting any of the men to follow her eyes. But she knew he was there, and wanted him to know that she had seen him.

A party this size would leave quite a trail, but saving Una now represented an entirely different challenge.

After the High Ones departed, Falon walked over to Carn's sorrow-riddled body. He grabbed Carn's shoulder and turned him over, the spitted sorrows snapping as they bent against the snow. Blood trickled out of the black holes where his ears had been. A cheek was split from the corner of his lips halfway to his eye, like some depraved smile branded upon him.

Then, as if he'd woken from the forever-sleep, Carn's chest began rising and falling. "Scarboy," he said, opening his eyes.

Falon stepped out of his reach and laid a sorrow across the stave, his hands finally steady.

"Did they take him?" Carn said, spitting out a tooth.

He nocked the weapon. "Take who?"

"Kaa."

"Who?"

Carn groaned, trying to sit up. "My boy," he said, the ripped meat of his cheek flapping as he spoke.

"I don't care about the boy. I'm going to find Una," he said, his confidence soaring now that Carn was incapacitated. "I wasn't going to let you take her, and I won't let them."

Carn turned sideward, head hanging, blood leaking from his wreck of a nose. "You need to save him."

"He's with his people now," he said, pointing the sorrow at Carn's face.

"Those weren't his people."

Carn coughed red into the snow, his chest crackling like it was filled with blood and broken leaves. He would suffer greatly before going to the forever-sleep, but Falon wouldn't honor him with an ascension. He lowered his weapon and walked away, Carn's gasps and gurgles fading in the distance behind him.

The baby's muffled wailing could be heard up ahead as Falon approached the hiding place. He reached into the gap, lifted Nunic, and held him to his chest with both hands. The child reeked of feces. Turning leeward, Falon laid a fur upon the snow and placed Nunic on top of it. The stench of his dressings roared into his nostrils when he removed them. He wiped Nunic's buttocks with his bare hands, smearing the filth against his irritated skin, the baby jerking and shrieking as if poked by hot cinders.

Barely able to feel his fingers, he washed his hands by plunging them into the snow, then cleaned the baby's dressings the same way. He folded the dressings around Nunic's waist still stained with stool and now spangled with a fine white dust that would surely melt cold against his groin, but there was no other choice in the little time that remained before the baby froze. He wrapped Nunic in furs and placed him into his shoulderpack screaming.

When Nunic finally quieted, Falon peeked into his shoulderpack to find him sleeping fitfully between the furs, whining and scrunching his features. Not ideal, but it would have to do for now. He put on his shoulderpack and left the hiding place with Nunic in tow. After passing Carn's unconscious but still-breathing body, he followed the High Ones' trail, evident as it was from the footfalls of so many men.

Before long, dark pillars of smoke rose over the treetops from what appeared to be a canyon in the distance, a gaping wound in the narrowland as if split by the axe of a God. The columns of smoke reached upward, melding into the clouds and drifting darkward toward j'Lok. As he drew closer, voices echoed far below. So many speaking at once that it sounded like the unbroken din of a single being. He crept to the edge of the cliff and peeked over.

High Ones.

High Ones and High Ones and High Ones.

At the base of the chasm was a horde large enough to destroy j'Lok many times over. They were set up like a war camp, a vast mobile host prepared for battle. There were no burdei, only fires.

Una had to be down there. It was up to Falon to save her. And to save Nunic, who still needed to be fed.

But entering the camp in broad daylight would be reckless, and Una's fate would be unchanged if Falon were slain. And what about Nunic? Would they receive him as one of their own? Or would they see him as a half-breed, or worse, a demon? He was not likely to be accepted, considering the High Ones' reaction the night of his birth.

I'm never going to see her again, he thought. As tears welled in his eyes, he feared they might freeze and shut forever.

The Highs Ones were gathering their weapons and moving darkward, joined by more howlers than he'd ever seen. They would reach j'Lok by nightfall. He knew what the High Ones did to women after battle. What would they do to the Gerent, considering her age and frailty?

The j'Lok were not ready. They would never be ready. Not for this.

Nunic shrieked again, and Falon slunk away from the cliffside; he had to flee before the howlers sensed him. He lumbered between the trees, clutching his swelling rib, fearful any misstep would send him tumbling. But where could he go? Back to j'Lok? To warn them? The j'Lok were about to be slaughtered.

But Nunic. Something had to be done for Nunic. He had to be fed. He needed milk. He needed it now.

Then he had an idea. The High Ones heading to j'Lok were all men. Where were the women? They must have been left behind. If the High Ones had taken Una prisoner, they'd probably left her in the camp. If Falon hid out until sunset, he could try to find her under cover of darkness.

He retreated deeper into the woods to find a place to rest until nightfall. After sleeping so little, he needed to restore his energy before entering the enemy camp. He continued into the forest, soon hearing what sounded like distress calls up ahead.

Just past a grove of everwoods was the aftermath of a battle of beasts, the ghastly remains of its participants strewn across the snows. A buck was face down in the embrace of an emaciated valleycat corpse, the two lying in a crimson blot where their wounds had soaked the white. The buck's neck was ripped open, and the valleycat had been gored by antlers sharp like talons. A few paces away was a crumpled doe, its throat torn and spread out in a spray pattern before it.

Nunic was growing restless again. If he didn't feed soon, he might not survive the day. Although the meat from this killing would be of no use to the toothless baby, there was an excess of blood—a substance with nutrition. While the blood soaking the snows had long since frozen, the carcasses themselves might still hold liquid within them.

He cut open the buck's belly, blood surging out in a cold red bubble. He dipped a finger into the cavity and brought it to Nunic's mouth. Once Nunic had consumed the blood on his finger, Falon gave him more. Did Nunic enjoy the blood? Or was he so desperate that anything would do?

As Nunic suckled the finger between his gums, Falon heard the distress call again—high pitched, like the screams of a bird being plucked alive. There would be danger up ahead, but some strange force, some need for discovery, compelled him to explore the cries exactly as he had the night before. He followed the sound to the hillside and found a valleycat cub, no taller than his knee, swatting a narrow breach in the rockface. The cub looked like it hadn't eaten in a sistersun, its bones and ribs bulging from beneath its tattered fur. As he closed in, the amber cub turned and whined at him, as if begging for help.

"What do you have in there?" he asked as if the cub would answer. It looked into the crevice and backed away to let him see. Inside was a fawn veiled in shadows, its back pressed against the stones behind it. Its flesh had been slashed and riven and one if its eyes hung off its face. Could it still see from that eye, which dangled from its socket by short white strands?

He wanted to help the creatures but was torn; was slaying them both the more merciful thing to do? With no parent to guide it, the cub would starve. Ripped and wounded, and with one good eye, the fawn might perish even sooner.

As Falon pondered this, the cub reassumed its position between the rocks, stretching its paws into the fissure, straining to reach the fawn. It was a pathetic display of two creatures desperate to survive—the cub toiling to feed, the fawn burying itself between stones to avoid the horrifying consequences of surfacing. He understood at once the plight of both beings and was unsure which he identified with more: the impotent hunter or its hopeless prey.

It was in this moment he realized they were all doomed to a life of pain. There might be bright spots, those brief, fleeting moments of sunshine where the beginnings of a smile might surface on one's face. But these moments were but oases in a sea of sadness, transient glimmers of hope in a world otherwise desolate and black. All things, strong and weak alike, would one day face the truth that the world was but the setting for a dark game, and they were all just passive pawns on some greater stage, some strange ephemeral shadow under which that game was played.

36

Green Eyes Cracked

W ITHERING HEARTHS pockmarked the grounds below, their contents barely glowing, but a few fires persisted in the semi-dark, their light reflecting across the valley in erratic waves. Beside the fires were clusters of nander women bound together by the throat. Falon must have missed them earlier amidst the commotion of soldiers departing for battle. Surely Una was down there among those women. She had to be.

The path down the cliffside was covered in snow, so steep Falon had to switchback and slide, wincing every time he hit a bump or rise. He paused on a ledge to check on Nunic, who slumbered in his shoulderpack, so exhausted from wailing that he was undisturbed by the chaos of the descent. He covered Nunic again and continued down the slope, his ribs burning inside him, then rested at the bottom while surveying the camp from ground-view. Since the High Ones had departed earlier in the day, the camp was mostly empty, but a few stragglers, possibly left behind to guard the women, skinned in the distance what appeared to be a colorless cavebear. A cloud of steam rose as they peeled the fur off the freshly killed beast.

He crept into the snowy camp, a stave in one hand and a sorrow in the other, the crunch of every step threatening to reveal his trespass. In the snow lay a pair of bodiless faces, their hair against their scalps like frozen brambles, their green eyes cracked and gazing away. The nearest firepit, surrounded by an eye-high arc of boulders, was hidden from the rest of the camp. As he approached it, the fetor of burning flesh choked the air, and the reason for its concealment became evident. He held his breath and turned away when he saw the charred remains of a female form snapping in the flames, the bones cut-marked and cleaved. His heart sank even though the body was too tall to be Una.

The women were past the next fire, and the sounds of crying children filled the grisly snowscape. Falon recalled the misery of the shivering masses as he passed the women, all showing the advanced stages of distress. One rocked her head as if overcome by dark spirits; another lay motionless in the snow. One had bruised eyes and blood caked on her flattened nose; another held in each hand a patch of torn-out hair.

As he scanned the grounds for any sign of Una, the women whispered amongst themselves. Some words he knew, others he scarcely recognized. Many women held crying babies, some at the breast and eerily resembling Nunic. If he couldn't find Una, perhaps another woman would feed him.

Just as he thought this, he saw her—curled on the ground, far from the fires, her hands and feet tied together.

"Una, get up, we have to go!" he said, running toward her with a listing gait. His shattered rib screaked with every step, scraping and grating inside his chest.

She lifted her chin, locks plastered against her forehead, cheeks softly red. "Is that you?"

"It's me." He stooped over with a hand on his chest, a reflexive but futile attempt to lessen the pain. "But we need to go before those High Ones over there see us."

"Nunic?"

"He's in my shoulderpack," he said, straightening his back. He sliced her binds. "Now stand up."

"I can't."

Her greyfur footwear was coated in a film of ice. He tapped her feet together, fracturing the coat into white flakes, then brushed off the remaining dust. He recalled how unsuitable his own greyfur had been the night before.

"Try to stand. We'll warm you by a fire once we climb out of this ravine."

"But I can't feel my feet."

"Please try."

He lifted her from under her arms and let go once she seemed secure, but she crumpled over at the knees. She looked up at him, shaking her head. "I can't."

Nunic started crying, but the High Ones in the distance didn't seem to notice. He was but one baby crying among many.

"He needs to be fed," Una said, extending her arms to receive the baby. "Leave him with me."

"Leave him with—what? No, you come with *me*! We'll leave this place together. I'll carry you."

"Carry both me and the baby? You're limping and hunched over and can barely even carry Nunic."

"Let me see your feet," he said, pulling off her footwear to reveal a gruesome scene. Her toes were swollen into dark knobs, her soles turning grey. Her overnight abduction and flight through the snow had been her ruin; there'd be no coming back from this. All Falon's energy, his hope and strength, flooded away in a single moment.

She looked up at him. "My feet have gone too far to heal."

"Let's try warming them by the firepit," he said, not knowing what else to say. "You can feed Nunic while we wait." He lifted her again from under the arms and dragged her to the black grounds around the fire, setting her feet before the flames.

Robert Scheige

She removed her breast and put Nunic to it, her expression blank. "They say the High Ones are taking us somewhere."

"Taking you where?"

"I don't know. No one seems to know."

The sounds of men rose in the distance. The bear-skinners were heading back to camp, carrying the bloody white fur.

"Just go, Falon."

"I won't leave you here."

"They'll kill you if they see you."

"What about you?"

"They didn't bring me here to kill me," she said, staring into the fire.

"Look at your feet! I won't leave you here alone."

"I'm not alone; there are other women here."

Tears welled up in his eyes.

"Falon, no, don't..." she said.

He took a deep breath, fighting to hold back his despair. "No, Una. We've been through too much. We found a way through everything; all these sistersuns of sickness and pain. We'll survive this too."

She looked down at her rotting feet and shook her head. "Not me," she whispered.

"What about Nunic?" he said, chin quivering and voice wavering.

She looked at the other mothers, then back down to Nunic. "No one will notice one more baby. When my feet worsen and send me to the forever-sleep, others here will bring Nunic to their breast. He won't survive out there; you have no way to feed him. He has to stay."

"Una, no. I can't go out there on my own. Not without you." An image of her frozen corpse flashed across his mind, sending tears down his cheeks. "I'm not going to just leave you here to face the forever-sleep alone."

She looked again at her feet. Below her knees, her legs were strewn in the rubble as if they were already lost. The deadness was spreading upward through her body and would soon consume her very being. "I'm never going to leave this place," she said. "You can only save yourself now."

A chorus of guffaws rose from down the gorge; the raucous bear-skinners were almost back at camp with their bounty. One well-placed glance and Falon would be seen.

"You need to go, Falon! Get out before they see you."

He looked up at the cliffs, unsure how he would climb them, then returned his eyes to her. "I'll come back for you," he said, standing tall to feign confidence.

"I know you will," she said, looking away.

He lifted her chin and looked into her eyes. "I will," he said. But even as he said this, he knew this was the last time he would see her. He had saved Nunic's life—for now—but no one could save Una. Her feet would never heal, and that meant only one thing. The thought of offering her ascension crossed his mind, but he could never bring himself to draw the blade.

As he held his thumb beneath her lips, she touched his scar with the tips of her fingers, for the first time looking at it directly and conspicuously. The corner of her lips rose almost imperceptibly for a moment as she ran her fingers across his face. She squeezed her eyes shut and opened them slowly before turning back to the baby.

"Our passage ends here, Falon," she said, refusing to meet eyes with him again.

37
Two Horns

F ALON'S FIRE-CAST SHADOW stretched before him as he fled, magnifying his every move. It warped and skewed against the uneven snows, shaped more by the vagaries of the surface than by his own form. He had not appreciated this sight on his way into camp when his shadows had been trailing behind him.

His sorrows were ready if one of the bear-skinners saw him. But the men were distracted by their plunder, one man stopping to harass a woman while the others hauled the dripping fur. The man cut the woman's binds, and with a blade held to the small of her back, led her into the darkness for what purpose Falon could only guess.

Powerless to help her, he went on.

He passed another fire and the women around it. He passed a shrieking infant and the woman who rocked it while staring into the flames. He passed the eye-high arc of boulders and the cracked green eyes behind it.

Then Falon saw him standing at the foot of the cliff.

The boy Carn had stolen from his people.

The boy who'd lured Falon into an ambush the night before.

He nocked the sorrow.

The boy stepped forward, his greyfur tunic torn and a dark arm hanging from it. He was skinny, gaunt even, and two heads shorter than Falon. The boy clutched in both hands a horn as long as he was tall. It shined black in the firelight, from its winding shaft to its needlelike peak, and had the markings of the horn that had killed Falon's father; the horn that had vanished during his dream.

"Don't come any closer," Falon said.

The boy looked confused, taking another step forward. One of his eyes was swollen shut behind a deep purple bruise and blood thickened below his nose.

"Stop!" he said, pointing the sorrow at the boy. It felt awful threatening someone half his size and in such bad condition, but he couldn't take a chance after what had happened the night before.

The boy halted, looked at the fires in the distance, and then back at him without a word.

"Put down the horn," he said, quickly pointing his sorrow to the ground, then back at the boy. The boy gently rotated the horn, then laid it in the snow between them.

"Where'd you get that?" Falon said.

"Father give me," the boy said, each word uttered as if carefully chosen. "I lose horn, then find again here."

"Your father?"

"Big man. You know."

"Carn? Where did he get it?"

The boy shook his head, sniffling. He wiped blood off his nose with a sleeve.

"That horn is mine. I took it from Kurnisahn," Falon said.

The boy considered this for a moment. "Aurochs have two horns," he said.

He loosened his weapon grip, no longer sensing a threat now that the boy was unarmed. "What's your name?"

"Kaa."

"Why didn't the High Ones take you with them today, Kaa?"

"They speak other words. They think I have broken mind," he said, pointing to his forehead.

"You don't remember how to speak their tongue?"

"Is more than one tongue."

Falon checked to see if the High Ones had noticed him, but they were busy cleaning the fur by a fire in the distance, flensing the grease and gore with flat black daggers. One man stood to survey the grounds and looked directly at him. Falon froze, hoping the man didn't see him, and the man leaned over to whisper in another man's ear before sitting back down.

He needed to get away before his luck ran out. He turned back to Kaa, his shadow stretching across the boy and onto the snow behind him. "I'm leaving," he said, then walked past him.

"Wait!" Kaa said.

He spun around and brought a finger to his mouth to quiet the boy. His ribs screamed from the sudden move, a reminder of the night before.

"I come with you," Kaa said, his voice wavering as if he was about to cry.

Falon looked back into the camp. Smoldering hearths. Burning bones. Tears. No place for a boy alone. Even though this very boy had conspired to assault Falon, none of this would have happened if Carn hadn't first taken him from his people and into the dark-ward wastes. Kaa was a victim too.

"My father is in forever-sleep. Please," Kaa said, a tear streaming down his cheek and dribbling off his chin.

He looked up at the cliff, straining the back of his neck to study the soaring escarpment. Sheer black rockfaces jutted from the snow above, wilted heathers dangled from its ledges. The tracks from his descent were barely visible from this angle, and the slopes he had slid down were too steep to climb.

"Mine is too," he said, putting the sorrow back into its bundle and strapping the stave to his back. "We can't climb this cliff. We need to find another way out."

"But to where we go?"

Falon picked up the horn and wiped off the snow, its shaft so wide that he needed both hands to hold it. "I don't know," he said, handing the horn back to the boy, and finally letting go.

Afterword
Notes on Historical Accuracy

B UT COULD THAT ACTUALLY HAVE HAPPENED?" one might ask. This afterword explains how I tried to balance the telling of a story while maintaining historical accuracy.

Since The High Ones is a work of fiction, I had to take some poetic license when writing it. I tried, however, to keep it as true-to-life as possible, as I view the novel not as fantasy but as historical fiction. Luckily, for the sake of the story, there are many grey and blank areas in our understanding of Neanderthals*. These unknowns gave me the freedom to construct plots, characters, and cultures without compromising scientific or historical accuracy to an unreasonable degree.

Two types of evidence informed my research when developing The High Ones:

1. Archeological evidence—bones, tools, living sites, etc.

2. Genetic evidence—taken from Neanderthal bones.

---

* For the sake of simplicity, I'll refer to Neanderthals throughout this section as *Neanderthals* and anatomically modern humans as *humans*. However, as members of the genus *homo*, Neanderthals were technically a type of human.

The history and science I've incorporated into The High Ones are based on today's understanding of Neanderthals. This understanding has changed dramatically over time, so many elements of this novel will likely seem outdated as more studies are conducted, and more archeological sites are found.

Although the first Neanderthal bones were discovered in what is now Belgium in 1829, the idea of "Neanderthal man" first emerged after the 1856 discovery of bones in the Neander valley in Germany (hence the name *Neanderthal*) by laborers digging for limestone. Coincidentally, Charles Darwin's *On the Origin of Species* was published a few years later, in 1859, and the discovery of Neanderthal bones contributed to the firestorm surrounding the book.

Neanderthals were initially purported to be brutish, simple hominins; more like gorillas than men. But our perception has changed since then, and contemporary anthropologists believe Neanderthals were far more humanlike than apelike. Many current thinkers, in fact, believe Neanderthals were nearly as humanlike as us.

Neanderthals were an intriguing type of hominin—the humans who were almost (but not quite) human. They were close enough to humans that they're sometimes taxonomically classified as a type of homo sapiens: *homo sapiens neanderthalensis* as opposed to humans' classification as *homo sapiens sapiens*. Due to strong evidence of interbreeding between Neanderthals and humans (more on that later), it can be debated whether Neanderthals were an altogether different species from us or just a subspecies. Some extreme views consider Neanderthals to be just another *race* of humans, although this is a view not widely held.

The premise of The High Ones came to me after reading a headline on nationalgeographic.com: *Digs Reveal Stone-Age Weapons Industry With Staggering Output.* The article discussed how millions of obsidian weapons, found as far west as the Aegean Sea and as far east as Ukraine, all originated from the same volcano in what is present-day Armenia. The production of these obsidian weapons dates back to the Lower Paleolithic age, which ended around 300,000 years before present (YBP); a time when Neanderthals were in the area (and humans probably were not). It is unknown who the producers of these weapons were, but since the quarries were active until roughly 1,000 BC, many different groups must have controlled this resource over its hundreds of thousands of productive years. Neanderthals likely represented at least one of these groups.

Neanderthal Intelligence and Language

THE HIGH ONES ASSUMES NEANDERTHALS were not only highly intelligent hominins but equally intelligent to modern humans. Biological evidence supports this view since their cranial capacity (i.e., brain size) was actually larger than modern humans—1500cm^3 vs. 1350cm^3. While this alone does not prove equal (or better) intelligence, a large set of evidence points to Neanderthals having been humanlike in many ways. Neanderthal archeological sites have included an assortment of tools, weapons, burial grounds, evidence of adornments (such as feathers and jewelry), and complex structures (such as a building of mammoth bones with 25 hearths inside). There is some evidence, though scant, that Neanderthals even used simple watercraft, such as canoes.

Despite such evidence of tool use, some argue that Neanderthals were cognitively inferior to humans. Many doubters point to the fact that Neanderthals seem to have undergone technological inertia for hundreds of millennia. While this is a strong argument, it does not close the case for cognitive equivalence due to the countless examples of humans experiencing technological stasis for extended periods. For instance, few pivotal technological breakthroughs occurred between Roman times and medieval times. If someone from ancient Rome stepped into a time machine and fast-forwarded 1,500 years, they would understand medieval technology. This is because humans reached a relative technological stasis until the Industrial Revolution, and only in the past 200 years did the world change enough to be technologically unrecognizable from that which came before. As a more extreme case, there are extant hunter-gatherer societies whose tools have not advanced for tens of thousands of years. Based on these examples, Neanderthal intelligence cannot be discounted simply because humans had a technological edge.

Studies of Neanderthal intelligence often focus on language. While the complexity of Neanderthal speech may never be known, evidence suggests that their language abilities may have been equally sophisticated to those of modern humans. Two chief discoveries support this view:

1. The existence of the FOXP2 gene in the Neanderthal genome. This gene is required for speech, not only in terms of brain development but also for the development of nerves that control the facial muscles used in speech. While the FOXP2 gene is found in many animals, the version found in Neanderthals is remarkably similar to that in modern humans.

2. The placement of the Neanderthal hyoid bone, a critical structure for speech since it supports the root of the tongue. In other primates, the bone is placed in a different position, leaving them incapable of humanlike speech.

Nature tends to select for adaptive traits, so it is unlikely these two characteristics existed in Neanderthals by coincidence. A more likely scenario is one where these traits had real-world utility—an enhanced vocal communication capability—i.e., language.

The High Ones posits that Neanderthals had sophisticated language, evident in both the dialogue and characters' physical expressions (e.g., shaking of the head, nodding, etc.). While no one knows what Neanderthal words and expressions were like, I wrote them as humanlike to better communicate the story and characters. In spite of this, putting words on the page often felt like I was writing with one hand tied behind my back. I wanted it to sound and feel real, but I had to ignore a large portion of everyday vocabulary to accomplish this. An incredible amount of contemporary terminology and colloquialisms sneaks into our vernacular, so it was challenging to write dialogue that sounded both realistic and authentic. Many modern phrases reference technological breakthroughs that occurred post-Neanderthal. A perfect example of this is the word *shoot* in terms of using a bow and arrow. Assuming Neanderthals had no projectile weapons other than those that are thrown (e.g., rocks and maybe spears), the idea of *shooting* would not come to them. As such, I had to replace the word *shoot* with *fling* or *throw*, both of which seemed more fitting. Also, they wouldn't *fire* an arrow since the concept of fire meant something particular (and important) to them.

For the sake of authenticity, I avoided traditional forms of measurement since Neanderthals wouldn't have had the concept of miles, weeks, minutes, etc. Instead, they probably would have used physical descriptions to quantify distance and time—the number of paces, sunrises/sunsets, cycles of the moon, etc. In the same spirit, I assumed Neanderthals had a basic numbering system, consistent with what extant hunter-gather societies sometimes use. Some of these hunter-gatherer societies have words for one, two, three—after which comes the vague number known as *many*. I added another word, *hand*, meaning *five* or *around five*, consistent with many numbering systems using fingers as a reference point (i.e., any base-ten numbering system).

One aspect of the novel where I took poetic license was that virtually all the Neanderthal characters—from the Ser-o to the j'Lok—spoke the same language. Since the story deals with groups of Neanderthals living possibly thousands of miles apart (it takes Falon and Una about seven months to travel from Kurnisahn to j'Lok), it is almost certain that such far-apart clans would have spoken different languages. Contemporary hunter/gatherer societies often speak unique languages in *each village*. In New Guinea, for example, over 700 different languages are spoken in an area roughly the size of Texas. It is thus unlikely that the various groups of Neanderthals depicted in The High Ones would speak a common tongue (and contrary to what's in the novel, it probably wasn't English). As an author, I had to pretend as if all Neanderthals spoke a common language for the sake of storytelling efficacy, although I drew the line by having humans speak a different language than Neanderthals.

Neanderthal Culture

NEANDERTHALS WERE HUNTER-GATHERERS and probably apex predators. They likely hunted a wide range of animals depending on what was available at a given time and place, but large mammals (such as aurochs and mammoths) seem to have represented a key component of their diet. One site in Gibraltar even features evidence of Neanderthals hunting marine fauna, including a seal skeleton with cut marks and, remarkably, dolphin bones. Hunting was also more than just a food source for Neanderthals since they used animal bones as building instruments and tools and almost certainly wore furs to protect against the cold. Nevertheless, some of their diet had to be vegetable-based, since plant matter has been found in their teeth and coprolites (fossilized feces).

Neanderthals were most likely organized in male-dominated societies (like most apes) and lived in small groups of a few families. One archaeological site in Spain features the bones of twelve Neanderthals apparently in the same social group. The three adult males had mitochondrial DNA (mtDNA) from the same matrilineal heritage, while the three adult females had mtDNA from different lines. This suggests the "marrying out" of females into other social groups, something I incorporated into the novel, especially with respect to Carn and Una.

There is strong evidence of symbolic thought in Neanderthals—including cave paintings, jewelry, makeup, and ritual sites. Neanderthal cave paintings, dating back 65,000 years, were discovered in Spain in 2018. Eagle talons apparently worn as a necklace (such as the Somm's) were found at one site in Croatia, and a site in Spain featured decorative shells with pigments mixed with different ingredients. In France, large circles made by Neanderthals and constructed from hundreds of stalagmites were found deep in a cave, apparently for ritualistic purposes.

Since human cultures can vary widely even over short distances, it is conceivable that Neanderthals, with their wide geographic range and considerable cognitive abilities, produced an array of cultures and beliefs over the hundreds of thousands of years they existed. In The High Ones, all Neanderthals believe in the same mythology: the sun god Vul-ka and the eschatology involving the High Ones. This I view as pure poetic license. While religion probably played a role in Neanderthal lives, it is unlikely the same mythology would exist in a pan-Neanderthal form. However, it is reasonable to assume that Neanderthal religions, like many primitive belief systems, centered around the sun (as they do in the novel).

The concept of *ascension* is a central component of The High Ones. This is another example of poetic license since no archaeological evidence supports Neanderthals mercy-killing the injured or the old. It is more likely that they *cared* for the injured and the old, as suggested by the discoveries of elderly, injured, and deformed Neanderthal skeletons. However, ascension-like practices exist in some hunter-gatherer societies *today*, so given the many independent Neanderthal cultures that must have developed, a custom like ascension may have existed at some point in time.

One last item worth mentioning is the physical development of Neanderthals vs. humans. Studies of Neanderthal teeth indicate they may have reached puberty a few years earlier than humans. If true, this would have had an impact on the Neanderthal parenting cycle and possibly culture and societal structure. As with most details about Neanderthal life, their development cycle is a matter of ongoing debate. For the purposes of the novel, I assumed Neanderthals' physical and cognitive development closely resembled that of humans. Otherwise, it might have been confusing to read a 14-year old character acting and speaking like an 18-year old.

Coexistence with Humans

GENETIC STUDIES INDICATE that human and Neanderthal lineages diverged from the predecessor species *homo heidelbergensis* ~500,000 YBP, although estimates vary by a few hundred thousand years. Neanderthals' habitat included most of Europe, and they seem to have kept humans out of their territory for most of their time there. Then, about 60,000-70,000 YBP, our human ancestors began rapidly spreading out of Africa into the Middle East, Asia, and eventually Polynesia. But for some reason, they stayed out of the Neanderthal range (mostly Europe) for a long time. Then, ~45,000 YBP, human and Neanderthal territories began to overlap, and by ~40,000 YBP, Neanderthals completely disappeared from the record. In other words, after their lineage split from humans ~500,000 YBP, it took only 5,000 years of coexistence to wipe Neanderthals off the map. It should be noted that these timetables are inexact and subject to significant debate in the scientific community. Additionally, strong evidence suggests that isolated pockets of Neanderthals, at least in the southernmost regions of their range, lasted until about 28,000 YBP. No matter the case, it is not likely a coincidence that Neanderthals went extinct so shortly after humans' arrival, and therefore humans play a central role in almost every Neanderthal extinction hypothesis.

It is widely accepted that Neanderthals interbred with humans during their brief coexistence. Genetic studies show that Neanderthal genes remain in the human population today, as 1-4% of genetic material in non-African humans is of Neanderthal origin. These studies also indicate there were at least three major interbreeding events (and possibly many more). Unfortunately for science, many inferences must be drawn from the limited genetic material available.

Such interbreeding is an important plot point in The High Ones, particularly with respect to Una's impregnation by the human raider. The wide-scale raping of a conquered population's females has happened innumerable times throughout the history of human warfare. This behavior is also seen in other primates (and mammals), so it is reasonable to assume it represents one source of Neanderthal genes in today's human population. The conduct of humans in the novel might be exaggerated for the sake of drama, since conquering males tend to rape and pillage but not necessarily enslave. Moreover, while slavery has happened in virtually every culture and corner of the world (even in modern times), it is unknown if this behavior existed on a wide scale prior to agricultural societies in which slaves could be more easily exploited and controlled. In other words, humans taking female Neanderthals as slaves probably did not happen, at least on a large scale, and thus represents another example of me (probably) taking poetic license[*].

It should be noted that human DNA of Neanderthal origin is all atomic DNA, as opposed to mitochondrial DNA (mtDNA). This is particularly interesting since mtDNA is inherited matrilineally. The

---

[*] The last scene, however, implies that human war bands may also have been using Neanderthal women for food in the increasingly hostile northern terrain. Paleolithic cannibalism, if humans eating Neanderthals can be deemed as such, is an idea strongly suggested by archaeological evidence.

simplest explanation is that all interbreeding was by human females reproducing with Neanderthal males, which would be a stunning conclusion since it seems to run counter to all situational evidence. Also, since the Neanderthal Y chromosome appears to have disappeared from the gene pool, any offspring of Neanderthal males and human females would most likely have been female. Alternative explanations are that:

a) Neanderthal mtDNA led to maladaptive mutations and was therefore selected against over the generations

b) Hybrid offspring of Neanderthal mothers were raised by Neanderthals and went extinct with them

c) Female Neanderthals and male humans produced infertile offspring (but not vice-versa)

Note that both a) and c) would be evidence for classifying Neanderthals as a separate species from humans (as opposed to a subspecies), as one definition of speciation requires the production of fertile, unmutated offspring. All this said, a large segment of Neanderthal research focuses on genetic studies, so our views are constantly evolving, particularly since current analyses draw from a small number of fossils.

Neanderthal Extinction

NEANDERTHALS SEEM TO HAVE GONE EXTINCT about 40,000 YBP, apart from isolated remnant populations. While the exact cause of their extinction is the focus of many studies, most hypotheses place humans in a starring role. There was likely more than one cause, and climatic, biological, and cultural elements all may have played a part. Among the leading theories are:

Rapid extinction by violence

The rapid extinction by violence theory argues that humans wiped out Neanderthals via massacres and/or other forms of armed conflict shortly after first contact occurred. This is the theory most strongly featured in The High Ones.

While the archeological record does not directly support the rapid extinction by violence theory (i.e., no sites contain an excess of battle-scarred Neanderthal bones), sufficient circumstantial evidence exists for it to be considered possible, if not likely. For example, whenever humans appear in a given region's fossil record, Neanderthals seem to have disappeared from that region shortly thereafter.

But why would humans have eradicated Neanderthals, rather than the reverse? Could human technology hold the key? History shows that when a technologically advanced culture confronts a less-advanced one, violence, or at least large-scale exploitation, is bound to occur. If humans had a technological edge on Neanderthals (as was the case with their bows and arrows in The High Ones), Neanderthals may have been wiped out much like Native American and Aboriginal Australian populations were decimated by European settlers. Few rational individuals assert that Europeans had a cognitive edge over other human cultures. Instead, most believe it was largely their technology—developed in response to a combination of geographical, cultural, and societal pressures—that facilitated European dominance.

Additionally, humans have a predisposition for xenophobia toward individuals unlike themselves (such as across racial boundaries). This phenomenon has occurred in almost every culture throughout human history. It is thus conceivable that contemporaneous humans would have viewed Neanderthals, who were so physically different, in a negative way. This provides potential motivation for the rapid extinction by violence theory.

Rapid extinction by pathogens and/or parasites

When a society carrying (and resistant to) a pathogen enters into contact with a society unexposed to that pathogen, it often wreaks havoc on the newly exposed society. An example is smallpox's role in the downfall of Native Americans. While anecdotal evidence suggests that pathogens and/or parasites are a plausible cause of Neanderthal extinction, no physical evidence supports this.

Climate change and competitive replacement

Neanderthal extinction coincided with both (a) a period of extreme cold and (b) what appears to be their first large-scale interactions with humans. Many scientists therefore believe a nexus exists between the two.

Neanderthals survived through several ice ages, and even seem to have had genes affecting metabolism. Such genes would have been adaptive since slower metabolisms could have helped avoid death by starvation*. However, for some reason, Neanderthals didn't make it through this last ice age, and a likely culprit is that, for the first time, they were not alone. It could be that humans simply out-competed Neanderthals for the increasingly scarce game, be it due to a technological or population density advantage.

Climate change plays a significant role in the novel, with mammoths being found further south than usual, birds exhibiting strange breeding cycles, and the rivers "turning to stone" for longer periods each winter. I nevertheless took poetic license by having the Neanderthals notice that each year is colder than the last. Climate changes on geological timescales, so even during periods of rapid climate change, meaningful differences would not likely be evident

---

* These Neanderthal genes survive in the human population today and are perhaps not coincidentally to blame for certain forms of diabetes.

from year-to-year. That said, some winters are naturally colder than others, so it is possible that the year in which the novel takes place represents an exceptionally cold spell during an overall downward temperature trend. It should be noted that most scientists believe Neanderthals were in population decline by the time extensive interactions with humans took place. Hence, the fertile hunting grounds depicted in The High Ones probably isn't an accurate reflection of the setting in which the first contact occurred.

Outbred by humans

Due to climate change, Neanderthals were probably undergoing a major demographical crisis when humans appeared on the scene. It is thus possible that the encroaching humans simply overwhelmed them. In this theory, "pure-breed" Neanderthal DNA disappeared because of their population deficit against humans. This cause, strongly supported by computer simulations, was likely combined with some of the other reasons listed above. An interesting inference of such thinking is that humans were not cognitively superior to Neanderthals; they were just, perhaps due to luck, located in a more favorable southern geography when the last ice age occurred.

The High Ones implies that rapid extinction by violence was the leading cause of Neanderthal downfall. While in reality, this may or may not have been the case, it is conceivable that massacres did indeed occur. Numerous stone-age human archeological sites evidence extreme violence. Could such violence have befallen Neanderthals? Maybe, but it is unlikely that this alone caused their extinction. However, it isn't beyond reason to assert that events similar to those depicted in The High Ones took place in the real world. In the novel, the human war party is going north for one reason—to control the obsidian mines. It is reasonable to assume that a group of humans seeking to take over a resource would annihilate the population controlling that resource. But why did humans have a scorched earth policy in the lowrock valley? The Bhatt massacre is unexplained, but the Kurnisahn and Ser-o may very well have been attacked as a consequence of Carn abducting their child (although this too is left open to interpretation).

In The High Ones, humans' ability to exercise such power over Neanderthals was mainly due to their technological advantage (bows and arrows). While the earliest extant bows are about 10,000 years old, other evidence suggests bow and arrow technology may have existed well before then. In the Sibudu cave in South Africa, archaeologists discovered a 61,000-year-old bone-point believed to be an arrow tip. Additionally, there are 30,000-year-old cave paintings as far apart as Western Europe and Australia depicting humans pierced by arrows. Such evidence suggests that bows and arrows are, at a minimum, not anachronistic in the novel.

Returning to the original question—why did Neanderthals go extinct? Their habitat constituted a vast area—from the Iberian Peninsula to Siberia. Different groups in different regions probably met different fates. After Neanderthal numbers went into steep decline, many remnant populations likely survived throughout the range, although only in the southernmost regions. The fates that befell each of these populations were not identical, as they occurred in different geographies at different times; thousands, or even tens of thousands of years apart.

Wolf domestication

IN THE HIGH ONES, dogs aid humans in their attacks on Neanderthals. This, too, is most likely an anachronism and is therefore another area where I took poetic license. While some theories about Neanderthal extinction feature humans using domesticated wolves (at least to out-hunt/out-compete Neanderthals), most genetic studies put the divergence of dog and wolf lineages at a maximum of 30,000 YBP. However, there is significant disagreement about when and where this domestication occurred, and the likelihood of multiple domestication events further muddies the picture. Either way, humans using dogs as a weapon against Neanderthals is inconsistent with our current understanding of the timeline, and I thus view this aspect of the novel as fictional.

Physical descriptions of humans

I DEPICTED HUMANS in The High Ones as taller, slenderer, having darker complexion, and with ridgeless brows and high foreheads. The only one of these descriptions not supported by direct physical evidence (i.e., skeletons) of first-contact humans is their complexion. It is not known what skin color these humans had, but it is conceivable that their complexion was darker than Neanderthals since they were coming from the south. Thus, to further differentiate them from Neanderthals, I described humans as having extremely dark skin. This is both consistent with human complexion in equatorial climes and supported by empirical evidence[*]. In contrast, most Neanderthals probably had fair skin, with genetic evidence suggesting red hair, green eyes, and freckles—features found more often in those with fairer skin.

Differentiating humans and Neanderthals in the novel was tricky. The easiest way to communicate their differences would have been to describe distinctive Neanderthal features (e.g., prominent brows).

---

[*] One study of Mesolithic human remains found in Britain showed that he had black skin. However, at ~10,000 years old, these remains are not evidence of what the first contact humans looked like.

Robert Scheige

But this was not possible because the novel is written from the perspective of Neanderthals, who wouldn't have described themselves as having pronounced brows since, for them, that was the norm. The novel's perspective thus required physical descriptions to focus on how humans looked different from Neanderthals rather than the reverse.

IN CONCLUSION, writing The High Ones was challenging. I aimed for a compelling story that was generally realistic based on today's knowledge of Neanderthals. While I had to take a certain amount of poetic license for storytelling purposes, I hope that readers find that the fictionalizations maintained an acceptable level of realism and historicity.

Sources

NUMEROUS SOURCES INFORMED my research of The High Ones. These are listed below for anyone who is interested in reading further.

- *The Humans Who Went Extinct: Why Neanderthals Died Out and We Survived.* By Clive Finlayson.

- *Neanderthal Man: In Search of Lost Genomes.* By Svante Pääbo.

- *The Neanderthals Rediscovered: How Modern Science if Rewriting Their Story (Revised and Updated Edition).* By Dimitra Papagianni and Michael A. Rose.

- *Sapiens: A Brief History of Humankind.* By Yuval Noah Harari.

- *The Third Chimpanzee: The Evolution and Future of the Human Animal.* By Jared Diamond.

- *The Sixth Extinction: An Unnatural History.* By Elizabeth Kolbert.

- *Digs Reveal Stone-Age Weapons Industry With Staggering Output.* National Geographic article by Frank Viviano. April 13, 2015.

- *Last of the Neanderthals: Eurasia was Theirs Alone for 200,000 Years. Then the Newcomers Arrived.* National Geographic Magazine article by Stephen S. Hall. October 2008.

- *Cheddar Man: Mesolithic Britain's Blue Eyed Boy.* Natural History Museum (of UK) article by Kerry Lotzof. February 2018.

- *Cosmosapiens: Human Evolution from the Origin of the Universe.* By John Hands.

Lastly, three books on writing and editing were extremely helpful in the creation of The High Ones. I'd be remiss to not mention them here.

- *Self-Editing for Fiction Writers, Second Edition: How to Edit Yourself into Print.* By Renni Browne and Dave King.

- *Stein on Writing: A Master Editor of Some of the Most Successful Writers of Our Century Shares His Craft Techniques and Strategies.* By Sol Stein.

- *The Emotion Thesaurus: A Writer's Guide to Character Expression.* By Becca Puglisi and Angela Ackerman.

Acknowledgements

THE HIGH ONES IS A NOVEL more than five years in the making; a project I started almost immediately after publishing my novella *Benjamin* in early 2015. Many individuals, both family and friends, provided feedback for either excerpts or entire draft manuscripts.

In no particular order, I would like to thank the following for their valuable contributions at different phases of the project: Fortuna Scheige, Steven Scheige, Susan-Lisa Gvinter, Jannalex Alviarez, Jeremy Nathan Marks, David Martinez, Erika Villoldo, Chris Cullen, Pouya Yousefi, Jessie Culotta, Nitin Gupta, John Zadlo, Stacey Parker, Kahina Aoudia, my photographer Michael Conan Wolcott, my cover artist Robin Vuchnich, and my editor, Kaitlyn Johnson.

A novel is never the end product of a single person, and every one of your comments, criticisms, and observations at varying stages of the project influenced the work.

About the Author

ROB IS AN INSURANCE/SPACE INDUSTRY professional, horror lover and former party kid. His father used to read him Tales from the Crypt as bedtime stories, which explains a thing or two. He loves all forms of art, playing chess, dancing in front of the mirror and is an avid reader of fiction and non-fiction alike. His first book, *Benjamin*, was published in 2015.

He lives in the Washington, DC area and can be reached at: bringbackbenjamin@gmail.com

Made in the USA
Middletown, DE
10 January 2021

31226856R00175